Sweetpea's
Secret

D1707759

Other Novels by Renay Jackson

Crack City
Peanut's Revenge
Turf War
Shakey's Loose
Oaktown Devil

Sweetpea's Secret

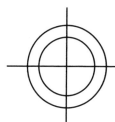

RENAY JACKSON

Frog Books
Berkeley, California

Published by Frog Books

Frog Books' publications are distributed by
North Atlantic Books
P.O. Box 12327
Berkeley, California 94712

Cover photograph by Peeter Viisimaa
Cover and book design by Suzanne Albertson
Printed in the United States of America

Sweetpea's Secret is sponsored by the Society for the Study of Native Arts and Sciences, a nonprofit educational corporation whose goals are to develop an educational and cross-cultural perspective linking various scientific, social, and artistic fields; to nurture a holistic view of arts, sciences, humanities, and healing; and to publish and distribute literature on the relationship of mind, body, and nature.

North Atlantic Books' publications are available through most bookstores. For further information, call 800-733-3000 or visit our website at www.northatlanticbooks.com.

Library of Congress Cataloging-in-Publication Data

Jackson, Renay, 1959–
Sweetpea's secret / Renay Jackson.
    p. cm.
   ISBN-13: 978-1-58394-224-6
    1. African American criminals—Fiction. 2. Oakland (Calif.)—Fiction.
I. Title.
PS3610.A3547S94 2008
813'.6—dc22

2008015037

1 2 3 4 5 6 7 8 9 Versa 12 11 10 09 08 07 06

Successful people profit from their mistakes and try again in a different way.

—ANONYMOUS

SHOUTS

All my readers—thank you very much.

Albert Hightower, Jr.—Dude, it's because of you that I can realize a twenty-year dream. Thanks, bro.

My mother—Mommie, you are the one person who believes in me thick and thin. I love you, baby.

The friends of Chester Himes—With the help of you all, my career took off. I will be forever grateful.

Alberta & Charlesetta, my musical sisters—thanks y'all!

For anyone missed—my bad, but thanks all the same.

TABLE OF CONTENTS

THE SKINNY

Sweetpea boarded the plane heading out of Vegas and slouched down in a window seat at the rear. His mind was at ease because the latest mission went off without a glitch. A professional hit man, he prided himself on quickness and efficiency. The mark, as he called them, had been none other than Big Ed Tatum, one of Oaktown's most notorious gangsters.

Initially, it was a job he never would have taken due to the fact Big Ed had been one of his best clients. In this case, however, he was left no choice because Big Ed not only wooed his sister Crystal into falling in love, he was responsible for his other sister Peanut's close encounter with death. She was shot at close range by one of his henchmen and almost died, leaving Sweetpea no choice but to get Peanut's revenge.

Adrenaline surged through his body as if he were a conductor viewing an oncoming train barreling down the tracks directly in front of him. Yet his outward demeanor was cool, calm, and collected. As the aircraft taxied down the runway, Sweetpea closed his eyes, replaying the past two days' events. No one aboard paid any mind to the dapperly dressed, distinguished-looking black man catnapping.

Decked out in beige Italian slacks, matching penny loafers, socks, and cotton button-down shirt, he seemed content to the stewardesses and fellow passengers. Many on board looked tired, run over and/or broke from what started out as an eagerly anticipated vacation. Sweetpea, they assumed, must have won big because the dude was at peace.

Replaying the hit, he rested his two-inch salt-and-pepper afro on a pillow propped against the window and prepared to doze off, oblivious to all. He remembered waiting in the parking lot of a casino then slashing one of the tires on Big Ed's Mercedes Benz. When the mark returned and noticed he had a flat, he pulled the spare doughnut tire from the trunk and went about the business of changing it. Sweetpea rolled his rental into an adjacent stall, with Big Ed paying him no mind.

The element of surprise, which hit men value as their best weapon, served him proper because Big Ed had never met him. All their transactions over the years had been made by phone and postal box payments. Getting out, Sweetpea made a simple statement to the intended victim about the flat. Before he received an answer, his hand covered Big Ed's mouth. With his knee pressed against the small of Big Ed's back, Sweetpea jerked his victim's head backwards, then slashed his throat from ear to ear.

Revenge was swift and family honor had been restored. Thinking about the murder caused his dick to get hard and his thoughts to turn to his woman Harriette. She would surely be served tonight because to him, murder was just as potent as any of the new sex drugs that had recently been introduced to the general public for impotent men, which he was *not*.

The plane touched down at Oaktown International. As passengers began scurrying about to retrieve their luggage from overhead compartments, Sweetpea sat comfortably in his seat, amused by it all. Since he was at the back of the plane there was no need to hurry. He never could understand why people were in such a rush when they would be standing still for another three minutes anyway.

Waiting patiently until his turn, he rose up, lifted his carry-on bag from an overhead compartment, then casually strutted down the aisle and off the plane. Now he would resume his life as Horace Boudreaux, mortgage broker and sometime playboy. It was a boring existence yet paid the bills, providing him all the comforts of life. He would assume the role well, until the urge to kill placed the monkey on his back and the roaring inferno inside his body.

When that happened, someone would be in trouble because it was the only way Sweetpea, assassin for hire, could exist. He had to kill.

THIRTEEN YEARS LATER . . .

CON GAME

Oaktown's City Center bustled with activity during lunchtime as workers scurried about for a bite to eat. Others rushed to appointments while many simply soaked in the sun around the plaza. Since it was Friday, the majority possessed paychecks, creating a somewhat festive atmosphere. People shopped, visited the farmer's market, or headed to that eatery they'd been dreaming of all week.

The weather was a nice eighty-five degrees, which was a welcome relief from the triple-digit temperatures of the previous three days. Inside bagel, coffee, and sandwich shops customers pecked away at their laptops while enjoying the cool air-conditioning units. To Northern Californians, used to year-round weather hovering around the seventy-five-degree mark, it was hot as hell.

One of the Bay Area's major selling points to out-of-state residents was always the decent weather. If you came from Vegas or another desert locale such as Arizona, it was scorching hot every day. In other places like Minnesota or Chicago, winter days were filled with bone-numbing cold. Most Oaktown residents only saw snow if they visited Reno or Lake Tahoe because in their neck of the woods, snow just didn't happen.

Once, and only once, did it occur. It was a rainy January morning in nineteen seventy-seven. For a brief five minutes snowflakes cascaded down onto the city, immediately melting into water the moment they touched ground. For many Golden State transplants, it amounted to simply a drop in the bucket, along with a subtle reminder of home. However, to Bay Area masses, it was like a Super Bowl victory celebration.

Children rushed out of classrooms, effectively halting school. Some danced around in circles while others tilted their heads to the sky with mouths gaped open, attempting to catch a taste. Teachers huddled in small groups, grinning from ear to ear as their charges frolicked about in glee. This act of nature could definitely be used in future lesson plans, be it math, science, biology, or history.

Located in the belly button of downtown, City Center was a collection of businesses that catered to the working set. Banks, credit unions, travel agencies, bookstores, health spas, and assorted eating establishments were everywhere. Nestled between Broadway and Clay with 12th and 14th serving as its borders, one could enter from all four sides. However, after six and on weekends, the place was a ghost town.

Hanging out at the corner of 13th and Broadway were three young boys who from first impression looked innocent enough. They appeared to be chillin' while casually waiting for a bus. But as buses whizzed by on their assigned routes, the dudes remained posted at the spot. No older than thirteen, each boy held two sheets of paper stapled together in his hand, along with pencils.

The top sheet displayed a crude computer-generated form showing a basketball hoop and court. Beneath it was a sad letter explaining that their team had won a trip to the national age-group tournament but due to lack of funds, they needed donations in order to compete. On the second page was a spreadsheet allowing donors to write in their name, address, phone number, email, and amount given.

Mario Hayes was the ringleader and really big for his age. Twelve years old, he already stood six feet four inches tall and weighed nearly two hundred pounds. Even though his height and girth resembled that of a senior linebacker, his boyish features and chunky figure told all. Baby fat surrounded his mid section. A low-cut fade covered his caramel-colored face, which was oval-shaped and smooth as a baby's butt. He, along with his sidekicks, were all dressed in black Dockers with matching hi-tops and white t-shirts.

Jamal and Bakari flanked the baby giant, giving him the illusion of even greater height. Just like Mario, the Foster brothers were twelve years young, but all similarities ended there. Each boy stood five-seven on tiptoes and weighed one hundred pounds soaking wet. Fraternal twins, Jamal was light, Bakari dark. Their heads were oblong and formed in the shape of peanuts, meaning their bodies had some catching up to do.

They had been friends with Mario since grade school and loved the fact that he chose them to be his road dogs. Mario was a bully who roughed up anyone who messed with him or his crew. Fearless, he'd often engage in fistfights with much older teens just to prove his manhood. More often than not, he came out victorious, which gave him a solid reputation on the mean streets of Oaktown's east side.

For his part, Mario respected Jamal and Bakari because they possessed the gift for gab, whereas he froze up while speaking to anyone other than his own circle of friends. Smart beyond their years, the Foster twins learned game from their Uncle David who, in his day, was one of the greatest con artists the city had ever known.

David Foster often sat around the dinner table on holidays boasting about some of his most successful scams. Jamal and Bakari spent many nights at his crib mesmerized by his vast knowledge of crime. He'd explain in detail the Jamaican Switch, three-card Monty, home repair scams, and using dope fiends to boost, just to name a few.

"Yeah boy," he would say, "I'd catch the mark before he went into an electronics store and tell him I could give him a two-thousand-dollar computer for three hundred, no questions asked."

"What did he say, Unc?" the twins chomped at the bit.

"First he will say no, but that's why you always go for the one with a hoe. The reason is simple: A lame with a bitch on his arm will want her to think he's in control and willing to do a little illegal shit from time to time if it saves them money. Now, he'll say no but the broad is curious and wants to see. Once that happens I pop the trunk and show 'em a gangload of computers neatly packaged and ready to go."

"Do you let 'em see?" Bakari would ask.

"Hell naw, niggah, if you let them open the package all bets are off and your game is blown straight to hell. What you do is tell 'em you work for a computer company and they have no idea you lifted some inventory. At that exact moment I'd have my boy Bernard come up and hand me three c-notes then carry one to his ride. Once the marks see this, they're sold hook, line, and sinker. Of course, when they get home and open the box they find it empty and weighted down with rocks." David would then let off a hearty laugh. "It also works with TVs, component sets, DVDs, and VCRs, but the money is in computers."

Jamal was first to strike with their basketball scheme, spotting a white dude wearing slacks, dress shirt, and necktie with cheap penny loafers. As he and his twin had explained it to Mario the night before, you had to choose your marks wisely. If they appeared to be athletic, more than likely you'd receive some scrill. On the other hand, if they were nerdish, leave them alone because those types asked too many questions and could care less about sports.

"Excuse me, sir. . . ."

Jamal ran the rehearsed spiel on the guy while Bakari headed for a sister with locks, dressed in spandex and toting an athletic bag. It was obvious that she was headed for the gym. Mario stood by watching as Jamal pointed him out to the dude. He knew his boy was telling the cat that he was the center and they were the guards. Once he saw the guy hand over money, and the woman do the same along with sign the second sheet, he knew the game would work. The twins returned grinning from ear to ear.

"Man, that shit worked just like my uncle said it would!" Jamal squealed. "We gone make a killin'!"

Before Mario could respond, the Foster twins were off to run more game. While they scored time after time, Mario remained stationary, simply letting folks read his paper. After two hours, the twins had made nearly forty dollars each while their overgrown friend had acquired nothing. He just didn't have the vocabulary for it. Deciding to take a much-needed break, the young bucks headed to Mickey D's for lunch. Jamal and Bakari each ordered Happy Meals. Realizing that the two dollars his mom had given him that morning would not go far, Mario scanned the dollar deal menu. Jamal came to the rescue, offering to pay his embarrassed friend's tab. Knowing his bill was covered, Mario ordered a Big Mac, double cheeseburger, large fries, and super-sized soda. The trio waltzed out of the joint, copping squats at a table in the courtyard next to Starbucks.

Like most twins, Jamal and Bakari thought and acted as one. Each boy knew what the other was thinking and they often finished sentences for each other. Nibbling at their meals while watching Mario devour his, Bakari spoke for the both of them.

"Mario?" Bakari said.

"What up, dawg?" his friend answered, lettuce dangling from the corner of his mouth.

"Man, you gotta rap for yours. The shit is easy as pie, homes." He sipped his soda.

"All you gotta do"—Jamal finished—"is represent! That means work dese muthafuckas, man, see what ah'm sayin'?"

"Yeah, ah know what y'all sayin. Just speak up like I really do need a donation fo mah road trip."

"Exactly," they chimed in unison.

"Okay," Jamal stated, "you get the next one and we'll watch."

"That'll work," Mario agreed, thinking that he at least owed for the meal. "I'll get him."

Mario got up from the table and walked toward a guy who had

just left the gym. He was dressed in gray sweats, white sneakers, and a very tight t-shirt, which displayed rippling muscles. A low-cut two-inch afro sat atop his smooth cocoa-brown face. Nary a whisker, Mario figured him to be in his mid twenties and an athlete. The twins attempted to warn him not to mess with that guy but were drowned out by the noise generated from the lunchtime crowd.

"Excuse me, sir."

Running down the spiel, Mario was shocked when the brother questioned him about his paper. "I don't see the police seal," the man said.

"Come again?" Mario asked.

"Look, young man," he began, authoritative in his demeanor and words, "I'm a coach and also a police officer, and I know for a fact that you're supposed to have an official police seal on this form before you can come out here begging people for money."

"Ah ain't beggin' nobody."

Mario glanced back at the table, but the twins were nowhere in sight. This caused him to panic and stumble over his words as the dude inquired about the coach, league, where the games were held, and names of opposing squads. With no other option, Mario bailed. The foot chase was on, with Mario quickly realizing that he would not outrun the guy.

Near the corner of 12th and Clay and without warning Mario made a grave mistake. He stopped on a dime, turned to face his pursuer, and swung wildly. The punch caught nothing but air then his stomach met full force with a thundering right hand. Doubled over in pain, Mario slumped down to one knee, only to find himself slammed face-first onto the pavement with a kneecap pressed to his back.

By the time beat cops came rushing up, a small crowd of onlookers had assembled. Gently lifting Mario from the ground, the cops cuffed his meaty wrists, smiling at the familiar black man who was busy wiping sweat off his brow. After escorting the kid to the back seat of a squad car that had just arrived, the pair rejoined their off-duty associate on the curb.

Dennis Branch stood chatting freely with the gawkers who would soon be returning to their jobs with an interesting street story to tell. A free spirit, Dennis had not set out to bust Mario, only to shut down his scam. Once the youngster ran, that meant evading arrest, and when he threw a punch, it escalated to assault on a peace officer. In less than two minutes Mario went from free adolescent to juvenile delinquent.

"Nice work, Dennis," said Chad Rowe. "What did he do?"

Rowe pulled a hanky from his shirt pocket and wiped sweat away from his perspiring forehead. A year from retirement, he volunteered for street duty because that represented a greater nest egg once his pension became official. Six-four with flaming red hair (though balding on top), with a potbelly falling over his belt line, this officer had not run any distance in years. A nineteen-year veteran, he had spent the past five in intelligence but also served in homicide, vice, and the gang unit details. Sergeant Rowe had basically performed desk duty for the previous decade, ruining what back in the day had been a chiseled physique.

"I approached the suspect, who was panhandling," answered Dennis. "Before I had a chance to tell him to scram, he took to the wind; then once I caught him, he swung at me."

"So he went from a 647C to evading arrest, then assault?" Rowe took notes.

"Exactly," Dennis responded. "People tell me there were three of them but I only saw this guy. The other two reportedly looked like brothers, so I guess they must have been working different parts of the plaza."

"Did they give a description of the perps?" asked the female cop.

"Yes, Rhonda, they did."

Dennis Branch eyed Rhonda Gentry with curiosity. He knew

she had recently graduated from the academy and secretly wondered why she chose law enforcement as a career. The girl was barely twenty-two, stood only five-six in heels, and possessed a mouth-watering frame. Even in her ill-fitting uniform one could tell she had body.

"Two juveniles, possibly brothers, twelve and thirteen, one light, the other dark, five-six or -seven and skinny, no distinguishing features."

Rhonda radioed the descriptions to central dispatch at the same time Jamal and Bakari peered out the windows of a passing bus. The twins felt pangs of guilt for their homeboy's situation, but what could they do? If he were sharp at his game he would have known not to bail from a cop. In the words of their Uncle David, rule number one of a player: Verbalize your way out of it!

Mario spotted his homeys, suddenly feeling sorry for himself. As he was transported to headquarters, tears flowed down his cheeks. He was taken to the fourth-floor Youth Services Division (YSD for short) and booked. Chad Rowe, who had ridden in the back seat of the cruiser beside Mario, filled out the paperwork then telephoned his mom. Mario hung his head in shame, knowing how disappointed his mother would be upon hearing the news of his predicament.

"Your mom wishes to speak to you." Rowe unlocked the cuffs then handed Mario the phone.

"Hello ... nuthin' ... I was just standing there talking to the dude ... I ran because I had to catch the bus ... Swing? I turned around an' almost fell, so my arms were flying in the air ... Man, you trippin'."

Mario returned the receiver to the cop then sat staring at the walls. Rowe talked another minute with his mom before ending the call. While escorting Mario to a jail cell he silently wondered why the youngster would refer to his own mother as "man." This boy was disrespectful, and that one singular action let Rowe know he was from a broken home.

Since juvenile court was booked for the day, Mario spent his first night of incarceration receiving no sympathy from the cops. Each shift arriving for duty was told of the conversation between him and his mom. Of course, after seeing how overgrown he was, and knowing he had no respect for his mother or himself, the kid was treated strictly by the book.

2

MAN OF THE HOUR

The liquor store at 8th and Adeline resembled a street party more than a mini market. Activity abounded as young black men peddled dope and stolen merchandise, or just chilled drinking hooch and smoking weed. With nightfall rapidly approaching, no one seemed to notice or care because there was money to be made. A large circle of dudes sat engaged in a high-stakes dice game on the side of the building, which faced a glass-littered parking lot.

Customers entered and exited the market seeming to be oblivious to the goings-on. Since it was none of their business, they pretended not to notice. The self-righteous Christians would make the trek six blocks down to a quieter location. Police were spotted blocks away, and upon cruising by they would find the storefront saturated with people drinking sodas and eating Chinese food, which was sold inside, and doing nothing illegal.

Across the street at the health clinic, homeless drifters began to set up camp for the evening. They were harmless, so no one paid them any mind. Their shopping carts, which housed their meager possessions, were parked in the bushes. The campers spread out filthy blankets and dozed off. Even though they owned nothing, they were territorial. Choice spots were hard to come by and even harder to keep, so strangers generally were unwelcome.

A very phine female wearing skin-tight jeans maneuvered through the crowd at the liquor store, attempting to enter. She was sassy and booty-licious.

"Girl, you look like a pot of gravy and I'm the biscuit, HOLLER!" shouted Ocie. Ocie Rivers stood in the middle of the action holding court. People really didn't care about his signifying nor what he had to say, but since he was buying they laughed at the square jokes he told. Born and raised on the west side of Oaktown, Ocie still found it difficult being accepted by his people. To most of the hoodrats he was considered an outsider. He just didn't fit in.

Six-feet-one on a slender hundred-and-sixty-pound frame, he wore straight-leg beige Dockers, penny loafers, and a solid white shirt with paisley tie. Thick black bifocals covered his angular mug, capped off by a flat-top fade. Twenty-three years old, his appearance made him seem five years younger. Ocie had been blessed with the proverbial golden spoon yet could not shake the elements of his environment.

Everyone in the community knew the story well. Fifteen years earlier the city's school district devised a plan to award the most gifted elementary students a chance to attend predominantly white schools in wealthy neighborhoods. Scholarships would pay the tuition, with yellow buses providing transportation. Ocie was selected for the program, becoming an instant celebrity and source of pride to his folks.

Initially things were rough due to the fact he had to withstand whispers behind his back along with subtle hints of racism on a daily basis. It wasn't long before many kids dropped out of the program, but Ocie toughed it out. By the time he reached Athenian High School he was not only a straight-A student, he was the star of the basketball team as well. He had been accepted by the snobbish whites, and if not for his skin complexion, could just as easily have been white himself.

After graduating from Saint Mary's College with a degree in accounting, Ocie began working for a paper manufacturing plant in the tiny city of Petaluma, which was a stone's throw from Santa Rosa, near the Sonoma and Napa Valley wine country. Luigi Russolini had met Ocie on the college campus, instantly becoming his homeboy. Over the years Luigi had told Ocie all about his dad's business and lifestyle. It was Luigi's dad who ran the paper business and hired Ocie.

Standing five-feet-six on a roundish two-hundred-pound frame, Luigi was fat and jolly. Coming from a family with money, he literally paid his way through college by getting other people to do his schoolwork. More often than not, Ocie was the beneficiary of his pal's generosity.

Knowing that his boss at the paper plant was a crook who had cheated numerous clients out of money made Ocie's decision to cook the books easier. Methodically, he began altering the spreadsheets and acquiring chump change. When the company secured a nationwide paper deal with money rolling out the ears, Ocie began taking more. The only way his game could be discovered would be for him to miss work.

That being the case, his attendance was perfect. He even worked on Saturdays in an otherwise empty office, diligently maintaining the ledger. Life was good. Ocie had an apartment located in a quiet upper-class neighborhood, a phat bank account, brand new Beemer, and super-fine snowbunny as a trophy. The boss frequently used him as an example to staff when discussing dedication. Then things began to crumble.

Ocie came down with a severe case of strep throat, which confined him to bed. Upon his absence the company hired a temp who immediately found discrepancies in the books and alerted the boss. When he returned to work Luigi, his dad Tony, and two goon types confronted him. The interrogation took place in an empty storeroom at the back of the warehouse.

It was both cold and damp, yet Ocie began to perspire from fear. Tony Russolini stood in front of him with body language that suggested both anger and disappointment. A fitness fanatic, his chiseled, muscular, five-nine frame seemed to swell right on the spot. Luigi posted himself in a corner behind his dad, not wanting to face his friend, because if he hadn't hounded his dad into hiring Ocie, none of this would have happened in the first place.

"Ocie, I trusted you and considered you a part of my family,"

Tony began, "and how do you repay me?" He held up the account ledger. "By stealing."

"I'm sorry, Mr. Russolini, but I didn't know what I was doing," Ocie repented.

"Didn't know, hell! You skimmed my books for forty grand and if not for your sickness probably would have ripped me off forever!"

"I'll pay you back—I still have most of the money."

"That's not the point. You betrayed me."

"I know and I apologize from the bottom of my heart—just give me one more chance."

Russolini gave his goons Sal and Vito the eye then turned away as they beat Ocie to a pulp. Blows rained down onto his head and body and he was defenseless to stop it. He had never felt such pain in his young life. Just when it appeared he couldn't take any more, Tony called off the dogs and watched calmly as they propped Ocie up in a chair.

"Since I always liked you and your work, I'll let you live. Now I want to know exactly what you did."

It was more of a statement than a request, leaving Ocie no choice but to divulge his scheme. Through eyes swollen shut plus a busted lip with blood flowing freely, Ocie sang like a bird. The only reason they let him leave was because he promised to immediately return the forty grand he'd pilfered.

Once home he called Mr. Russolini, informing him that he knew about many of his dirty secrets. Bluntly, Ocie told the man that he wasn't giving back a dime, and if anything happened to him the police would be receiving a letter that would reveal all. Of course the Italian promised him death, but Ocie was not worried. He felt the man had too much to lose behind what he considered a drop in the bucket.

Still in all, he returned to his roots. Selling the Beemer, Ocie bought a twenty-year-old El Dorado, rented a shabby apartment, and spent his days hiding out until his face and body healed. For those dumb enough to ask about his gruesome mug he'd simply say that he was involved in a car accident. Sal and Vito set up surveillance at his old Petaluma crib for a few weeks but came up dry. His woman was just as miffed about his whereabouts as they were. Ocie Rivers had disappeared.

Meanwhile, down at the liquor store, he was working another game: "Hey sugar dumpling, let me tell you something...."

The female laughed not only at Ocie's squareness but also at his correct pronunciation of each word. As she switched away the crowd roared. Unfazed, he continued his showboating to the peanut gallery. Spending his money freely, Ocie Rivers thought he was a kingpin. They all liked him, or so he assumed.

Travelle and Moon, two losers who had spent their entire lives looking for the easy way to make a buck, watched that fool with more than a passing fancy. Rivers had cash and they aimed to get it. Since his return to the streets those two had secretly trailed him each day. They knew who he was and were just as surprised as everyone else when he returned. However, Ocie only recognized them by face and couldn't possibly know the danger they had in mind.

"We get dat fool ta-nite foe he spin da scrill," Travelle whispered to his road dog.

"Dass a bet," Moon responded.

Travelle Spencer resembled a tank, standing five-seven on a two-hundred-pound frame. Powerfully built from years of pumping iron, he possessed a nasty attitude along with no conscience. Size twenty-nine in the waist, he wore thirty-four Old Navy jeans that sagged below his butt, displaying colorful boxer shorts. A sky-blue Magic basketball jersey hung down to mid thigh; twisty braids covered his scalp. He had no jewelry and couldn't even tell you what time it was due to not owning a watch.

Ronnie Moon stood six feet even, weighed two-thirty, and resembled a free safety. Ruggedly handsome, his hair was cut low to the scalp, which accented his perfectly round dome. The white tee shirt he wore was stretched to its limit by his bulging arms and chest. Faded blue jeans along with dirty white sneakers completed his wardrobe. Dark as black ink, Moon's facial expression caused one to think he was passive. However, the dude was a very violent man, never thinking twice about hurting another human being if he could gain financially from it.

Travelle and Moon had been partners in crime for more than ten years. Like most hoodrats in the ghetto, those two considered going to jail a badge of honor that they wore proudly by showing off their muscular physiques. Blending in with the crowd, they continued to keep close tabs on Ocie, whom they considered lamest of the lame. As nightfall rapidly approached and the street corner freeloaders began to dwindle, they remained stationary, watching as Ocie downed one beer after another.

"Now his ass drunk," said Travelle. "We gone do it tonight."

"He'll never know what hit 'im," chimed Moon.

Ocie staggered out of the store carrying a twelve-pack of beer as he argued with the owner, a middle-aged man of Asian descent who stood in the doorway cursing Ocie out in his native tongue. Everyone on the corner laughed heartily at the scene, knowing that only squares like Ocie Rivers received this sort of response from the store proprietor. When danger loomed, the man would just smile and pretend not to know what the hell they were talking about.

"And once I buy this shack you'll be working for *me,* you tight-eyed son of a bitch, HOLLER!"

Of course before he could open the box people lined up to get their brew. Incorrectly assuming the laughs were due to his wit, Ocie handed out the freebies, along with popping the tab and guzzling one of his own. Tired, high, drunk, and beat, he said his goodbyes, hopped inside his Caddy, and drove home. Little did he know he was not alone.

3

JUDGE'S SCORN

Crystal Hayes sat on a bench outside the juvenile courtroom impa-
tiently waiting for her name to be called. She was upset for having
to take the day off from work, but it bothered her more that her son
Mario had finally done something stupid enough to bring shame to
the family. Heaven knows she did everything in her power to keep
him on the straight and narrow, but without a male role model at
home, the streets would surely gobble him up whole.

His father had been murdered shortly after she became preg-
nant, and since no man could satisfy her the way he did, she chose
to remain single. Many of the men she dated on occasion never
returned because first, Mario would treat them rudely at the crib.
Second, once they realized she wasn't giving up the pootnanny no
matter how much scrill they spent, they chose to spend their time
and hard-earned bucks elsewhere.

Glancing down the packed hallway at families awaiting their
turn, Crystal was mortified. The only faces she saw were either
African American or Chicano, nearly all represented by a single
parent. A huge majority were mothers who from first impressions
appeared to be living a life of poverty. There were a few men scattered throughout who sat or stood stone-faced and angry.

With every bench occupied, the latecomers stuck to the wall
with feet propped against it for support. Attorneys and public
defenders were easy to spot due to their attire, grooming, and
attaché cases. Generally speaking, they were the only white faces
in the crowd.

"Hayes!" shouted the deputy.

Snapped out of her trance, Crystal rose and glided toward the
open door. Instantly the hallway became silent as women stared

with envy and the men devoured her frame. To say jaws dropped would be an understatement to the highest degree because Crystal Hayes was all that, then some. She wore blue high heels that caused her to appear even taller than her five-eleven height.

Bone-colored stockings gripped her toned legs without sag, giving the illusion they were bare. Although it was a business suit, the skirt on her navy blue two-piece displayed hips and ass for days. Its matching jacket covered a white blouse with ruffles in front, accented by awesome boobs whose nipples strained the fabric to its limit.

Crystal eased past the ogling deputy resembling Pam Grier's body double. As he closed the door, the Sheriff gave a few men that lustful eye they all knew so well. Try as they might to player hate, the females grinned along with everyone else because they knew Crystal deserved all the props she received.

The only people allowed inside juvenile court were staff, attorneys, the court referee, probation officers, sheriff's deputies, and immediate family. Crystal now understood why the hallways were packed to the gills. Taking her seat on the front row, she watched without blinking as Mario was led into the courtroom from a side door. He had on the same clothing she remembered he had worn the day before, although he was much dirtier.

Mario kept his head down, refusing to look at his mom. Peering up at the court referee (who would be called a judge in adult court), he awaited his sentence. She was a black woman in her mid thirties with a very pretty face. An older white clerk read off the charges as the referee's eyes zoomed in on Mario.

"Any family present?" she asked.

"Yes, I'm his mother," answered Crystal.

"Who's representing?"

"I am, Your Honor," stated a young college-type white man.

"Young man," she spoke to Mario, "you know that you have committed a serious offense by attempting to strike an officer of the law, don't you?"

"Yes, Your Honor," Mario answered solemnly.

"Normally I would grant you probation, but in consideration of the seriousness of your offense, I have no choice but to sentence you to three years at the California Youth Authority complex in Stockton."

"But Your Honor, I slipped."

"Look, young man," she snapped, "you seem to have a problem with discipline. I hope by the time you're released your attitude will change. Next case."

As bailiffs escorted Mario to the back room he glanced around, only to find his mother's head hanging with tears flowing freely from her eyes onto her blouse. Once he was out of sight, Crystal Hayes gathered herself, rose from her seat, and exited the courtroom. The elevator couldn't come fast enough because she felt ashamed and embarrassed. Her only child would be gone for three long years, meaning that she now would return home from work to an empty house. Like all parents, she lived and breathed for her child.

Five hours later the prison bus rolled up to the gates of YA, which is the moniker everyone used when speaking of the Youth Authority. Mario along with eight other teens got off the bus and walked in a single-file line to the admitting room. The first thing he noticed was that everybody wore blue jeans, white t-shirts, and cheap tennis shoes. The recreation yard was brimming with activity on the basketball court and football field, along with ping pong and dominoes being played near the housing units. Suddenly the action ceased as all eyes were on the new arrivals.

Many in the crowd assumed Mario to be around fifteen or sixteen years old due to his extraordinary size. Soon they would be shocked to find out that he was actually a twelve-year-old man-child. Mario observed that all the juvenile delinquents were standing in groups with their crews. The Latinos were huddled up in two separate packs consisting of Norteños and Sureños. Blacks congregated based on city or hood affiliation, with whites and Asians off to themselves as well.

Everyone in line seemed to know somebody, with most greeted respectfully by their hoodrat friends. Although he did see a few Oaktown dudes he knew, Mario felt alone because they were all older and he wasn't close to any of them. Out of the corner of his eye he saw one guy staring him down. Try as he might to ignore it, he couldn't help but look.

The dude was bigger than Mario, and something about him seemed familiar. After three or four glances in that direction, homeboy mouthed the word "trick" to Mario, who looked away quickly, knowing that he would have a problem with that dude. He was surrounded by a gang of fools. It was obvious he was the ringleader, so that meant double trouble. Mario trudged on to the receiving room with his head down.

4

PLAN IN MOTION

Sweetpea pushed his shopping cart to a spot on the side of the clinic then laid out a blanket on the dirty ground. All of the homeless drifters eyed him from head to toe because he was new to them. They secretly wondered about the elderly stranger in coveralls torn at the knee, dirty beenie cap, and run-over shoes. Butter, who considered himself the landlord of the encampment, strutted over to Sweetpea as everyone sat up from their resting place, anticipating a possible rumble.

Butter's six-three frame towered over the smaller Sweetpea by two inches, and whereas Sweetpea's body appeared soft and slender, Butter's was a rock of granite. Dark as midnight, he had sloppy cornrows, yellow teeth, a horrible body odor, and was very dirty. Standing directly in front of Sweetpea he initiated the conversation.

"Hey OG, you know dis camp is already occupied."

"Oh really? Ah wadn't aware of it." Sweetpea talked ebonics.

"Yeah it is, and da only way you can stay since nobody knows you is ta pay a fee."

"What kinda fee?"

"I'ont know," Butter scratched his dome, "but you gotta have sumptun."

"All ah got is dis weed plus fifty-dollah bill ah stole from a white dude downtown."

Sweetpea displayed five phat joints along with a wrinkled-up fifty, which Butter gladly accepted.

"Dass what ah'm talkin' 'bout, shidd. Man, what's yo name, dawg?"

"Dey call me Preach 'cause back in da day it was either that or pimpin' an ah didn't wanna do dat."

"Man, you awight—hey yaw, dis heah's mah new friend Preach and ah wont everybody to treat him right," Butter said to the group. One by one they introduced themselves after trying out some of the weed Butter fired up freely. There was Henrietta, Butter's woman, who looked just as pitiful as her man. Very petite, she stood five-two on a skinny one-hundred-pound frame with a nappy fro, ashen charcoal face, and dirty wrinkled clothes. Melly Mel greeted Sweetpea, displaying a mouth full of crooked rotten teeth, with the same terrible odor as Butter emanating from his body. Sir Charles ambled up, hitting a joint then choking on it, his rolls of fat jiggling with each cough.

Sweetpea stood in the center of the pack answering all questions and spinning fantastic tales of how great he used to be. Butter ran across the street to the store and returned with liquor for all. He was just as mesmerized as the rest of his friends by Sweetpea's gift for gab. They could hardly care that he did not want either booze or dank; matter of fact, they were surprised and happy that he passed. This meant more for them.

It was certainly obvious that the brother had stories to tell, so each person knew he probably was a wonderful preacher in his day. What the bums didn't know was that they were in the company of a professional hit man who was using them as a prop. All the while he talked, Sweetpea kept one eye on the corner across the street, his attention squarely focused on Ocie Rivers, the mark.

Upon seeing Ocie hop inside his ride and drive off, Sweetpea noticed two thug types trailing a block behind. Rubbing his crotch while hopping from one foot to another, he stated for all the derelicts to hear, "Man, ah gotta take a crap. Where should ah go?"

"Behind da buildin'," Butter answered.

Grabbing a half-used roll of toilet paper from his cart, Sweetpea headed around the side of the clinic then proceeded to march across the parking lot to 7th Street and a waiting Neon rental car. Pulling off, he trailed Travelle and Moon as they shadowed Ocie. Nearly twenty minutes later Butter went around back to find out what happened to his newfound friend, only to return to his crew flabbergasted.

"He gone," Butter stated while tilting his beer can and showing them the tissue paper.

Like the vultures they were, they emptied "Preach's" shopping cart, helping themselves to all the cans and bottles he'd left behind. They didn't care about his possible return because if he did, everyone would develop sudden cases of amnesia regarding his possessions.

Ocie parked on the corner of 7th and Campbell then entered "The Barn," a soul food establishment. Located directly across the street from the main post office, The Barn was where west-side residents went to get their grub on. Since its only competition came from Lady Ester's or Walt's Hickory Pit out east, Soul Brother's, Nellie's, or Lois the Pie Queen to the north, The Barn was the spot. Its setup was similar to a hofbrau where you could view the food, set up buffet style, but could not touch due to glass partitions that were scorching hot.

Moon parked mid block and watched as their mark went inside. Little did they know that two hundred yards behind them Sweetpea observed it all, sitting in front of the old Ester's Orbit Room nightclub. Common sense told him that those two clowns had robbery on the mind, so his plan now changed dramatically. First he would let them do their dirty work, then take care of them as an after-the-fact hit.

Sitting in front of the Orbit Room led Sweetpea to reminisce about the good old days when 7th Street was the hub of Oaktown's nightlife. You could always find off-the-hook blues along with soul food, and at Ester's place, liquor was added to the mix. All the heavyweights hung out there, such as Slim Jenkins—the pimp who had a stable of whores parading up and down the strip—and Raincoat Johnson, the owner of a pool hall and pawn shop. No matter what the weather, Johnson always wore a raincoat, so naturally people tagged him with that nickname. The memories caused a broad smile to crease Sweetpea's face.

Glancing across the street at the post office made Sweetpea's face switch to a frown, because that government building was the reason Earl's Barbeque was forced to move—ejected from its site for construction of a new post office. Throughout the hood, Earl's had a reputation for having the best barbeque on the planet.

A stickler for anonymity, Sweetpea neither knew nor had ever heard of Tony Russolini. Vice versa for that matter. However, being the number-one hit man in the region, Sweetpea's reputation was legendary. Two days earlier he had received a call on his untraceable cell phone from an unknown voice.

"Hello," Sweetpea answered.

"Yes, I don't know if this is the right number, but I was told I could get a job done."

"It's the right one—what do you need?"

"Ocie Rivers, black, twenty-two, slender, whereabouts unknown, and from the west side."

"That'll cost you ten grand cash, which is to be hand-delivered in a plain envelope to 408 13th Street, Box 785."

"Anything else?" Tony asked.

"Once I get the money, I'll handle your business."

Sweetpea hung up the phone then began calling all his contacts throughout the city in order to get a line on Ocie's location. Before the day was over he knew that his mark was spending money like it was hot on the west side and was holed up in a rundown apartment on 8th near the Campbell Village housing projects. Two days later Sweetpea received his payment, which had been routed by the mail attendant to two more postal boxes.

With his to-go order of fried chicken along with macaroni and cheese plus collard greens, candied yams, and cornbread, Ocie walked out of the soul-food joint ignoring his growling stomach.

He would soon be satisfying his yakking belly. Travelle and Moon smelled the sweet aroma emanating from the eatery and realized that they too had gone hours without eating.

"After we fuck him up, ah'm eatin' da niggah's food," Travelle told his partner.

"Shidd, niggah, you ghin half dat shit ta me," Moon chimed. "Ah'm hungry too!"

Zooming off ahead of Ocie, Travelle and Moon pulled up in front of his apartment. They entered through the back door by breaking one of the many windowpane squares covering the upper half of the door. Sweetpea had watched them pull off, instantly realizing their plan. Following behind Ocie, he parked down the block, got out of his rental, and headed to the back of the building. If he had guessed correctly—and judging by the broken window on the back door, he felt he had—the robbers would exit the same way they entered. If he was wrong, then he would have to track down the culprits and do them in.

Either way, Sweetpea had a reputation to uphold so all three men were as good as dead. Since he was still dressed in his homeless outfit, he scoured through one of the garbage dumpsters in the parking lot, lifting out cans and bottles. This position gave him a clear view to both the front and back of the unit. With darkness hovering above, no one gave him a second look. Sweetpea knew it was on.

5

EAST VERSUS WEST

"Next!" Junior hollered, smiling as Willie and Marcus stepped onto the court.

Junior, Rick, and Dread awaited the next set of fools stupid enough to challenge them on the hoop court. They had annihilated the competition for the past two hours but not because of their skill level. More to the point, it was how the threesome played the game. Their style could best be compared to a scrum football practice due to the way they hacked and fouled opponents blatantly. Oaktown Three, as they called themselves, had no rules, and since they continually won, you had to beat them at their own game.

Wiping sweat off his six-foot, five-inch frame with a towel, Junior laughed loudly when it became obvious that no one other than Willie and Marcus wanted to play. He was the ringleader and a towering, solidly built seventeen-year-old. Convicted for selling drugs on east-side street corners, Junior would be released in a matter of months after serving nearly three years. No one would miss him due to the fact he had caused nothing but pain and misery to everyone incarcerated. Junior Grissom ran YA, plain and simple.

Ricky Lowe waited at mid court, palming the ball while Dread headed for the water faucet. Rick was a gangly six-two eighteen-year-old who was his family's "coulda been" pro. All blacks have at least one, be it a son, cousin, or nephew. The boy had game but lacked severely in discipline, respect, and willingness or ability to follow instructions.

On his fifteenth birthday, Rick along with two homeboys attempted to rob a bank. Their plan was ruined before it got off the ground due to stupidity. First, Rick's mug shot was recorded on the bank's surveillance camera. Then secretly, the teller placed a dye pack inside the bag of money so when it exploded, all the cash was ruined. Last but not least, once the rollers gave chase, Rick's partners bailed from the vehicle, leaving him alone. He drove to a secluded street and crouched down in the driver's seat with his foot planted firmly on the brake pad.

The capture was easy because as soon as Five-O hit the block and noticed the brake lights on, his goose was cooked. Captured with the red money, on tape, and in the getaway car, Rick received a sentence of ten years. He would be locked up until age twenty-five, which was the maximum age for juvenile delinquents. His friends wore Halloween masks of dead presidents and were never caught. Rick never snitched, but his dream of a future in the NBA died that day.

"Yaw need one moe playa, Willie," stated Dread. "The game is three man."

Courtney Adams returned to center court and stood next to Rick, drenched with a combination of water and sweat. The eighty-degree Stockton heat forced him to wash down his head and face at the faucet. Just like his teammates, he was shirtless. In hoops this is known as "skins," meaning that your opponents have to wear shirts, resulting in a game of "shirts versus skins."

Built like a weightlifter at five-foot-eight and one hundred and ninety pounds of pure muscle, Courtney had game, as well as a bad attitude and even nastier temper. Nicknamed "Dread" due to his lock hairstyle, he was a fairly decent-looking eighteen-year-old. Caramel-coated brown, Dread had a smooth complexion that accented high cheekbones, budding mustache, and piercing jet-black eyes. Lifelong road dogs with Junior, he was arrested for drug dealing too and also would be released in a matter of months.

"Man, nobody else wants to go down, so we gotta play two-man!" yelled Willie.

"Look fool, dis a three-man game—see what ah'm sayin'? If you can't find nobody else, then step yo monkey ass off the court."

As Dread spoke he snatched the ball from Rick's hand, flinging it directly at Willie, who caught it and just as swiftly flung it back. Willie Glasper was afraid of no one, and coming from the west side of Oaktown, he couldn't stand east-side niggahs, which the Oaktown Three represented. He possessed a similar build to Dread, and since their height was identical, he knew that would be the man he would guard.

Marcus Rivers stepped between the two before violence erupted. The last thing anyone needed was for a fight to occur because the end result would be no more hoops today. Willie and Dread continued to stare each other down, ready to rumble, but Marcus, joined now by Rick, was not about to let that happen. Junior stood on the sidelines watching with an amused look on his face.

Seventeen years old, six-foot-one, skinny, and a pretty boy, Marcus took on the role of negotiator. Also from the west side, he knew their problem was the fact that no one wanted to be responsible for holding Junior. There weren't that many dudes tall enough, and those who were did not have the bulk. Junior was a baby Shaq. Spotting Mario participating in a game of flag football, Marcus spoke to Rick.

"Give us a minute, boss—we'll be back."

"One minute is all you got, homes, then we rollin'," Rick responded.

Marcus grabbed Willie by the arm and headed toward the football field. Dread began shooting at the rim, playing an imaginary game of one on one. Sideline spectators along with Rick and Junior watched as Marcus and Willie pulled Mario to the side, speaking in hushed tones. Once they began walking back toward the court joined by Mario, all other activity ceased.

Junior took it as an insult that Mario had the nerve to agree to play with those west-side clowns, so his body swelled up with anger. He never did like Mario, and once everyone began saying how the young guy reminded them of him, his hatred grew stronger. No one could stop his game, but what Junior failed to realize is that the only reason they played so poorly against him was out of fear.

"Let's rock," Marcus said, stepping onto the court.

Dread rolled the ball to Willie, who assumed his point guard spot at the half-court line. The crowd of onlookers swelled as bets were placed on who would win. Since the inmates only had money on their books that could not be transferred, items such as candy bars, potato chips, and soda were wagered. Willie shot a beeline two-handed pass to Dread with such force that it appeared to have been released from a cannon.

"Check!" he yelled.

Dread flicked the ball back just as strongly then squatted down in a defensive posture. Willie tossed the ball to Marcus and the game was on as Marcus dribbled to the right baseline and fired up a shot, which bounced off the rim into the waiting arms of Junior. He passed it out to Dread near the top of the key then accepted a return pass.

Junior received the ball, threw a head fake on Mario, then went up for a finger roll. What happened next surprised even the most casual observer because Mario soared upwards and blocked Junior's shot into the waiting hands of Willie. The crowd let out a loud "ooh" as Willie calmly sank a basket from the free throw line.

"Check, muthafucka," Willie growled, flinging the ball at Dread. "Yeah, we 'bout ta get in dat ass—see what ah'm sayin'?"

"Check back, bitch." Dread returned the ball like a bullet. "Yaw jus got lucky."

"Luck ain't had shit ta do wit it, see what ah'm sayin'."

Willie passed the ball once again to Marcus on the right base-line, only this time Marcus lofted it over Rick's head to Mario, who faked left on Junior, causing him to leap into the air. Dribbling to his right while his airborne foe came down, Mario skyed toward the rim, slamming the ball home one-handed. The crowd went ballistic as new bets began to take shape. Those betting for the Oaktown

Three either felt that Mario was fearless or a fool, and knowing Junior as they did, thought the latter.

The ones in favor of Willie, Marcus, and Mario felt as though Junior had finally met his match. Everyone knew it was really a contest now, and they were astonished that the young guy had skill. Mario was more than Junior's equal. Junior slammed the ball to the pavement in disgust then bodied up on Mario closer. Now that he realized the young fool had game, he would have to pull out all the stops. This meant the roughhouse play would be instituted with full force.

Marcus inbound the ball to Willie, who dribbled a few times along with talking head to Dread before lobbing a pass to Mario. Junior, anticipating the play perfectly, pulled the back of Mario's shirt, causing him to fall down as the ball fluttered harmlessly out of bounds. Willie and Marcus were pissed but remained tight-lipped, knowing that if they cried foul, they would be accused of being whiners.

Dread put the ball in play from the sideline, passing to Rick who fired a rainbow jumper over Marcus' outstretched arms. The ball hit nothing but net. Taking it to the top of the key, Dread bounced a pass to Junior, who snatched it while simultaneously hooking Mario's shoulder blade. This trick gave him a free lane to the hoop where he dribbled twice before slamming the ball home with authority.

Junior raised both arms to the sky then pounded his chest while Mario got up from what was becoming a familiar place, the ground. The remainder of the game was nip and tuck with neither team leading by more than four points at any given time. Rick and Marcus continued hitting long-range bombs while Mario played Junior on even terms. Willie and Dread spent more time fouling and mouthing off to one another while basically taking on the role of assist men, meaning they did more passing than shooting.

Whoever reached twenty-four first would be declared the winner, and since you had to win by at least four points, it was no surprise that the contest went well past those digits. Each resulting lead change increased the drama, with play becoming more vicious by the second. Tied at thirty-all, Marcus lost the ball and a scramble began. Willie wound up with it and drove uncontested to the hoop for a lay-up.

"Where you at, fool?" he clowned Dread. "You cain't hole me, niggah, shidd."

"You keep talkin' dat shit an ah'mo bust yo ass, niggah, see what ah'm sayin'?"

"Game point," Willie stated, firing the ball at Dread. "Check."

"Play ball, bitch, and cut out all lat jaw jackin'." Dread flung it back.

Anticipation mounted as Willie passed to Marcus, who attempted to blow past Rick to the hole. It seemed like he would succeed when suddenly Rick stuck out a knee as soon as Marcus began elevating. Caught off balance and in an awkward position, Marcus threw the ball toward center court past everyone except Willie, who snared it on the fly. Willie lobbed a pass over Dread's outstretched arm to Mario.

Junior, who by now had been flagrantly fouling Mario all game, used his giant paw of a hand to push Mario's backside further away from the basket. The next sequence of events stunned the entire prison population because Mario passed it to Willie near mid court then clapped his hands twice demanding the rock back, which Willie obliged.

Dribbling a few times while facing Junior, Mario turned his backside to Junior, still pounding the ball on the asphalt. Spotting Marcus streaking toward the goal, Mario whisked a no-look, behind-the-back, one-bounce pass that Marcus retrieved in step, casually laying it in off the glass. Shirts had defeated Skins with the crowd going wild. Willie resumed berating Dread as Junior, feeling humiliated, threw a wicked right hand to Mario's mouth, knocking him down. Before Junior had time to finish his ambush Mario was on his feet throwing several rapid-fire punches at Junior's head, many of which connected.

The prison guards, who had enjoyed the contest too, rushed in immediately to break up those two, but before anyone had time to move, Willie and Dread were engaged in a ferocious battle at center court. Marcus and Rick squared off too, but not really wanting a part of the other man they were happy when the guards interceded, marching them off to solitary cells.

Now Willie and Dread were rolling around the pavement in a wrestling match, seeking to gain advantage. Everyone looking knew that whoever came out on top would be victorious, but staff broke up the rumble before it had time to escalate. Mario, bloody lip and all, had now gained the respect and admiration of the prison population by standing up to the reigning bully.

At dinner that night he received several gifts of milk, rolls, and fruit from his newfound admirers. To the teens incarcerated, the game was like a heavyweight boxing match, and Mario was the new Lennox Lewis.

"Man, ah'mo chrome his dome, soon as ah get the chance!" Junior promised a definite ass-whipping for Mario as he and his boys Rick and Dread watched him accept all the freebies bestowed upon him by fellow prisoners. Of course Junior kept tabs on who was kissing ass, and they would pay too. Their crime: taking the other side. Due to the rumble, all basketball activity was cancelled for Junior, Dread, Rick, Willie, Marcus, and Mario. However, every day the two groups of three would converge on separate sides of the court, watching the action and each other.

Mario now had associates whom he could hang out with and be accepted. Once he settled into the juvenile delinquent routine at the YA, time seemed to move along rapidly. Three months flew by and before he knew it, Junior and Dread were released. Willie and Marcus got to go home one week later, but Mario now had many friends who flocked to him, eventually including Rick. Junior never did get the chance to rumble with Mario again but left the prison vowing revenge.

"See you on the outside, trick," Junior told Mario while walking to the bus that would take him back to his old stomping grounds.

"Whatever's clever," Mario responded just as icily.

Not really worried about Junior's threats of physical violence, Mario felt that since they roamed different turfs in Oaktown, they would probably never see one another again unless Junior returned to jail. Mario himself surely had no intentions of ever coming back.

6

OUTFOXED

Balancing the bag of food in his left hand, Ocie inserted his key into the lock with his right. Pushing the door open with his foot then reaching for the light switch, he felt a strong hand clamp around his wrist. The light went off just as quickly as it came on while Travelle jerked Ocie inside. In one motion he twisted his arm behind his back like a chicken wing, along with clutching his throat in a choke hold. The dinner bag fell to the floor while Ocie struggled to get free. Moon shut the door then hit Ocie upside the head with a gun.

"Break yourself," Moon hissed.

"W-w-what?" Ocie stammered.

Street people know that phrase means "empty your pockets," hand over all your cash, but Ocie, being square, had no clue. Travelle flung him violently to the floor face first, then he and Moon beat Ocie down savagely. Blows rained down on his body from all angles as he attempted to cover up. Satisfied with their handiwork, Moon rifled through Ocie's pockets and lifted out several hundred dollars from his wallet.

"Gimme all yo money, niggah—where it at?"

"That's all I got, I swear to God!"

"You a goddamn lie punk—yo ass been spendin' money like it's hot."

"I'm not lying, man, that's all there is."

"Kill his ass then we'll find it," Travelle stated matter of factly.

Moon, in a fit of rage, kicked Ocie in the face then stomped his kneecap while Travelle retrieved the bag of food off the floor and set it on the table.

"We gone give you one mo chance, fool." Travelle did the talking. "Now tell us where the scrill is 'cause we know you got a stash. Either way it goes, you ain't gone be the one spending it."

Ocie looked up through swollen eyelids terrified. His body shook uncontrollably as his brain tried to figure out what to do. Lumps formed all over his face and head. His body felt as though it had been in a train wreck. Knowing he was a defeated man, Ocie gave up game.

"It's in the bedroom, under the nightstand."

Moon jetted for the bedroom while Travelle opened the bag, helping himself to a piece of yard bird. Taking a squat at the rickety kitchen table, Travelle would watch Ocie as Moon searched for the cash.

Sweetpea saw the lights go on then off and knew the action had begun. Placing the cans and bottles collected inside a grocery bag in case anyone was watching, he swiftly headed for the back stairwell and quietly crept up the steps.

Peering through the broken windowpane he saw Travelle stuffing his mouth with a fork full of collard greens and Ocie balled up in a fetal position on the musty carpet. The third guy was nowhere to be seen, so Sweetpea would wait in the shadows until he revealed his location. His wait took no more than ten seconds when Sweetpea heard loud noises coming from what he knew to be the bedroom. Deftly reaching inside the broken windowpane, Sweetpea opened the door and eased in.

Travelle thought he heard a noise coming from the back door and turned around, only to see a stiletto rotating directly toward him. The knife caught him in the throat, killing him instantly as his face fell with a thud onto the dinner plate. Sweetpea flicked it in the manner of a person tossing a frisbee, and since he could hit a running target from fifty feet away, he knew Travelle was dead the moment greens flew out of his mouth and splattered onto the table.

Moving like a ninja, Sweetpea pulled the weapon from Travelle's throat then tiptoed over to a horrified Ocie. Initially he intended on slitting Ocie's throat from ear to ear, but with Ocie making eye contact he allowed the guy to think for a moment that he had a guardian angel. Calmly placing a finger to his mouth, Sweetpea set the knife on the carpet then lifted Ocie's head up with one hand, grabbed his chin with the other, and twisted, violently snapping his neck like a pretzel.

Picking up the knife from the floor, Sweetpea crept over to a spot just outside the bedroom door. He knew from experience that the element of surprise was an assassin's best friend because the mark didn't have time to think. Therefore, they couldn't react and thus had no chance to develop a defense. Moon continued to ransack the room then yelled out to a very dead Travelle: "Ah got da cash, homes—save me some uh dat grub."

Hearing no response from his usually talkative road dog caused Moon's extrasensory perception to go on full alert. Something was wrong, or so he thought, because Travelle always answered back.

"Velle." He got silence.

"Velle, ah got da scrill."

Silence again.

There was no exit door, and with the window nailed shut Moon was left without an escape route. Desperate and scared, he devised a plan on the spot. Taking one of Ocie's shirts on a hanger he stuffed it with clothing, tied the bottom into a knot, then grabbed a discarded wooden back scratcher off the floor. When he had initially seen the back scratcher he'd thought to himself, "What full-blooded black man would need some shit like this?" Now it came in handy and could possibly save his hide.

With the swiftness of a matador flicking his cape at a charging bull, Moon plunged the stuffed shirt through the door opening. Sweetpea bit on the play, grabbing what normally would be the face then looking dumbfounded at the home-made contraption that produced only a coat hanger. Moon seized the opportunity, diving through the doorway like a safety in a head-on collision with a quarterback for a sack. He tackled Sweetpea as the knife floated through the air, resting near Ocie's corpse.

Before Sweetpea hit the floor he found himself being pummeled by a barrage of punches, courtesy of Moon's fists. Dazed and punch-drunk, Sweetpea's right hand snaked into his coveralls searching for a backup knife that was stashed away inside a pouch on his belt. Gripping the handle tightly, he suddenly felt his left arm pinned down by Moon's knee.

Moon jerked the right arm out from under Sweetpea's clothing with the intention of clamping them both down, which would free up his hands along with leaving Sweetpea at his mercy. That meant a serious beat-down would follow due to Sweetpea being defenseless. The arm came up with Moon seeing the knife, but before he could move, the blade slashed his face from cheekbone to chin. Sweetpea attempted a back-handed slash to the other side of the face but missed because Moon was on his feet and running out the back door to safety with the money in his pocket.

Blood poured from the wound on his face, drenching his shirt, yet Moon fished the car keys from his pocket on the dead run. Hopping into his bucket, he sped away. One thing he knew for sure was that he would not be attending Travelle's funeral because whoever the hit man was, he would surely be there waiting to finish the job.

Sweetpea, still groggy from the ass-whipping he'd just received, returned the blade to its holder then stumbled down the back porch and across the street. To anyone looking, he seemed to be a drunken bum staggering toward his next bottle, which was nothing new to west-side residents. Heading down the block, he took refuge behind a row of rose bushes separating Prescott Elementary School from its lawn and the sidewalk. Pulling out his cell phone along with Tony Russolini's number, he dialed.

"Tony here."

"Mission accomplished," Sweetpea whispered.

"Thank you," Tony responded.

The phone line went dead, and ten seconds later, Sweetpea was out cold.

7
OLD PROS

The double murder scene at Ocie's crib was organized chaos, which was normal for Oaktown. Fire trucks, paramedics, coroner's staff, and the media were all present outside on the street, along with a throng of neighborhood residents. Television crews waited patiently as newscasters stood off to the side rehearsing their lines. Officers cordoned off both front and back entrances with yellow "Do Not Enter" tape while evidence technicians methodically searched for clues.

Inside, more officers huddled in groups, speaking in hushed tones while Nathan Johnson and his partner Manny Hernandez viewed the two dead bodies. To these detectives who had worked as a team for nearly twenty years, it was business as usual. Johnson, a strapping six-foot, six-inch black man with a bulging waistline and shades of gray covering a one-inch afro, had less than four months until retirement. In two weeks he would be reassigned to a desk job, so he knew this probably would be the last murder case of his career.

Hernandez, once a solid two-hundred-pound bundle of muscle, had less than eighteen months until retiring also. With his jet-black shiny hair now solid white and physique robust, he had also requested voluntary reassignment to a desk job. Hernandez just couldn't see himself working with anyone but Johnson, much less breaking in a young whipper-snapper. The seasoned detectives, like most long-time employees, knew the ropes and all tricks of the trade. However, one criminal continually eluded them, which left a bitter taste in their mouths. He was "the Knifeman," as they called him.

"Looks like the Knifeman is up to his old tricks, eh, Nate?" said

Hernandez while gazing at the precision hole in Travelle's neck.

"That dude needs to do like us, Manny, and retire."

"I agree, amigo."

The detectives knew this killer's M.O. without knowing his name, because he always left no clues, cut up his victims with the precision of a surgeon, and escaped without a trace. It would be an understatement to say they were surprised when an evidence tech produced what appeared to be the murder weapon—the knife left near Ocie's dead body. They immediately thought the hit had been carried out by an amateur. Then Johnson saw something that seemed odd.

"Get a look at this," he told his partner.

"Blood." Hernandez stated the obvious.

What they viewed was Moon's blood trail on the floor leading outside, along with two sets of bloody footprints. Following the trail to the sidewalk where it ended, they conversed.

"It isn't the Knifeman," Hernandez said.

"I know," Johnson responded. "He would never make a mistake like that."

"Let's go take another look at the crime scene."

Upon returning to the apartment they saw the stuffed clothes hanger, back scratcher, and ransacked bedroom. Evidence technicians busily bagged and labeled the knife and blood samples from the floor, dusted for fingerprints, snapped photos of the shoe prints, and searched for hair fibers. Every item would be DNA-tested, with the shoe sizes providing an idea of the suspect's height and weight measurements.

"What do you make of it?" Hernandez asked his partner.

"I'm not sure," Johnson responded. "If it is indeed the Knifeman, then I would say he's getting old or careless."

"Well, let's go face the media."

"Then grab a bite to eat."

"You got it."

The detectives marched out the front door to face the eager crowd of waiting reporters. Instantly the nighttime darkness took on a carnival atmosphere and glow as lights focused on the two of them. Johnson stepped out first while Hernandez stood one step back to his right. Microphones were shoved so close to his face that if Johnson had leaned in, one of them would have busted his lip.

"Detective Johnson," one reporter began, "what can you tell us about these murders?"

"Not much. We won't know until all the facts are in and clues have been examined."

"How many were killed?" shot another.

"There are two victims."

"Was it drug-related?" asked yet another.

"I cannot speculate on that."

"Does the trail of blood on the back stairwell and parking lot mean that someone who was injured got away?"

"It's possible, then again, I'm not at liberty to say." Johnson thrust his palm up. "Until all facts are in and the investigation is complete, I will make no further comments or speculate on the crimes committed."

Bulling their way past rapidly firing flashbulbs, Johnson and Hernandez hopped inside a blue Crown Victoria sedan and cruised away to their favorite eatery. The spot was a restaurant located one block from headquarters called Mexicali Rose. While waiting for their meals they dipped tortilla chips into salsa bowls and engaged in light-hearted conversation regarding what was quite likely their last case together.

When dinner arrived all talking ceased as they ate in silence, which was normal for these two.

During the course of the meal Johnson's cell phone began to vibrate. Removing it from the holder attached to his belt clip, he viewed the number on display. It was from Jimmy Chang, an evidence technician in the office, so he answered the call.

"What's shaking, Jimmy?"

"Boss, I got something for you."

"We're on our way."

Hernandez was already fishing a dove from his pocket while wiping his mouth with a napkin. Dropping the twenty on the table, which covered the tab and tip, the detectives bounced. They both knew that for Jimmy to call so soon, it had to be good. Two minutes later Jimmy greeted them as they entered the evidence room. On the force for nearly two decades, Jimmy Chang had acquired a reputation as the most astute and thorough evidence tech in the department.

Now graying slightly at the temples along with wearing dark-rimmed bifocals, Chang smiled and extended a hand as the two detectives marched through the swinging doors. Each man shook his hand, noticing that his flat-top hairdo, which covered a pyramid-shaped dome, had recently been trimmed.

"What's up, Jimmy?" Johnson asked.

"Sorry to disturb you guys' meal," Jimmy laughed. "I know how you like to eat!" He patted his washboard stomach.

"This better be good, my friend," Hernandez said, smiling.

"I think it is. I found a set of car keys at the crime scene that had a rental car tag on them. It really didn't add up, so I drove back over there and, sure enough, the rental—a compact Dodge Neon—was parked on the street. I called to have it towed, and it should be arriving any minute."

"Good work, man—let's go check it out!" Johnson boomed.

The three men headed out of the building and across the street for the tow yard just as a navy-blue Neon was being pulled into the lot.

"Have someone dust it for prints," Johnson ordered.

"OK, boss," Jimmy answered.

"Dust the key, too."

"Prints smudged." Jimmy was one step ahead.

"DNA?"

"I know, hair samples, cigarette butts, soft drink containers—don't worry, boss."

"Don't forget to check with the rental company for a name, address, anything we can use."

"I already did, Sarge. It came back negative. Customer used a fake name and ID."

"Sorry, Jimmy, I forgot who I was talking to."

"No problem, boss, you're just doing your job."

Jimmy let out a hearty laugh as Johnson and Hernandez went back across the street to their office. They knew he would do fabulous work and there was no need to instruct him, but Johnson was a creature of habit. He also knew that, unlike most technicians, Jimmy Chang would not be offended by his instructions. The dude was a pro.

Once inside the homicide office, the detectives sat at their desks typing reports of the murder on their computers. Often checking with each other to make sure their facts of the case were similar, they completed the task then reviewed notes.

"All signs—from the precision cuts on the corpse at the table to the snapped neck of the victim on the floor—point to the Knifeman," Hernandez stated without a doubt.

"I know, Manny, but the sloppiness of the crime scene doesn't back it up."

"Maybe he's getting old."

"It's a possibility, but let's wait for Jimmy's report."

Dropping their own reports into the boss' mail slot, Johnson and Hernandez walked out of the office, heading home. Tomorrow, which was a normal Saturday off day, they would be back to work on an overtime basis with—they hoped—a clue from Jimmy.

RECUPERATION TIME

8

Sweetpea awoke at five in the morning due to all the noise generated by garbage trucks. The sanitation workers hurried about, completing the task at hand. Head still groggy and body wracked with pain, he shed the coveralls and left them hidden behind the bushes before stuffing his phone inside the front pocket of his trousers. With his head pounding as if slugged by a sledgehammer, Sweetpea sat still for a moment, hoping the pain would ease.

Stumbling toward the spot where he left the rental, he was surprised to find it gone. Searching his pockets for the keys proved fruitless as he came up empty-handed. Returning to the bushes, he rifled through the coveralls, still finding no keys. Unknown to Sweetpea, they had flown out of his pocket when he was tackled by Ronnie Moon. He never imagined that Five-O had the keys *and* the car, and instead assumed that youngsters were probably in it joyriding.

Realizing that he had to get away from the area in a hurry, Sweetpea dialed the one person whom he knew he could trust. She answered on the first ring.

"Hello."

"Baby, it's me and I need a favor."

"What is it, dear?" Her voice was hoarse from being awakened at such an early hour.

"I can't locate my keys so I need a ride home."

"Where are you?"

"On the west side, 8th and Campbell. I'll meet you in front of the elementary school."

"Is everything alright?"

"I'm fine, just hurry."

"I'm on my way."

Sweetpea ended the call then wiped the cell phone free of prints. Noticing the garbage men heading in his direction, he hurried across the street and placed the coveralls and phone inside the same dumpster he had pulled cans out of the night before. Hiding in the shadows of one of the apartment complex's buildings, he waited then watched as a garbage man wheeled the dumpster into the street and the truck lifters mechanically emptied its contents. Now he could peacefully wait for his ride, as all evidence was gone.

Harriette Colbert lifted her six-foot frame out of bed and pulled on a white summer dress covered with brown flower designs. She'd worn it the previous day but could care less about the wrinkles it now displayed. Sliding her feet into a pair of brown house slippers, she grabbed her purse and rushed out the door, failing to brush her teeth, comb her hair, or check the mirror to see what she looked like. Her man needed help and that was all that mattered.

Even without makeup she was still highly attractive, with blond locks cascading down to her shoulder blades, aqua-blue eyes, pointy nose, and full lips, which was unusual for a white girl. Her legs resembled turkey drumsticks, complemented by muscular country-girl thighs, wide hips, nicely shaped round behind, and large breasts. Using her remote to activate the garage door, she slowly backed her 2007 Camry down the driveway then sped off.

Hitting the corner of 8th and Campbell, at first Harriette found the block deserted, which caused her to slow down. Scanning the area, she still didn't see him; however, when she glanced sideways Horace was at the passenger door. Harriette had no idea where he came from but her heart skipped a beat when she saw his face. It was obvious he had suffered a terrible beating, so a million questions rushed to her brain.

"What's up, Juicy?" he said while getting inside.

"Honey, what happened to you? How did you get here? Look at you—you look a mess! Are you in trouble?"

"Baby, just drive. I'll fill you in on the details later."

"Juicy" was the nickname Horace had given her years ago, largely because she was always ready, willing, and wet for his dick. It was love at first sight when she met him nearly twenty years earlier while working an entry-level position for the mortgage firm where he was employed. He was ten years her senior and at the time a married man, but she didn't care because there was an aura about him that engulfed her.

The moment he walked into the office and introduced himself, her heart skipped a beat. The thought of hooking up with a negro had never entered Harriette's wildest dreams, yet there was something about her new boss that made her body quiver. When he shook her hand, her vagina poured out fluids, ruining her silk panties. Of course no one knew but her; however, after that she spent many lonely nights masturbating, with her brain imagining it was Horace pleasing her stout frame instead of her fingers.

Horace was just assuming the title of first-line supervisor, and as he rose in the organization, so did Harriette. That meant she was now an executive secretary for Horace, who had become district manager. Over the years and as their relationship grew, Harriette realized there was something secretive about Horace and his unexplained jaunts around the country. Add that to the fact he always chose to live in his own crib while she maintained hers, even though she wanted to live together as a bona fide couple.

Whispers of their relationship eventually turned to shouts around the firm, but Harriette refused to acknowledge them with a response. Forever professional, she carried herself with dignity and grace even while being labeled by haters as a man-stealing slut. She drove home with her man reclining in the passenger seat. To all passersby, it appeared that she was riding alone.

With a million questions running through her mind this morning, she remained silent, knowing he would only talk when he chose to do so. Pulling up into the driveway of her home, Harriette shifted the gear into park and they both got out. Walking through the garage door, which was attached to the kitchen, she tossed her purse onto the counter then turned around to face her man.

"Get naked and I'll run your bath water."

"Don't make it too hot."

Going to the refrigerator, Horace lifted a bottle of water from it, unscrewed the top, and gulped it down. It was both refreshing and seemed to ease the pain in his head. He entered the bathroom to find the tub half full of soapy bubbles, with Harriette busily brushing her teeth. After stripping down he gently placed one foot inside the rapidly rising bath water. Harriette finished brushing then helped him by clutching his underarms while guiding him slowly downward.

After soaping his back she bounced out of the room. Closing his eyes, Horace replayed the previous night's events through his mind. No matter how hard he tried to imagine a different ending, the thought of getting beat down continued to rear its ugly head into the mix. Maybe if he hadn't bit on the hanger play? Or waited for the mark to show his face? The strategy was sound but he never anticipated his foe's crude escape plan. It was the first time in his career he had been outfoxed by the hunted, and now there was no doubt that revenge would be had.

The sweet smell of bacon frying interrupted Horace's thoughts and reminded him just how famished he was. After drying off his body, he entered the bedroom and lifted a black silk house robe with a huge lion on the back from the closet. Putting it on, he went into the kitchen and took a seat in the breakfast nook. Harriette placed their meal, which consisted of swine, eggs, toast, coffee, and orange juice, on the table along with the morning paper. She said a silent prayer blessing her food then spoke.

"There's an article about two people being killed last night on the same corner I picked you up from—"

"And...?"

"You know I never question you about your affairs but I was just curious."

"Curiosity killed the cat." He began eating.

"Honey, quit being evasive. I was just wondering if you knew anything about it or, God forbid, were involved."

"Listen, Juicy, and listen close, because I'll only say this one time. After the police arrived people started cursing them out, which blacks are known to do. Next thing I know fists were flying and with me trying to be a peacemaker, a few knuckleheads in the crowd waited until the police left then turned on me."

"Honey, why would they do that?"

"Stupidity, that's why."

"Well, I know it's none of my business, but what were you down doing there and where is your car?"

"You're right, it is none of your business."

"I'm not hungry."

Harriette pushed her plate to the center of the table then stormed out of the nook. Horace resumed eating along with reading the article about the double homicide of Ocie Rivers and Travelle Spencer. Once done, he dumped her food into the trash can then put their dishes in the sink. Walking gingerly into the family room of her tastefully decorated home, he plopped down on the sofa. She lived on Mandana between Lakeshore and Park Boulevard in Oaktown's Trestle Glen neighborhood, which consisted of homes priced at half a million dollars and up. To say it was her castle would be an understatement, for Harriette's house was her most treasured possession.

A family landmark for nearly five generations, the crib was passed to Harriette, an only child, with nary a word from relatives and extended family. The family room had a beige-colored L-shaped leather sofa with seven or eight fluff pillows scattered about. Against the wall was a fifty-two-inch flat plasma television screen connected to an entertainment center complete with dual DVD/VCR, component set, and floor-to-ceiling compact disc movie rack. The coffee table was white marble, placed on a Persian rug displaying a giant lion underneath, matching magazine rack off to the side of the sofa, fireplace on the center wall, and vertical blinds covering a sliding glass door directly behind that.

Ten minutes later Harriette entered the room freshly bathed and wearing a pink negligee that just barely covered her wide hips. Horace was stretched out on the sofa enjoying a peaceful sleep and did not realize what was going on until he felt familiar sensations in his loins. Slightly lifting his head up he saw Harriette's mouth slurping on his rapidly stiffening pole.

As her tongue began flicking the tip of his penis, Horace made a feeble and half-asleep attempt to lift her up by the shoulders but she was having none of that. Even though oral sex caused her vagina to get soaking wet and crave his thick eight-inch dick stuffing her to the limit, she really enjoyed giving her man a blow job.

"I love having your dick in my mouth," she whispered while sucking.

Feeling his body stiffen, Harriette sped up the assault on his manhood, clamping down with her lips as he let off a powerful load of cream. She began making noises that resembled a pig squealing *oinks* while swallowing every drop. His toes curled and legs started shaking from the wonderful sensations flowing through his body as his woman continued slurping his now-sporadic drops.

Lifting his head once again to see what she was doing caused his dick to regain its hardness because her head lay off to the side gasping for breath. One of the straps on her negligee had fallen off her shoulder, revealing a delicious-looking milk-white breast with its bright pink nipple surrounded by a brown areola jutting out at attention.

Manhood now at full force, he eased her down on the carpet and mounted, slowly inching his way further inside. With each thrust her head snapped back, causing Harriette to grit her teeth and moan out loud. Horace's dick, while being average in length, was fatter than an oversized cucumber and stretched her juicy hole to the max.

She loved the way he fucked her because he always did it slow and in rhythm. The buildup leading to her orgasms would bubble inside until violently erupting like a volcano. After what seemed like hours but in actuality had only been a few minutes, he blasted off another load of cream, which spurred her body into releasing one too. Almost instantly, they both were sleeping like babies.

9

NEW PLAYER IN THE HOUSE

Ronnie Moon wheeled his hoopty to the curb with rims spinning and music blaring loudly from the sound system. Many in the crowd hanging out in front of the store stopped whatever they were doing to admire Moon, who had quickly risen to the level of major player in the lucrative drug trade. Of course, rumor had it that he got his start by offing neighborhood lame Ocie Rivers and stealing his money, but no one dared bring up the subject around Moon.

The fact that he now possessed a long scar on his face, which ran from cheekbone to chin, only caused the whispers to flourish. Moon could care less what people thought as long as they knew he was large and in charge. After momentarily admiring his ride, which was a navy blue '98 Intrepid complete with tinted windows, whistlers attached to the tail pipes, thousand-dollar paint job, and ultra sensitive alarm, he strode over to a few of his boyz.

Once he completed the customary hugs, handshakes, and pats on the back, Moon casually pocketed the fat stacks of cash they turned in. To passing motorists he looked like a walking billboard with a matching t-shirt/cap combination, which displayed the history of the negro baseball league along with team logos and insignias. He also sported a red and black athletic coat covered on both front and back sides by sewn-on patches of Nabisco snack items such as cookies, cakes, chips, and cereal.

True to his nature, the blue denim jeans that Moon wore displayed back pockets sagging down well beyond the bottom hem of his coat, along with brand-new three-hundred-dollar tennis shoes. With several gold ropes dangling from his neck, expensive diamond rings on his fingers, Rolex watch on his wrist, and studs in both ear lobes, the dude was draped, to say the least. The eye-catcher of his entire getup, however, was when he spoke because one was blinded by gold covering his grill.

Although he looked like a fool on Halloween, to the idiots on the corner of 8th and Adeline Ronnie Moon was fly. Taking a seat in one of the few rickety chairs that were usually occupied by OGs, a slang phrase for "original gangsters," Moon spotted a couple of familiar faces across the street.

"Save my seat," he spoke to no one in particular.

He knew nobody would dare sit on his throne until he left the scene entirely, so the request was basically to inform everyone that he was not leaving. Strolling across the Avenue with little regard for traffic, Moon pulled out a cell phone and placed a call. Deep in conversation by time he reached the other side, he ended the call then approached a crowd of young teenagers, ignoring all but the two he had eyed moments earlier.

The teenyboppers who had up to now been enjoying themselves on their corner in front of the Acorn housing complex became silent. They hoped he wasn't coming their way to clown because Ronnie Moon had a reputation for violence. Watching intently, everyone let out a sigh of relief once he spoke.

"Ah see dey let you two fools loose, huh?" he said, grinning.

"Fa sheezie," responded Willie.

"Shoulda tole me, boy, an ah woulda gave yaw a party."

Moon grabbed Willie in a bear hug as both men grinned broadly. The crowd of youngsters all smiled along with them, happy that no one would get beat down. Next, Moon hugged Marcus just as forcefully then resumed his rap while sizing up their now-muscular physiques.

"Man, look at you niggahs, done got big as me!"

"Well, cousin, what can I say? You know how it is wit clean livin' plus all the meat an potatoes you can handle."

"How long you been out?"

"A couple uh days."

"Need work?"

"Hell yeah, cuz—dey tole us you da man now."

Ronnie Moon and Willie Glasper were maternal first cousins due to their mothers being sisters. Although three years apart in age, they had always been close, not to mention career criminals seeking the easy way to get ahead. The relationship and bond they had developed while growing up was more like brothers than cousins, in large part because they were raised up in the same housing complex.

"Well, ah ain't the man yet, but ah am workin' mah way up."

"Man, tell dat to a fool who don't know—look at you, boy! Got a propah ride, fitted to a tee, and I know, a phat bank."

"Fa sho, cousin, let's take a ride."

The three felons headed across the street, hopped into Moon's hoopty, and pulled away. As Moon drove his hand subconsciously rubbed the long scar on his face. It was a habit he'd developed but was unaware of. Willie had noticed and, until now, didn't want to bring up the subject although he had heard the rumors of how it came about.

"What up wit da scar, cuz?"

"Man, dis niggah tried ta cut me up one night; ah kicked his ass, dough."

"Oh yeah?"

"Damn skippy."

"Now if you wasn't mah cousin. . . ."

"If ah wasn't yo cousin what?" Moon snapped.

"Ah heard you got dat shit robbin' Ocie—they say that's how 'Velle got kilt."

"Man, you of all people should know not to believe everythang you hear."

"Ronnie, where you takin' us? We was just 'bout ta get some pussy, niggah."

"Muthafucka, aftah ah'm done wit yo ass, you gone be turning pussy away."

"Oh yeah?"

"Hell yeah, niggah, ah'm 'bout ta hook you fools up propah."

Moon shot down the on ramp of the 980 interchange, merging with traffic on 580, better known as the MacArthur Freeway. Heading east, he exited at Fruitvale and made a left, rolling through the heart of the Dimond District, which consisted of stores, eateries, banks, and assorted businesses. Hooking another left at MacArthur then a right at the next corner, he pulled into a covered parking lot at the end of the dead-end street.

"So dis where you live at, huh?" asked Willie.

"Yeah, dis da crib, dawg."

The Poolside Apartments, located near a walk-in entrance to Dimond Park, were painted white with brown trim. Moon had lived there only three months yet managed to create several enemies during that time, a result of constant blasting of rap music, loud verbal arguments with his women friends, and a non-stop flow of traffic coming to and from the door. Exiting the car with his road dogs trailing behind, Moon bounced up the stairs and unlocked the door to his crib.

Surprisingly, the unit was spacious and roomy with a nice view of the neighboring park's swimming pool, picnic area, and hoop courts. The elegance ended there because the apartment was so sparsely furnished, anyone entering would assume it to be vacant. Announcing their presence in case his lady was naked, Moon yelled out, "Baby, I got company!" Getting no response, he went into the bedroom. Upon returning he handed both Willie and Marcus giant ziplock bags containing several smaller baggies of base rock ready for sale.

"Bitch always in da street—ah'm thankin' 'bout firin' her ass."

"Like dat, playa?" smiled Willie. "Tole you who da man was, niggah." He grinned at Marcus.

"Naw, it ain't even like dat," he snarled. "Ah told da hoe ta clean dis muthafucka up 'fo she left. Look at dis shit." He waved his arms in magic-wand fashion toward the kitchen before going in there.

Willie and Marcus took note of the crib while copping squats at an old wooden table with folded sides hanging down and four scarred-up chairs surrounding it. The living room was virtually bare, with just a thirteen-inch color television sitting on an additional chair, hooked up to a video game player on the floor. A mattress and box spring rested on top of a rusted frame in the bedroom, which reeked of smelly socks. There was also a badly worn nightstand/dresser combo to house his drugs and clothes.

Although white vertical blinds had been installed to cover the window facing the park, old blue navy blankets full of lint balls served as drapes throughout the rest of Moon's crib. Moon retrieved three beers from the refrigerator and served them to Willie and Marcus at the kitchen table. Marcus grimaced at the sight of Moon's filthy kitchen, which displayed several empty food containers along with beer cans on all counter tops.

Trash was positioned like a pyramid being built from the garbage can, rising up along the wall. It looked as though the next item placed on top would result in everything tumbling over. Moon set his own beer on the table and headed back to the bedroom, returning with a small bag of weed, shoe box top, scissors, and rolling papers. After deftly chopping up a few buds he rolled three joints, fired one up, inhaled deeply, then grunted that familiar stifled sneeze sound that potheads know so well.

"Dis some good shit, dawg," he said before passing the joint to his cousin. "Now, dis how it work—yaw got fifty bags each dat you sell fo twenty a pop. Do it right an you make a gee. Ah 'spect yaw should be ready ta re-cop tamarraw, no later dan Friday."

"What we get?" asked Willie as he began choking on the reefer.

"Brang me back seven-fifty an da other two-fifty is yours; den we do da same thang again."

"Check dis, Moon," Marcus said while accepting the dope from Willie. "Why cain't we just spin two-fiddy wit you an get our own shit?"

Willie glanced at his boy Marcus with pride because even though the same question swirled around in his brain, he never would have asked it. Moon was just as direct with a response.

"'Cause ah'm frontin yaw asses. Now, since you be family an all, ah'll let you do dat, but remembah, if you lose yo scrill in a dice game or let dem hoes have credit an come back shoat, all bets is off. See, wit me as yo sponsor, all you gone do is get paid. Once ah know you ready, den we can do dat shit."

Moon's cell phone began vibrating so he lifted it from his belt clip and answered the call. Speaking in hushed tones, he rose up from his chair swiftly, heading for the bedroom. To both Willie and Marcus' surprise, he closed the door behind himself.

"What you wanna do, dawg?" Marcus asked Willie.

"Ah cain't call it, dude. If we re-cop wit da profit from somebody else an fuck off da money gamblin' or wit dem bitches, Cuz ain't gone deal wit us no mo. But if we keep workin' fa him, we keep gettin' paid no matter what, feel me?"

"Fa sho."

"So we'll just play it by ear an hustle wit Ronnie til sumptun bettah come up."

"I'm in."

Willie and Marcus remained seated at the table, smoking weed and guzzling down beer. Each boy was deep in thought about the offer of instant money from Moon, along with the respect and admiration they'd receive on their turf. It was only a matter of time before they would be living large. Moon stormed from the bedroom, obviously upset.

"Let's bounce," he snapped.

"Everythang alright, Cuz?" asked Willie.

"Ain't shit ah cain't handle."

The three felons rolled back to the west side with Moon quiet the entire way. Marcus and Willie counted their dope while developing plans on how they would distribute it. Letting them out on the same corner where forty-five minutes earlier he had picked them up, Moon drove off with the pedal to the metal. Instantly, Willie spotted a crackhead named Jonezy heading for the crowd at the store. Deftly intercepting him, he sold Jonezy three twenty-dollar packs of base rock.

For the next several hours he and Marcus made sales to neighborhood fiends as they passed the Acorn. When the dealers posted across the street in front of the store realized what was happening, a call was made to their supplier, Moon. He informed them that the two youngsters were on his payroll and had the same rights as everyone else to make money. He also reminded them that since everybody knew Willie and Marcus were family, no violence should come their way.

Suddenly what had been a smooth corner operation turned into total chaos, with dealers catching buyers half a block away, creating their own spots to grind. Cars pulling up were bum-rushed by three or more hustlers thrusting packages in their face, practically demanding that they purchase. Just like any business in competition with others selling the same thing, a price war resulted where deals were made for every sale. There was now more supply than demand, and with prices dropping rapidly, the fiends benefited most by getting more dope for their money.

10

ROUSING SEND-OFF

The concert hall at the Marriott Hotel overflowed with people decked out in their finest attire. It was a black-tie affair with men sporting tuxedos and women elegantly dressed in evening gowns. Unlike most events at the venue that occurred in smaller banquet rooms, the size of the crowd dictated the more cavernous main hall.

Outside the building on the street, police officers in squad cars and on motorcycles directed traffic and sent motorists detouring away from both 10th and 11th Streets. Cops were everywhere in their finest "Grade A" uniforms complete with white gloves, shiny shoes, and neatly pressed outfits. Passersby knew something big was going on at the hotel.

Inside, every available chair and table was rolled in from throughout the premises, with choice seating at a premium. To the casual observer, it had to mean that an important dignitary or VIP such as the governor was in town. In actuality, the guest of honor was none other than Sergeant Nathan Johnson, who was retiring from the police force. The turnout surprised even Johnson, who had no idea that so many people respected him.

With more than a thousand well-wishers in attendance, the lobby and concert hall bulged at the seams. Many guests were drinking cocktails from one of the five bars strategically placed around the room. One hundred circular tables covered with white cloths were neatly decorated, displaying eating utensils, napkins, wine and water glasses, plus floral arrangements strategically placed in the center. Giant placards with bold numbers identified each table.

A normal setup consisted of eight chairs per table, but for this event hotel staff had managed to squeeze ten seats around each. There was a rhythm and blues band quietly tuning their instruments center stage, while a disc jockey set up to the left side played slow jazz that reverberated throughout the room. As the soft music provided a nice atmosphere, the DJ listened intently through headphones to future songs he would play.

The main tables sat connected atop a makeshift platform in front of the stage, with twenty chairs stretching the length of the head table. Johnson, his wife Gladys, and three adult children were seated front and center, with the smile on the detective's face capable of illuminating the room without electricity. To Johnson's immediate right sat his long-time partner Manny Hernandez with his wife Heather. The remaining chairs were occupied by the chief of police, mayor, city manager, and high-ranking sworn staff, along with neighborhood bigwigs and prominent church ministers.

Directly in front of the head table was the dance floor, empty now but sure to be packed by evening's end. Edgar Lewis, emcee for the affair and Johnson's current supervisor, stood at the microphone decked out in a black tux with tails, red cummerbund and matching tie, black shoes, and top hat, clutching a program in hand.

Lewis had been more than honored by receiving the request to emcee Johnson's retirement party since he considered the man a father figure. He was ecstatic, not only because Johnson served as his training officer along with showing him the ropes as a rookie, but because the man never said a begrudging word when Lewis got the job he knew his "boss" coveted. Gently tapping the microphone to make sure it was on, then nodding at the DJ to lower the music, Lewis addressed the crowd.

"Ladies and gentlemen, could I get everyone to please take their seats. The program is about to start."

The crowd didn't seem to hear so Lewis spoke louder and more forcefully than the first time. "May I have your attention, *please*. Everyone take their seats so the program can begin. We have a long night ahead, people, so let's get the ball rolling."

Still with no cooperation from the crowd, Lewis walked over to the building engineer and instructed him to dim the lights. Returning to the microphone Lewis waited as the room went dark with a bright spotlight focused on his slender six-foot two-inch frame. Now he could initiate the proceedings because the sudden darkness caught everyone's attention.

"Could you all please be seated so we can start," he requested then waited patiently as the crowd followed instructions with people noisily claiming their spots. Once everyone was finally seated, Lewis addressed the audience in earnest.

"Good evening," he said to a now-silent room, then added: "Now, I was always told by my mother that when someone addresses you, proper etiquette calls for a response, so let's try it again—good evening."

"Good evening," the crowd responded.

"For those who don't know, my name is Edgar Lewis and I'd like to thank you all for coming to what will be a great send-off for an even greater man." Thunderous clapping greeted his opening remarks so he continued, "We have created a souvenir program that we intend to follow, but first I'd like to tell you a little story about the man of honor. I met Sarge on my first day out of the academy and needless to say. . . ."

As Lewis told the story of his and Johnson's relationship, wait staff served mixed green salad appetizers. By the time he was done, what had been a festive atmosphere was raised several levels, for not only was Lewis' story funny, it was obvious to all that he possessed a fine sense of humor. One by one dignitaries approached the microphone and displayed their wit, toasting and roasting the guest of honor. What was to be a retirement celebration quickly turned into an uproarious roast, with Johnson laughing louder than anyone else.

Last on the program of speakers was Johnson's long-time crony Manny Hernandez. Rising up from his chair on the platform, Hernandez shook hands vigorously with his now ex-partner, covered his plate with a napkin, then ambled down to the podium. Johnson sat watching with pride because he knew this one would be good. Over the years he and Manny had seen and done everything, so he prayed that his boy wouldn't reveal too many skeleton bones hidden in his closet.

"First I'd like to say that the Nathan you guys have been hearing about is someone I don't know," began Manny. "The man I served the last twenty years with was stubborn, mule-headed, and always wanted his way." The crowd roared. "I remember a classic case we investigated which will give you an example of what I mean. . . ." Pausing for emphasis, Manny then resumed: "It was a cold chilly night in November of two thousand and four, and the case involved a double homicide resulting from Sydeshow activities. . . ."

Manny continued to tell the story of Johnson being convinced that a potential witness knew more than he was letting on. The tale had many humorous parts along with several punch lines, with Manny seeming to know exactly how to deliver. "Now, as Nathan gave the guy his familiar stare-down, I played good cop but it didn't work, because the guy was so scared of my partner that he urinated on himself right then and there."

Johnson sat reveling in the moment as his partner related one of the funnier episodes of their times together. When Manny concluded his speech everyone in the house rose to their feet for a standing ovation in honor of Nathan Johnson. Tears streamed from the detective's eyes but they were tears of joy, not sorrow. God knows there were too many times where cases were not solved due to an eyewitness refusing to cooperate.

The final speaker listed on the program was none other than Johnson himself. Slowly heading for the dais he was bear-hugged by Hernandez then waited off to the side while Lewis grabbed the mic. Johnson knew Lewis would give him a rousing introduction, so he pulled out his prepared speech to re-read it for the umpteenth time. He secretly said a prayer asking the Lord to walk him through it, for this was not the time to break down.

"Folks, we have a surprise," Lewis crooned. "Unknown to Sarge, we invited a special guest because we felt no one should be left out of this joyous occasion." Looking directly at Johnson, Lewis continued, "I'd like you all to join me in giving a warm welcome to Lieutenant Norman Johnson from the Tampa police force. He's the detective's brother who made the trip here from Florida, and they haven't seen each other in years."

The crowd went wild but Johnson's entire body stiffened as his brother Norman walked out a side door and headed to the stage. They, like many siblings, had not spoken to each other due to a rift that developed when their father passed away. Of course it was created by the division of property and cash. Norman's six-foot, five-inch, three-hundred-and-twenty-five-pound frame towered over Lewis, who was tall himself. Just like his older brother, he was huge. Nathan watched now with anxiety and apprehension, for he had no idea what his brother would say.

Norman stood waiting for the applause to cease with a stoic expression on his face. It was obvious to all that they were siblings due to similar massive builds and cocoa-brown complexions. One noticeable difference was that Norman had a large afro with thick sideburns and a full bushy mustache. Failing to look at his brother, who was on pins and needles, he spoke, not surprising anyone by his deep baritone voice.

"First, I'd like to thank Manny for inviting me and also to tell you all why I chose to come. It's true Nathan and I have not spoken in two decades for reasons I choose not to divulge. As I contemplated the invitation my mind drifted into why I had distanced myself from not only Nate, but also my sister-in-law and nephews.

Every reason I gave myself not to show up was cancelled by the fact that I miss my brother dearly. We have put more years behind us than we have ahead, and now I've realized that material possessions aren't that important." Turning to face Nathan he continued, "Brother, I apologize for acting like a juvenile. Judging from the size of this crowd, it's obvious many people adore you. If you will agree, I ask that you accept me back into your life so we can make up for all the lost years."

Tears flowed freely down both men's cheeks as the audience sat transfixed, caught up in the moment. It was magical. Women and men dabbed their eyes with tissue, napkins, and handkerchiefs. Some cried openly once the brothers embraced. They held each other tightly while both of their bodies shook from uncontrollable sobs. Lewis, sensing the emotion, nodded for the DJ to play a song.

"Everybody, the dancing will now begin as Sarge does some catching up with his brother. We'll have him speak later." Lewis wiped his own eyes then grabbed a partner to boogie on the dance floor.

Johnson's family joined the two long-lost brothers as hugs were given freely. Nathan and Norman took seats off to the rear of the stage and engaged in deep conversation, with each man apologizing profusely to the other. All was well now and they vowed to spend as much time together as possible. This was surely a night Nathan Johnson would never forget, for it reunited him with his little brother. Of course he would be forever grateful to Manny for pulling it off.

Two hours flew by with the siblings still conversing when Derrick Boston and Maria Jimenez approached. They had taken over the few open cases still remaining on Johnson and Hernandez's ledger. Looking more like a couple than Five-O partners, Boston spoke for the both of them.

"Sergeant, we hate to cut a wonderful evening short but duty calls."

"Have you met my brother?" Johnson asked with pride.

"Nice to make your acquaintance, sir. I'm Derrick."

"And I'm Maria."

"Norman Johnson." He shook hands with each one.

"What's the deal?" Nathan asked as if still on duty.

"Got a call about a double homicide in the Dimond District," said Derrick. "All signs indicate that your Knifeman may be up to his old tricks."

"Go do your job, Derrick—that guy has given me fits for years. Nab him for me."

"You got it. Norman, it was our pleasure, so glad you could come."

"Thank you," Norman responded.

Boston and Jimenez strutted to the exit as Nathan began filling Norman in on the Knifeman. As well-wishers came and went, Nathan couldn't help but think that this night reminded him of old times, with him and Norman discussing crime-fighting. By the time he did eventually speak, it was anti-climactic because the unexpected reunion with his brother had stolen the show.

11
UNFINISHED BUSINESS

"Preach, where you been, man?" said Butter.

"Man, ah must be gettin' old," answered Sweetpea. "You know da day ah went ta take a crap?"

"Yeah, ah 'membah dat."

"Well, fo ah could do mah do, Five-O rolls up an arrests me fo stealing da cash an dope off dat homeboy ah tole you 'bout. Fool claimed he ain't knowed nuttin' 'bout no dope."

"No shit!" exclaimed Butter through yellow teeth.

"No shit, dawg, dey had a dude in the car an he identified mah ass own da spot. Of course ah tried ta play it off lack ah ain't did shit, but dat didn't work an dey hauled mah ass off ta jail. Man said ah spent da money on drugs; fool lied an said he had three hundred."

"Blood, ah tried ta keep deese fiends from takin' yo shit but aftah 'bout an hour, ah couldn't hole um off," Butter lied.

"Man, ah ain't trippin' off no cans and bottles, shidd, ah was just glad dey only gave me thirty days in North County, not da three strikes mah black ass shoulda got."

It had been exactly one month since Sweetpea used his Preach routine on Butter and his band of homeless humans. While he and Butter engaged in loud talk, the pack of down-and-outers gathered around listening intently. Once the man they knew as Preach pulled out several joints of weed plus two twenty-dollar bills and handed them over to Butter for rent, he was accepted back in the fold.

Of course his only concern was to watch the corner and wait for his mark to make an appearance. The next four hours were spent with Preach spinning fantastic tales of hoes, game, hustlin', cons, and the good life with his new-found admirers. When Ronnie

Moon finally arrived on the opposite side of the street and Sweetpea laid eyes on him, he knew that was the dude who'd savagely beat him down, nearly killing him. Ronnie Moon hopped out of his Intrepid resembling a walking billboard as Sweetpea excused himself from Butter and the gang to go pee.

"Yaw 'scuse me fo a minute while ah go to da labratory," Sweetpea stated eloquently as his audience erupted in laughter.

Instead of urinating, he stood off to the side of the building studying Moon. Instantly he recognized the slash he'd put on Moon's face, but the telltale sign was Moon's physique. Sweetpea could never forget the powerful build his assailant possessed because of the devastating blows his face had absorbed. When Moon began punching the lights out on a guy standing near the store, Sweetpea felt every blow as if they were directed his way.

The viciousness of Moon's attack left no doubt that he was the same dude. This hit would be Sweetpea's last and serve as an early retirement party from a life of murder and mayhem. Unknown to him or his intended victim was the fact that an all-points bulletin had been initiated for Moon's arrest due to the results of his DNA sample lifted from blood on Ocie's apartment floor.

After peeping out the scene for a few days whereby he would hang out with the bums during the day with an excuse that he had a bed in a homeless shelter at night, Sweetpea began trailing Moon. A few weeks later Sweetpea was sure he had the hoodlum's routine down pat. He'd gotten a line on Ronnie from one of his many informants after placing a thousand-dollar bounty on a guy he described to his connections as having a fresh scar on his face and possibly selling dope. Within days information came pouring in from everywhere with all trails leading to Ronnie Moon, who had recently moved to the eastern side of town yet suddenly taken on the role of major player on the west end.

It was a cold December morning when Sweetpea decided this would be the day. The weather would serve as his accomplice, along with the element of surprise. His game plan was fairly simple: wait in the shadows until Moon took off on his daily rounds, then kidnap his woman. Sitting in a navy blue minivan parked on the corner of MacArthur across from Nation's Hamburgers, Sweetpea knew Moon never left the crib before noon. Today he would settle the score with the scar-faced bandit once and for all. Camping out down the block from Moon's apartment, Sweetpea watched as he left to make the first of his normal drop-offs.

Dapperly dressed in beige slacks with matching shoes, socks, and shirt, Sweetpea's outfit was accessorized by a blue blazer, paisley tie, and navy blue fedora. Horn-rimmed spectacles and black walking cane provided the distinguished gentlemanly first impression he hoped to give off. In his left hand was a folder containing assorted official-looking documents. His game would be that of a door-to-door salesman.

The two months he had trailed Moon resulted in Sweetpea knowing that he changed women like a player changes cologne brands. Most of his honeys usually lasted a week, but the new love of his life had been hanging around for nearly a month now. Sweetpea felt as though Moon had been "caught up" in the love game, which was the parley card the assassin needed. If the scheme didn't work, then he'd have no alternative but to revert to plan B, meaning a flat-out violent assault. Since that was not his style, Sweetpea hoped his deduction of Moon being struck by the love bug was correct. Driving to the Poolside Apartment complex, he parked in a visitor stall then got out, gingerly walking up the stairs.

Dashaunda Bryant heard a knock at the door, and thinking it was Ronnie—who always seemed to forget his keys, dope, or cash—opened it without checking the peephole. Upon finding a well-dressed elderly man standing there, she addressed him.

"Can I help you?"

"Yes, my name is Leonard Daniels and I was wondering. . . . Oh, excuse my manners. How are you, ma'am?"

"I'm fine, what do you want?"

Dashaunda stood posing with hands on hips, agitated by the interruption. A ghetto girl, "Shaunnie" was a beautiful five-feet, seven-inch dynamo. Her stomach was washboard-flat, accented by a nice round behind and hips for days. She possessed country-girl features with thick legs and thighs, strong cheekbones protruding from her oval face, pearl-white teeth, and braided singles covering her dome. Normally, her cocoa-butter complexion complemented by thick lips warmed the coldest of rooms when she smiled, which was often.

However, today she was having none of that. Shaunnie was sick and tired of the daily interruptions by Witnesses, newspaper sales reps, and kids selling candy. Sweetpea couldn't help but notice her physique from the short mini skirt she wore and thought about fucking her before doing his damage. Remembering the beat-down he'd suffered, and noting the girl's disposition, brought his hormones back under control.

"I wondered if you ever heard of pre-paid legal service?"

"Yeah, I heard of it but you know what, I ain't interested."

"Tell me, do you own a last will and testament?"

"No and don't need one."

"Life insurance?"

"Look, man, I ain't interested."

Shaunnie slammed the door in his face then turned to resume cleaning up, unaware that Sweetpea's foot blocking it was too fast. He stepped inside, slamming it behind him along with dropping the props on the carpet. Like a cat he pounced on his victim, grabbing her in a carotid chokehold. She attempted to scream but no sound emanated from her vocal cords. In a panic, she tried back-kicking him in the nuts, which proved unsuccessful because his legs were pressed together.

Slowly he lifted her off the carpet, applying more pressure as her body went limp. Laying her gently down on her back, he conducted cardio-pulmonary resuscitation (commonly known as CPR). Squeezing her nostrils closed, he blew air into her mouth then clamped one hand over the other, interlocking the fingers. Mashing down with violent pumps on her chest, Sweetpea pulled his switchblade from the inner pocket of his sport coat and watched as she began coughing up a storm.

"Now you'll do as I say, or you die," he spoke softly through clenched teeth. "You do understand?"

"Y-Y-Yes." She coughed some more.

Satisfied with her attention span, Sweetpea helped her off the floor, clamping one of her arms to her side with his left hand. The knife he held in his right arm rested lightly on her throat.

"What do you want?" she cried.

"You to help me get that scar-faced motherfucker you call your man."

"I can't, he'll kill me!"

"You don't have a choice," he warned, "'cause I'll kill you right now if you refuse."

"Okay," she whispered.

"Let me show you something." Sweetpea sat Shaunnie down at the kitchen table. "See that cable wire connected to the television?"

"Yes," she answered, still gasping for breath.

With a quick flick of his wrist the knife rotated in mid air, striking the cord dead in the center. Shaunnie nearly choked seeing the blade pin the cord on the wall. It happened so fast and with such accuracy that she now knew she was in the presence of a killer. Pulling the blade free while keeping an eye on her, Sweetpea placed it flat on the side of his face, boring into her eyeballs with his own.

"This is what we're going to do. You'll walk out with me as if we are close acquaintances. One false move and your life is over, understand?"

"Y-Y-Yes, I understand."

With that, he clutched an arm and led her to the bedroom where she retrieved her purse and cell phone. Pulling the door closed behind them, Sweetpea gripped her waist possessively with his left arm while hiding the knife in his right hand. To the casual observer it appeared as if she were sharing a loving embrace with her father.

Sweetpea deactivated the alarm on the minivan using his remote control then escorted Shaunnie to the passenger door. "Put your hands behind the seat," he ordered. Opening the sliding passenger door, he secured her wrists together with some handcuffs that were lying on the floor. Casually walking to the opposite side, he slid into the driver's seat and started the ignition.

As he rolled away Shaunnie tried desperately to free her arms by raising them up backwards over the headrest. Her body was not flexible enough to succeed in this maneuver, yet with her head down to her knees she managed to develop an on-the-spot ab routine. Sweetpea smiled at her failed attempts as he continued to drive on. At the corner he made a right turn and while doing so spotted Moon heading home with two occupants in his Intrepid.

This sudden turn of events was not part of the script, catching Sweetpea totally off guard. Shaunnie was too busy wiggling in her seat to notice her man drive past. Hitting another right at the next light in front of the Southern Café soul food restaurant, he cruised down a narrow winding road, parking just before the basketball courts on the far side of Dimond Park.

"You put that scar on his face, didn't you?" Shaunnie shouted.

"I could take credit for that." He reached inside her purse, retrieving the phone.

"You're dead, motherfucker. I hate you!"

"Now now, Lady, what's his number?" He was calm.

"I ain't tellin' you shit!"

Like a rod out of a cannon, Sweetpea slapped her several times across the cheeks, turning them crimson. Startled by the onslaught, Shaunnie broke out in tears, with large droplets pouring down her face. The second time he asked for Moon's number she willingly obliged. After the second ring he answered.

"Yeah, who dat?"

"Ronnie Moon?"

"Who wanna know?"

"Wait a minute." Sweetpea placed the phone's receiver to Shuannie's mouth.

"Ronnie, don't do nothin' he say, he gone try to kill you!" she blurted.

"Now, Ronnie"—Sweetpea was casual—"dump the two goons then hightail it back to the house for further instructions. If you're as smart as I think you are, you won't call Five-O."

"Who in the hell is this?" he growled. "Ah'mo peel yo cap, mutha. . . ." The line went dead.

Sweetpea reached over Shaunnie's seat and lifted the recline button, which caused her body to drop out of view from passing motorists. Once she began kicking her legs in his direction he shot a wicked elbow to her uplifted hamstring, causing excruciating pain. Shaunnie next felt a gloved hand cover her mouth with the index and thumb fingers clamping down on her nostrils. Try as she might, the girl was helpless to counter. Within minutes her body went limp. She was dead.

Initially, Sweetpea had decided not to kill her but with her nasty attitude plus smart mouth, the girl just rubbed him the wrong way. Now he was faced with a new dilemma that left three options to ponder. One would be to dump her body in the bushes directly in front of the van and guardrail, which could be risky in broad daylight. Two, abandon the van and dead body there, leaving no getaway vehicle. Or three, drive back around the corner to Moon's crib and wait for him inside to complete his mission. He chose the latter.

12

PAYBACK

Moon pulled away from the curb peeling rubber. Marcus and Willie barely had time to let their feet hit the ground. They had no idea why he was so upset, but instead of worrying about his problems, their minds were on what they hoped to be lucrative drug careers.

As he streaked onto the 980 interchange, Ronnie replayed the phone call over and over in his brain.

He knew instantly who the perpetrator was because although he had many enemies, only one would be bold enough to carry out a dastardly scheme like kidnapping his woman. The image of Travelle's face lying in a plate full of soul food reinforced his belief that the old guy who'd cut him was the one responsible for this mess.

Well, he thought, since the fool wants war, then war it is. Hitting his block like a bat out of hell, Moon crookedly parked in his assigned stall and bounced up the steps on the dead run.

"Shoulda killed his ass lass time," he told himself.

Fumbling with his key he finally inserted it into the lock and entered his unit cautiously. "Shaunnie!" he yelled, receiving no answer. Moon looked around. The apartment appeared to be in the same pitiful shape as he remembered. For the umpteenth time he dialed his woman's cell phone and got her answering machine. Slamming the phone down in a fit of rage, Moon stormed into the bedroom to get his gun. When he opened the nightstand drawer where he kept his weapon, he found it missing.

"Damn!" he shouted out loud before another thought crossed his mind. Rushing over to the dresser drawer that housed his stash of dope, he found that gone too. Now irate, Moon jerked open every drawer in front of him, cursing out loud all the while. Heading to the closet, he snatched the sliding door open so hard it nearly came off track. Instantly his eyes grew wide as silver dollars as a lump formed in his throat.

Moon made a feeble effort to close the closet but Sweetpea was too swift. Plus, he had the element of surprise in his favor. The knife plunged into Moon's chest at the exact moment he broke for the door. That quick move temporarily saved his life, allowing him an escape route. Sweetpea stepped from the closet clutching the now-bloody weapon. His latex-gloved hand held the tip of the blade firmly, ready to fling it the moment he entered the hallway.

The next sequence of events could only be described as *déjà vu* because the second Sweetpea stepped out ready to fire, Moon, who had stopped in his tracks just outside the door, threw a violent forearm shot to the assassin's throat, knocking him down. This time, however, Sweetpea did not drop his knife. Moon noticed and ran into the kitchen for a blade of his own.

Normally, with blood pouring from his chest and ruining his clothes, Moon (or anybody, for that matter) would have been sapped of all their energy. However, the adrenaline rush going through his body caused Ronnie to gain an added boost of vitality that not even he knew he possessed. He ripped the knife drawer open so savagely that all its contents dropped to the tiled kitchen floor, leaving him holding the box. Spotting a giant meat cleaver, he scooped it up then turned to face his assailant.

What he saw instead was Sweetpea's body in the familiar position of a baseball pitcher who had just released a fastball and the knife rotating rapidly in his direction. Moon's natural reflex mechanism instructed his body to duck, but there was no time. The knife struck him square on the forehead, boring through until part of it could be seen sticking out the back of his dome. He died instantly while his body plopped to the floor with a sickening thud like a ten-pound sack of potatoes.

Sweetpea, who now held a second weapon in the strike position, just in case the first didn't finish the job, quickly put it away while gliding over to Moon's dead body. Kicking some of the scattered pieces of silverware to the side and clearing a path, he knelt down above the prone figure and removed the blade from his forehead with the precision of a surgeon. Lifting a dirty rag off a pile of dried-up plates in the sink, he wiped Moon's blood from the blade before snapping it shut and putting it away.

Still feeling the pain inflicted from Moon's violent forearm blow, Sweetpea rubbed his jaw while heading for the bedroom mirror. Double-checking to make sure he would be presentable outside the apartment, he straightened up his clothes then marched out the door. After closing it he removed the latex gloves, folding them like tube socks while walking gingerly down the stairs.

Once at the minivan, which was parked under the carport, he scanned the area to be certain no one was looking before pulling Shaunnie's body out of the vehicle. There was a car parked right next to him, so Sweetpea laid her body between it and the wall, out of view. It would not be discovered until the owner moved the ride, and by then Sweetpea would be long gone.

Hopping into the minivan, he drove to the rental agency, returned the vehicle, then caught a shuttle bus to the airport. Instead of heading inside the terminal he boarded another shuttle that took him to long-term parking and his awaiting Mercedes 560SEL. Getting into the passenger seat, Sweetpea lifted a large brown grocery bag from the back containing a silver nylon jogging suit along with socks and sneakers.

Removing his business-like attire, the assassin donned the warm-up sweats then carefully placed the brim, outfit, gloves, afro wig, fake mustache, and goatee inside the brown bag. Now he looked nothing like the man who would be described to police in case someone spotted him. Exiting the Benz, he walked over to a trash receptacle, stuffed his getup inside it, then returned to his ride and drove off, paying the cashier with a smile on his face.

Once again Sweetpea had completed a dastardly hit leaving nary a clue. Now he had revenge on the scar-faced robber and could finally take a much-needed vacation. Removing his personal cell phone from the glove box, he called Harriette to let her know dick was on the way. Killing always made him horny, and he would definitely serve his woman today.

13

FREE AT LAST

Mario walked through the yard at the Youth Authority complex, accepting good wishes from all his boys who still had plenty of time to mark their calendars. The three-year stint he'd served saw him develop from an overgrown man-child into a strapping six-foot, five-inch tower of strength. Unlike most of those being released who headed for a bus to take them near home, Mario had a family member to drive him home. His mother Crystal waited patiently just outside the compound for her only son to reach her.

He could see even from a distance that his mom still had it going on, and the whistles along with catcalls amongst those being left behind reinforced the fact. Crystal stood at the entrance wearing hip-hugging blue jeans with Phat Pharm pink tennis shoes and a matching spandex tank top that highlighted her awesome frame. Mario grinned broadly at the attention she received. Not to mention that each step brought him closer to being free once again.

"My baby!" Crystal shouted while attempting to bear-hug him.

"Momma, you're embarrassing me," he stated weakly, eyeing his cronies.

"Boy, I don't care about your reputation—you are my baby!"

Crystal marched arm in arm with her son to a black Acura Legend that he had never laid eyes on. It was a two-door convertible and clean as a whistle. Mario instantly envisioned himself cruising the streets with the top down and some fine honey riding shotgun, or showing off his driving skills at the Sydeshow (a late-night idiotic affair where revelers spinned doughnut circles in their cars leaving tire tread marks plus clouds of black smoke).

"Boy, look at you, you've grown an awful lot," Crystal smiled while getting in the car.

"Momma, that ain't the half of it," he cheesed. "Got mah grades back up to bar."

"You mean up to par, son."

"Yeah, up to par, so ah'm back in da 'leventh grade now. Know a little bit 'bout computers, passed mah written test to drive, and took some anger management classes."

"That's good, baby."

She pulled away after Mario placed his meager belongings in the trunk. Reclining the seat to its limit, Mario stretched his large frame to the max, enjoying the scenery. He felt the time incarcerated had done him well yet had no intentions of ever coming back. Being told what you could or could not watch on television, when to eat, what time to bathe, along with so many other rules that generally were enforced on a guard's whim, reminded him that freedom was the real bomb.

"So, Momma...."

"Yes, honey?"

"When you gone let me drive? What happened to the Camry anyway?"

"When you graduate from high school and get a job, or go to college. Still playing basketball?"

"Yeah, ah still ball a little—what happened to the other car?"

"I still got it—it's sitting at home waiting for you."

"COOL!" he shouted.

"But you're gonna have to earn the right."

"What?" He didn't understand.

"Listen, Mario"—she got serious—"nothing is free in this world. You have to earn what you get. Now in order for you to drive you first have to do well in school, show me that you've learned respect, and stay out of trouble."

"Is that all?" he laughed.

"It may not sound like much, but it's hard to do. You down with that?"

"Yeah, ah'm down."

"Good. Now tell me, what are your plans?"

"Ah'mo enroll in school an mind mah bidness."

"I see you still haven't learned proper language."

They both roared as Crystal zoomed down the 205 highway heading for home. The majority of their forty-minute ride was spent traffic-free, with Mario giving his mother vivid descriptions of life behind bars. She had informed him by letters and in her biweekly visits of moving into a new crib, but he had no idea how fabulous their new digs were until she eased up into the driveway.

The house was a giant three-bedroom located in the heart of Maxwell Park on Best Street, which was sandwiched on a steep grade between Birdsall and Fleming. It looked like a castle to Mario's sixteen-year-old eyes. As they got out, he viewed first the home then his mom with newfound admiration. She had really come up this time.

Further up the block he spotted at least eight fine females practicing what appeared to be a cheerleading dance routine. Crystal opened the trunk then eyed Mario wickedly. "Your speech may need work, but your vision is 20/20," she laughed. "Help me get your things." Mario hoisted his bags from the trunk, taking keen notice of all the females eyeing him.

Heading up the steps with his luggage, Mario ignored the girls watching his every move. He would get to know who was who later because right now his mind was on grub and all the delicious meals he remembered Crystal burning in the kitchen. Jailhouse food was both decent and served its purpose, but now he could pick and choose his own meals, along with eating until he was stuffed.

The house was painted sky blue with white trim, and although the front yard was small, consisting of a tiny patch of grass and rose bushes, it was immaculate. Red-colored stairs with black railings on each side escalated upward from the sidewalk to the front door, and a large window in the front room faced the street below. Inside, Mario's feet were greeted by plush white-shag carpet with runners streaming throughout the house.

In the living room sat a white baby grand piano, glass-encased fireplace, white leather sofa that looked like it had never been sat on, and a glass-topped coffee table. The dining room was just as elegant, with a large brown curio in the corner displaying several expensive figurine pieces along with fine china plates and cups plus sterling silver eating utensils. In the center sat a humongous oak table surrounded by six stately padded oak chairs. Similar to the living room, this one appeared unused and decorated simply for show.

"Well, what do you think?" Crystal asked her son.

"It's cool, Mom, but I'ont see no TV, or component set."

"Follow me."

Mario set his bags down and trailed his mother as she gave him a scenic tour of their new home. To the right was a hallway with a door at the end leading to the master bedroom, which she had graciously given him. It provided a splendid view of the street below and housed a king-sized bed with matching cabinets and drawers. A huge brown entertainment center rested alongside the wall in front of Mario's bed and came complete with a twenty-seven-inch television, VCR/DVD combination, mini component set, plus a video game player.

Down the hall next to that room was a bathroom, which Mario could tell had been recently remodeled. The door to Crystal's sleeping quarters was already open and, just like his own, Mom's room was tastefully furnished, only smaller. It was obvious he was more than impressed but the big surprise came when they marched through the kitchen into a third bedroom that had been converted into an office. At the rear was a sliding glass door to a room addition that served as a family room. Mario's jaw dropped at the sight of a giant fifty-two-inch plasma monitor with towering five-foot-tall speakers on either side.

He could care less about the built-in fireplace with white marble mantle above, showcasing his numerous trophies, or the semi-circular sofa in the middle of the room. All Mario could picture was the life-sized figures that would be coming out of the screen directly into his den. He stood there with eyes fixated on the monster appliance, smiling from ear to ear.

"Well," Crystal asked, snapping him out of his trance, "what do you think?"

"Momma, you came up phat. Dis sh—, oh 'scuse me, da crib is da bomb."

"I'm glad you like it. Now what would you like to eat?"

"I'ont even know, maybe a burrito or sumptun."

"A burrito?" she arched her brow.

"Been dreamin' uhbout um."

Crystal shook her head from side to side while leaving the den as Mario grabbed the remote and poked the power button. Seconds later she reappeared, dangling her keys on her pinky finger. He was already sprawled out on the couch, peering intently at the sports center newscast.

"Let's see if I remember—steak burrito with everything except guacamole. Right?"

"Yeah, Momma. Let me get a couple uh tacos, too."

"I'll be right back, Your Highness."

She took a bow then headed for the front door, but he was too occupied by the images on the screen to notice her snide remark. Mario's first few weeks home were spent with him doing his best to make his mom proud. He enrolled in school, joined the basketball team, helped out around the house, and displayed the sort of respect his mother always felt was in him.

However, after only a month things began to sour. He started hanging out with what Crystal labeled undesirables, skipping classes or school altogether, and coming home all hours of the night, if at all. The final straw came when she unexpectedly opened his bedroom door one day and found him packaging up dope for sale—cocaine, to be exact.

"What the hell are you doing?!" she yelled.

"Man, you trippin'," he responded.

"Oh, so you're right back into taking the easy way out, huh, Mario?"

"Momma, dem lil' nickel an dimes you give me ain't enough."

"Get that shit out of my house."

Crystal pounced on him like a cat and tried to grab the dope, but he was too quick. The next thing she knew, he had blocked her path, clutched her blouse together by the lapels, and was drawing back his beefy fist.

"Oh!" she screamed. "You're gonna hit me!" Mario let her go, calmly picked up his product, folded it neatly back inside its newspaper wrapping, then walked out. Crystal had never felt that much fear in her life and stood there gasping for breath while shivering like a leaf. Resigned to the fact that her son was a bad seed, she lay across his bed crying her eyes out.

14

HE'S BAAACK

A huge crowd of gawkers anxiously strained their necks for a peek at Shaunnie's dead body. Word travels fast in the hood, and death always brings out the masses. Business owners, concerned citizens, and curious onlookers gathered in a crowd covering the entire dead-end street. The grisly find had been reported by the Jacksons, Sylvia and Ted, who were leaving in their car for a dinner engagement with friends.

Sylvia spotted the body first as Ted backed out of their parking stall, immediately calling 911 on her cell phone. Once police arrived on the scene Ted informed them where Shaunnie resided, along with pointing out that the Intrepid parked haphazardly in another stall belonged to her boyfriend. As additional backup officers swarmed the block, the sergeant in charge ordered them to kick in the apartment door due to no response from the loud knocks delivered to it.

With guns drawn Five-O prepared to bum-rush the joint in the exact manner they would a drug bust—meaning they would be ready for whatever fate held in store, or more to the point, what or who was on the other side of that door. Right before the raid was to be conducted, the complex manager emerged from the crowd informing Oaktown's finest that he possessed a key. Still in an attack mode, the officers positioned themselves at the ready as one of their associates quietly inserted the key and deftly pushed the door ajar.

A collective hush hovered over the onlookers as television news cameras zoomed in on the proceedings. Daily programming on local stations had been interrupted for a special news bulletin, and now the entire region could watch the drama unfold. Reporters stood at safe distances describing the action, which viewers did not need due to the fact their eyes were riveted to boob tubes. This only intensified the drama as citizens held their breath.

When officers exited the apartment putting their guns away while calling for evidence technicians, it was obvious that someone else had been killed. Derrick Boston slowly eased the navy blue service vehicle past the mass of humanity while Maria Jimenez applied makeup and lipstick in the sun visor mirror.

Derrick still sported his black tuxedo but had replaced the red bow tie and cummerbund with a more traditional black paisley necktie. Maria, on the other hand, now wore a gray two-piece skirt/jacket combo that she had slipped into in the ladies' room at the banquet. She had changed outfits at the Marriott by stripping out of her gold-sequined evening gown down to her panties and bra, then changing clothes as if nothing were unusual about what she was doing.

Of course, most of the females in the restroom found it odd and whispered among themselves regarding her boldness. Once she walked out they openly hated on her with a vengeance, especially fellow female cops. Many were jealous of the fact that since she now served as a homicide detective, the girl was always in the news discussing cases. They all secretly craved the limelight Maria reveled in, and because she enjoyed it tremendously they hatefully classified her as a prima donna.

"You'd think these people would have something better to do with their lives than ogle at a dead body," she said to Derrick while putting away her compact.

"Yeah, I feel you, baby," he answered, pulling over to the curb. "Guess they ain't got it like that."

"They need to get a grip."

"You ready?"

"Always," she laughed.

Boston knew that her answer to his question referred to being ready to get fucked, which he had done less than three hours earlier. Gazing at her chiseled legs as she exited the vehicle caused his penis to swell with blood. Instantly he wanted to dick her down, still feeling his rod bang away inside her willing cunt. Boston and Jimenez had engaged in a secret affair shortly after becoming homicide partners, which now was closing in on ten years.

As time passed her husband Jesús had become increasingly suspicious of Boston, whom he frequently referred to as "that asshole partner of yours." On the rare occasions when they met at a department function with spouses in tow, the body language they displayed only increased Jesús' ire. He couldn't stand the handsome negro who spent more time with his wife than he did.

While Boston was both good-looking and fit as a fiddle, Jesús was short and fat. His main hobby was guzzling beer while eating humongous meals and watching television. On the rare occasions when they did have sex, he knew something was wrong because once her pussy got wet, his short thumbnail dick slipped and sloshed around in her vagina like a fish out of water. He had no doubt she was receiving a regular dose of "sweet meat" and knew exactly who was feeding her.

Once his bickering and accusations became unbearable, Maria left him, taking their two children with her. Now she was free to openly be with her man, but for that to happen he would have to leave his wife, which proved harder than they imagined. Boston's wife Naomi was beautiful, intelligent, and had a blossoming career as an attorney. She was just as fine as Maria and her equal in bed. However, the more time Derrick spent with his partner the deeper he fell in love.

It was Naomi who initiated the breakup due to her husband's frequent trips to out-of-town conventions that his partner also attended, his lack of interest in marital lovemaking, and water-cooler gossip at her job. Although Derrick and Maria tried to play it off at work, the reality was that everyone knew they were an item, and in the world of law enforcement, gossip spreads like wildfire.

Since attorneys are in frequent contact with cops, many of Naomi's coworkers learned of the relationship long before she did. She found out by accident while having lunch one day at Kincaid's on the square. After reviewing notes from a particularly difficult case as she picked at her seafood salad, she stuffed her papers inside the folder, paid the tab along with leaving a tip, then headed for the powder room to freshen up.

Seconds after the restroom door closed behind her, Derrick and Maria walked through the eatery's front door. Minutes later, Naomi reappeared ready to leave, but right as she passed the maitre d's podium she glanced one final time into the dining area. Her heart sank when she saw her husband holding hands with his partner while gazing lovingly into her eyes. Grabbing a water pitcher off a tray at the bar, she marched over to the startled twosome and emptied the contents on top of his head, then gracefully walked out.

By the time he got home she had his bags packed and sitting on the front porch. He inserted his key but nothing happened, because she'd also had the locks changed. The marriage was over.

"You talk to the neighbors, I'll question beat cops," said Boston. "I'm on it."

Walking side by side, closer than they realized, the detectives headed for the crime scene as a team before branching off in different directions. Boston began gathering statements and facts from beat cops while Maria questioned the Jacksons. Returning to her partner, she viewed Shaunnie's corpse while Jimmy Chang verbalized his initial findings.

"Preliminary findings indicate the victim was killed somewhere else and dumped here," Jimmy said while crouching over the body.

"What facts back this up, Jimmy?" asked Boston.

"No sign of a struggle, along with position of body, plus"—he continued—"victim's wrists had been handcuffed before her death."

"Mode?" queried Maria.

"Asphyxiation," Jimmy responded without looking up.

"There's ano—"

"Yes," Jimmy answered before hearing Boston's question. "Black male victim upstairs. Would you two care to join me?"

The threesome marched up the steps, stopping at the front door before placing latex examination gloves on their hands and booties on their shoes. Since Maria was wearing high heels, she took them off and covered her bare feet with the paper booties normally worn by nurses, doctors, and medical personnel. Once inside the unit, Jimmy immediately noticed the trail of blood running from the kitchen to a bedroom. After casually glancing at Moon's lifeless figure Jimmy, with examination bag in tow, followed the drops, which were more like blotches and splatters.

Boston and Jimenez huddled up with a few uniformed officers stationed inside the living room engaged in small talk. It was there they would wait until Jimmy finished his solitary task of dusting for prints, bagging and labeling evidence, securing blood samples, drawing chalk outlines, snapping photos, and other assorted duties like checking underneath Moon's fingernails for skin fragments that could have belonged to the suspect. Twenty minutes later Jimmy called the detectives into the kitchen.

"I still have a lot of work to do, but it looks like we'll get nothing here," he said, then shouted, "Wait a minute!"

"What is it?" asked Boston, staring at the open hole on Moon's forehead. "The murder weapon?"

"No, not that," Jimmy answered, failing to look up. "You see this wet spot on his shirt sleeve?"

"Yes," the detectives responded in unison.

"It's possible it could be the suspect's saliva. Judging from the mess here, there was definitely a struggle of some sort. I'll take a sample and run some tests for DNA."

"And if it matches up—" Jimenez pondered.

"We have a suspect," Jimmy assured her. "Although I wouldn't bet the farm because my preliminary findings indicate this hit was professional."

"The Knifeman?" Boston stated, more of an answer than a question.

"Looks that way," Jimmy resumed, "judging from the girl downstairs and this guy here." He pointed at Moon while rising. "It had to be a pro because how many people can pull off a hit such as this one, leaving only a drop of saliva—which could be water for all I know—and get away in broad daylight?"

"Not many, Jimmy, not too many," stated Boston.

"One more note of interest . . ."

"What's that?"

"Driver's license identifies the victim as Ronnie Moon."

"So Sergeant Johnson's belief that the hit on the west side a few months back was done by the Knifeman proves to be correct."

"Yes," Jimmy concurred, "he made a few mistakes in that one but atoned for it today."

"Thanks, Jimmy. Let us know if you come up with something more."

"No problem. I'll let you know the results of my tests as soon as I get them back."

Boston first then Maria shook hands with Jimmy before heading outside. She slipped off the booties and replaced them with high heels. The once-bustling crowd of onlookers had dwindled down now to a handful of residents eagerly awaiting permission from cops to return to their apartments. Driving off, Jimenez gave her partner the address to Shaunnie's parents' home.

They rode in silence because the task awaiting was one cops hated the most—informing relatives that a loved one had been murdered.

15

PURSE SNATCHER

Yolanda Lopez walked briskly away from the tortilla factory at 38th and Foothill, heading home. She had purchased both corn and flour tortillas, along with other staple items such as cheese, refried beans, tomatoes, cilantro, and jalapeño peppers. A recent immigrant from Mexico, "Yo-Yo," as she was called, spoke very little English.

She worked as a housekeeper for a nationwide hotel chain in Emeryville, a tiny city sandwiched between Oaktown and Berkeley whose population growth was bursting at the seams due to the dot.com boom plus smart management from elected officials. Big-box department stores migrated there for cheaper rents, especially after being turned away by elected officials of neighboring cities to the north and south.

Having to catch two buses to reach her job on the waterfront meant Yo-Yo would arise at three in the morning to get there at six. She, along with her husband Julio and two small children, lived in a home owned by her aunt Isabel, who served as their sponsor. The house was crammed with other relatives and, just like blacks had done before them, everyone worked their asses off chasing the American dream.

What she didn't know (and what the negroes found out later) was that while you worked your butt off to attain prosperity, your children were busy becoming Americanized. Meaning the Latino children learned the English language along with American culture. The latter included disrespect, sassing their parents, and placing material value before family morals.

Today Yo-Yo had put in three hours overtime due to a coworker calling in sick, so her dawgs were aching and talking back to her.

Standing a smallish five-foot-three while lugging nearly two hundred pounds of flesh on her portly frame, Yo-Yo huffed and puffed her way home. With darkness rapidly descending, she trudged along to her aunt's home on 36th Avenue.

There was a Latino Baptist church by the entrance to Cesar Chavez Park, and on the other side, a taco stand specializing in take-out orders. Next to that sat a used appliance repair shop sandwiched in by yet another liquor/grocery store. Young Mexican hoodlums used the park as a hangout to drink liquor, sell dope, and beat down any rival with the nerve or stupidity to enter their domain.

Salvadore "Loco" Lopez was the leader and, just as the name implied, was stuck on stupid. The boy was both crazy and fearless, with a bad attitude and quick temper. Standing a mere five feet, eight inches on a one-hundred-and-fifty-pound frame, his appearance was deceiving. That was due in large part to the oversized clothes he wore such as sagging size thirty-eight blue jeans, extra large white t-shirt starched and pressed to a crisp, covered by a 3X blue and white checkerboard shirt/coat. The only button fastened on his coat was the top one, fulfilling the typical "Mexican thug" stereotype.

Brand-new royal blue sneakers adorned his feet; dark sunglasses covered his eyes. Loco's hair was full, thick, and slicked down onto his scalp in the manner of a rock 'n' roll idol of the fifties. The distinguishing mark that caused you to take a second look was a tattoo stenciled on his neck: *Loco*. Taking a swig from his forty while his boyz bobbed their heads up and down in rhythm to a crudely made bedroom studio beat, Loco swayed and gyrated, simultaneously jutting out one finger back and forth on a closed fist.

Pedro "Pepe" Gonzales and Juan "Chito" Guzman stood alongside Loco drinking beer while grooving to the cut they had arranged on Chito's four-track recording unit. They were members of the Norteños, and their enemies were called the Sureños. Mexicans representing Norte or Sur (North or South) were just as violent amongst themselves as blacks representing East or West Oaktown.

With so much mayhem and havoc they wreaked on themselves, it was clear that each race limited the number of crimes perpetrated against one another. There were isolated and scattered incidents, few and far between, and the reason was simple: nobody wanted a race riot. Yo-Yo felt safe in her neighborhood, which was heavily saturated by her own kind.

Pepe was small, five-foot-three to be exact, but he had the mindset of a killer with his affinity for guns and violence. He was not afraid of anyone or anybody and represented his race with fierce pride. Dressed in blue saggy jeans, white t-shirt and kicks along with a bandana neatly wrapped around his head, he considered himself a future rap star. Pepe's plan was to mix English with Spanish on a cut, blend it all in tastefully, then sell it to the masses.

Chito was slender, a six-foot-tall walking clothes hanger. However, he had a natural ability to figure things out. The unofficial mastermind of their set, he was the one who provided Loco with plots and plans for success. Decked out in the same fashion as his compadres, Chito wore no t-shirt underneath his shirt/coat, proudly showing off a giant dragon tattoo on his belly. Even though it was nighttime all three men wore dark shades over their eyes. The street was quiet yet they were engaged in a serious party amongst themselves.

A few hundred yards down the block, Mario sat silently on a bench at 38th and appeared to be waiting for a bus. The buses came and went yet he remained stationary, contemplating his next move. The most pressing issue was where he would rest his head for the night, because over the past few weeks he had basically worn out his welcome at each location. Since barging out of his mother's house, he spent nights with friends, never staying more than two or three nights at a time.

It was a rather rude awakening for a teenager because Mario

discovered that his homeboys' families, and quality of life, were much worse than the one he had given up. Add in the fact that he could not eat when he chose, sleep comfortably, nor bathe on a regular schedule, and he realized home was the place to be. However, his bullheadedness and inflated ego would not allow him to head home and apologize to his mom. In his mind that amounted to "punking" out and admitting he had made a mistake. Much like kissing ass (which for a youngster ranked in the same category as being "dissed") confessing to a mistake and asking forgiveness was taboo.

Spotting a portly Latino female lugging a bag of groceries, he noticed her purse dangling just below the sack. With nightfall descending and the streets rather quiet, Mario seized on the moment, bouncing up from his seat and running down the street. He waited for the light to change in front of a taco truck that sat on the outskirts of a car wash detail shop. The detail shop overflowed during business hours with black customers having their autos cleaned by a staff whose majority of employees were black. It was now closed for the day and deserted.

Once the light changed Mario took off in a dead run right in front of a bus dropping off passengers at a bus stop situated in front of the closed garage. Yo-Yo approached the chapel carrying the food and clutching her purse tightly, for it contained a measly twenty dollars that would be used to tide her over until Friday's payday. Hearing rapidly approaching footsteps, she wrote it off as someone running down the street. Stepping to the side in order to give the jogger a passing lane, she suddenly felt extreme pain to her head and back from a forearm shot.

Her body sprawled to the ground in one direction, with the grocery bag and purse flying off in the other. Its contents splattered across the sidewalk, with the canned items rolling into the streets. Yo-Yo, bruised and suffering a busted lip, began screaming at the top of her lungs. Mario scooped up the handbag on the dead run, resembling an offensive lineman who'd just picked up a quarter-back fumble and was now lumbering toward the end zone.

"*¡Ayúdame! ¡Me está robando!*" ("Help, he's robbing me!")

Loco, Chito, and Pepe heard the screams coming from a voice that sounded all too familiar. Instantly they dropped their liquor bottles and sprinted to the park entrance, where they spotted Yo-Yo struggling to get up. Looking in the other direction, they saw a black guy running down the street carrying Yo-Yo's purse. All three burst out in full sprint, and even though they had not exercised in years, you would have thought they were soccer stars.

Mario had a block and a half advantage, but as he neared 35th Avenue the distance had decreased to only half a block. Turning on 35th he was both surprised and startled as a vehicle pulled to curb with its passenger window rolling down. "Get in!" shouted the driver, who zoomed off the moment Mario slammed the door. His pursuers hit the corner in full stride but were dumbfounded to find Mario nowhere in sight.

They figured he must have taken refuge behind a house and began scouring the area in search of their suspect. Twenty minutes later the three gang members returned to the park and gave statements to police, who had arrived a few minutes after the assault. Once quiet resumed, they continued what they knew best—drinking, listening to homemade beats, and selling dope, only this time engaged in boastful conversations about what they would have done had they caught the nigger.

16

STILL WITHOUT A CLUE

Boston and Jimenez entered the office, immediately noticing a hand-written message on the bulletin board. It was from Jimmy Chang, asking them to come to the lab because he had valuable information. They knew it must be a bombshell, for Jimmy was always in the habit of coming to them. Taking the elevator, they headed straightaway for the basement and Jimmy's domain.

"Good morning, Jimmy," greeted Jimenez while Boston shook his hand.

"Hey you guys, have a seat." They did as told. "I have some really good news and some bad—which would you like first?"

"Pick your poison," said Boston.

"Okay, first the good. We have a DNA match on the knife found at the murder scene on Campbell Street." This perked them up but Jimmy wasn't done. "I also have a match with the fluid on the murder victim's shirt last night. Get this: both samples come from the same person."

"Jimmy, that's wonderful!" gloated Jimenez. "That means we have a suspect."

"Not so fast." He held up a palm. "That's only the good news."

"What's the bad?" asked Boston.

"The bad is that we don't have a name, so whoever it is must have never been arrested or fingerprinted, because I cross-referenced the sample into the national database and still came up empty."

"So that means unless the suspect slips up, which is highly unlikely, we really don't have a thing," said Jimenez, her voice now sounding deflated.

"From the looks of it, I would have to agree, but you never know."

"Thanks, Jimmy, and if you find out anything else let us know," Boston said.

"Sure will."

Jimmy again shook hands with the detectives as they rose to leave, then he turned to resume his duties. Before they reached the door a call blared over Jimmy's radio transmitter regarding a shooting death on the east side. Upon hearing the announcement, Jimmy packed up his bags and was out the door. When Boston and Jimenez re-entered the homicide unit, they found Edgar Lewis in front of the coffee machine filling his cup.

"Good morning," he stated.

"Morning," they replied in unison.

"Call just came in about a murder on the east side, 38th and Foothill at Cesar Chavez Park."

"How many victims?" asked Boston.

"Just one—his name is Salvador Lopez. Goes by the street tag 'Loco.' By all accounts it was gang-related because Loco is a high-ranking member of the Norteños."

"We're on our way."

The pair of detectives headed out the door to yet another crime scene. In this case Jimenez would serve as the lead detective because normally when Hispanics were murdered most of the witnesses spoke only Spanish. It was also one of the reasons their crimes were very hard to solve because in addition to the language barrier, many had the fear of being deported, as well as an unwillingness to be labeled a snitch.

The entire drive was spent with the two engaged in conversation about the Knifeman.

"Think we'll ever get this guy?" asked Jimenez.

"It's like Jimmy said, you never know, baby. Maybe he will slip up somewhere along the line. He is starting to make mistakes."

"Yes, he is getting a little sloppy, if that truly is him and not some copycat."

17

POINT MADE

Junior sat in his customary top-shelf seat on the bleachers at Arroyo Park, watching highly entertaining basketball games. Often signifying after someone was slammed on or fooled out of their socks by a wicked cross-over dribble, he loved being the center of attention. His rapid rise in the Eastside Drug Empire, better known as the EDE, surprised no one simply because his deceased father had been the gang's leader until his untimely death.

Now enjoying the luxurious fruits of his labor, Junior had it all: a nice sporty gold and white Navigator, closet full of the latest fashions, and bankroll fat enough to choke an elephant. Dread sat next to Junior sipping on a screwdriver while alternately hitting then passing the weed to his lifelong dawg. Arroyo was packed with an assortment of colored people enjoying nice weather and the festive atmosphere engulfing the park.

Dopefiends shot up heroin or smoked crack in the men's restroom while hookers sold pussy in the women's. Alcoholics drank their poison within the comforts of their hooptys in the jam-packed parking lot, while street peddlers swarmed every car, cruising by in an attempt to make more scrill. On the baseball field, Little League games were in full swing, the bleachers overflowing with family members, friends, and casual observers.

Scattered throughout were picnic areas where families basked in the aroma of ribs grilling as smoke wafted through the air, invading nostrils and reminding many how hungry they truly were. Junior was the unofficial ruler of the park, with all of the d-boyz on his payroll raking in their share of cheese. Situated on three rows directly beneath him and Dread were soldiers in his army, strapped to the gills with weapons, all willing to risk their lives in order to protect his. This provided him a sense of invincibility, which only helped to swell his already massive ego.

"Man, smellin' all lat food got me hungry," Junior said.

"Know dass right," co-signed Dread.

"Shidd, ah thank ah might hafta go get me a plate from somebody."

"Get a plate? Yo ass could buy the whole fuckin' park!" Dread once again kissed ass—"have all lem muafuckas workin' fa us!" Junior roared with laughter, spurring his sidekick on: "Hell, half dem niggahs prolly uh give us da shit fa dope, fuckin baseheads. . . ."

"You a fool!" Junior cried.

"Man, you know I ain't lyin'—dem clowns uh give us da pits, tay-duh salad, bake beans, an hot lanks fa a muthafuckin hit, shidd!"

Junior was laughing so hard that all his boyz turned their attention to him, pleased that their boss was in a good mood. They, like everyone in the park, knew that his jovial mood could turn into a furious rage at the drop of a hat. So even though it was cool at the moment, they were still cautious. After sitting around discussing food for the next twenty minutes, Junior and Dread finally decided on burritos. He felt ribs would have been cool but didn't want to be licking his fingers today or getting sauce on his brand-new gear.

What normally was a one-minute walk to his Navigator took fifteen due to everyone wanting to shake his hand, give pats on the back, or be seen conversing with him. As Junior stood there reveling in the limelight Dread sipped on his screwdriver, along with casually scanning the grounds for rivals. In their world an ambush was always right around the corner waiting to happen, and Dread's senses remained on full alert even on their home turf.

"Junior, dare go dat fool Wendell! Niggah crazy showin' his face 'roun here."

"Man, go brang dat niggah ta me."

Dread marched over to the edge of the parking lot, summoning a few of his goons along the way. Wendell McCoy stood with two other dudes watching the Little League game from a distance. Wendell owed a rather smallish drug tab of fifty bucks yet had been avoiding the park and paying his bill for nearly a week. He had come across the money during that time but, like many dopefiends, instead of paying up and remaining broke, chose to cop from other dealers.

Before entering the parking lot he had watched from a distance for twenty minutes to make sure Junior was not around, but with the fear of being spotted, Wendell failed to check the basketball area, which had to be done on foot. He felt safe because he knew Junior was always highly visible, and the thought never crossed his mind that he would be inside the park. The lot was where all the money was made and Junior's normal hangout location.

Wendell had been friends with Junior and Dread since elementary school, and if not for his fear of prison and love of the base pipe, would have been on their payroll. A former high school football star, his athletic five-foot, ten-inch, two-hundred-and-thirty-pound frame was now a distant memory. Wendell weighed no more than one-seventy soaking wet, had not visited a dentist or barber in years, and could care less about his appearance.

Wendell needed to be at the park because that was where money could be made from being a temporary delivery driver or taxicab, coming up big in a crap game, or selling stolen merchandise. Besides, he was tired of being holed up inside his room with his mother constantly clowning him about getting a job. He knew fifty dollars would not make or break Junior and truly believed that since they had known each other all their lives, he would be allowed a few extra days in which to pay off the debt.

With his attention riveted to the action on the field Wendell was the last to know what was going on behind him. Suddenly he felt alone and turned to find himself staring into the face of Dread as his friends slowly backed away. Dread gripped his elbow in a vice lock and roughly escorted him over to an awaiting Junior.

"Wendell, where you been hidin' at, bro?" Junior greeted with his deep baritone voice.

"Aw, ah been around, man. Hey, ah'mo have yo money tomorrow."

"You said that two days ago."

"Naw, on da real, Junior, ah'll have it tomorrow, man."

Just from the way the scene unfolded, everyone knew Wendell owed money and they anxiously waited to see how the results of his face-to-face with Junior would turn out. All parking lot activity seemed to come to a standstill, with Wendell now the center of attention.

"Man, if it wasn't for the fact that I've known you damn near all my life, I'd kick yo ass right now, niggah!" Junior was talking loud enough for all to hear. "See, if ah let you go, all these fools gone thank dey can do the same thang."

"Ah'mo pay you, Junior, that's a promise."

"Awight Wendell, ah'll give you til tomorrow, but just to make sure you understand...."

Without warning Junior fired a vicious right to Wendell's jaw, dropping him in a heap on the dirty concrete. Blood spurted from his mouth as he got up, only to be greeted by a thundering blow to the nose, which returned him to the pavement. He was knocked out cold, with Junior standing above him massaging his knuckles. Then shouting loud enough for everyone to hear, he stated, "And that goes for anybody else who tries to welch on a tab. Let's raise, Dread."

Dread followed Junior to his ride, hopping inside the passenger seat while the park returned to its normal chaotic tempo. Wendell groggily arose from the ground and stumbled out of the park, with most of the people watching feeling pangs of sorrow for him. They knew that if his bill was not paid by tomorrow, he may as well move out of the hood. The overriding consensus was "better him than me" and reinforced their belief that if you can't pay, don't get credit.

"Yeah, ah did dat shit so all da rest uh dem fools gone know not ta try an play me," Junior boasted.

"Niggah deserved it," Dread stated dryly.

The seven-minute drive to High Street was filled with the two men passing weed back and forth in order to get their munchies on. By the time they arrived, their stomachs were growling and appetites enormous. Of course the hallucinating effects of the dope had them cracking up while replaying Junior's antics at the park.

"Man, dat niggah dropped like a sack uh potatoes!" Dread joked. "Ah started ta holler T-I-M-B-E-R but his ass was already on the ground!"

"Ah really didn't wanna clown his ass like dat, but the rest uh dem fools need ta get da message."

"Shidddd, they got the message alright. Dat punch made dey ass remember Mike Tyson, you know how he use ta knock niggahs out then dey get up an staggle all over da rang!" Both men laughed.

"Yeah, ah did pop his ass, huh?"

"Dat ain't da word, bro, you destroyed da muafucka! Thank he woke up yet? Ah'm surprised you didn't break yo hand!"

"Man, you crazy!"

Junior laughed so hard his stomach hurt and eyes became watery as Dread continued with the comedy routine. The restaurant parking lot was heavily saturated with cars, and since Junior did not want any scratches or dings on his ride from other car doors, he opted to park at the back near a grocery store. Riding with the air conditioning unit on low and the windows up resulted in a thick cloud of smoke escaping the vehicle once they opened the doors. Junior stood on the ground and stretched his massive frame, ready for the walk inside, before a sneer crossed his face.

"Dread, look over there." He pointed to the eatery's entrance. "Ah'll call the boyz," Dread stated, pulling out his cell phone. "Aw yeah, it's own now."

Junior cracked his knuckles and marched to the restaurant entrance while Dread followed behind, barking orders into his phone. Once he hung up, they stood outside waiting.

18

UNCLE STEPS IN

"I see you're still stuck on stupid."

"Just tryin' ta get money for food," Mario responded.

"We call that a job—now toss the purse."

"What?"

"Throw it out the window."

The window jetted downward with Mario flinging the purse as far as he could manage. It slammed against a building facade where it would remain until some lucky soul found it. Mario had no idea it only contained a measly twenty bucks, thinking instead that someone else would profit from his hard work.

"Where you headed, Unc?"

"I was on my way to your mother's house; heard you're supposed to be a dope dealer now."

"Dope dealer—man, yaw trippin'."

"Look son, I know you don't deal because if you did, then you wouldn't be out here snatching purses for money."

"You can just drop me off then 'cause ah ain't goin' ta Momma's house an listen ta yaw talk about me."

"What's this about you threatening her?"

"Threaten her?" Mario's voice rose. "Is that what she told you?"

"You did grab her by the throat, right?"

"That was an accident an ah only did it 'cause she was tryin' ta throw away sumptun dat didn't belong to me."

"So that makes it okay?"

"Naw it ain't okay, juss a natural reflex."

"Oh, so if I go upside your head because of your smart mouth, it would be fine because I could write it off as a natural reflex?"

Mario failed to give a reply and watched in silence as his Uncle

Horace pushed a speed-dial button on his phone. Mario was physically bigger than his uncle and, like all youths, felt invincible, yet there was something weird about him that sent warning signals throughout Mario's soul. He had an uneasy feeling about Uncle Horace but just couldn't put his finger on what it was.

Uncle Horace never came around the family too much except for holidays, and even then was not much of a talker. To Mario, it wasn't what his uncle said but the manner in which he said things that frightened him. Uncle Horace had a low baritone voice, eyes capable of melting iron, and a very direct manner of talking. There was something mysterious about his uncle that almost seemed criminal.

"Hey Crystal," he spoke into the receiver, "I'm with Mario now, picked him up off a street corner. . . . Yes, I can do that . . . not a problem."

"What she say?" Mario asked.

"She asked if it was alright for you to stay with me for a few days."

"I heard you say it was not a problem."

"You heard correct." His voice was flat.

"Well then, why you goin' to the house anyway?"

"Are you gonna wear that same outfit tomorrow?"

"Oh, uh. . . . Naw."

When Horace pulled up in front of Crystal's home, Mario remained stationary while his mom brought a bag of clothes outside, meeting her brother at the top of the stairs. They talked for a few minutes but Mario was unable to hear with the windows rolled up. He really was not ready to face his mom anyway because (like most teens) he felt his mom was too controlling and didn't understand that times had changed since she was growing up.

Finally Horace returned to the car and placed Mario's belongings in the trunk. The entire ride was spent in silence, with Mario unable to think of anything to say. He was more than relieved by the time they reached their destination because the soft and easy jazz oozing out of the stereo was killing him. Once they hit Fairmont Drive, Horace punched the garage remote clipped to the dashboard. They slowly entered the underground parking lot.

Directly to his right in the visitor's stall sat Harriette's Camry, a sight that caused a slight smile to cross Horace's face. He knew she would be waiting to suck on and get fucked by his sausage-sized dick until having one of her body-shattering orgasms. After twenty years they still had the most incredible sex, and she still knew the bare minimum about him. He was just as strange to her as he was to his nephew.

Horace popped the trunk, handed Mario his bag of clothes, then activated the car alarm. Inside the elevator he gave his nephew ten crisp twenty-dollar bills then inserted his key into the penthouse slot and turned it. The only other elevators Mario had ever seen that needed a key to operate were the ones in jail, where the key opened a lock box allowing cops to travel to their desired floor. It was a crime-fighting tool intended to help prevent prisoner escapes.

"Thanks for the money, Uncle Horace." Mario pocketed the dough.

"You're welcome. Spend it wisely and not all in the same place."

"Hey? Why you need a key for the elevator?"

"You don't need a key for the elevator, just the penthouse."

"So I finally get to see the penthouse, huh?"

"Consider yourself special, boy. I don't have people at my place."

"Yeah, ah know, dis is the first time ah ever been here."

They entered the house, with Horace instructing Mario to remain posted near the door while he yelled out his woman's name. He knew she would probably be naked and did not want his nephew receiving any free eye candy, nor spend the night with raging hormones, for that matter.

"Harriette?" he called again.

"Yes, honey?" She appeared from the bedroom just as he'd imagined.

"Go put something on—my nephew's here with me."

"Oh really?"

"Yes, he'll be staying here a few days."

Harriette quickly backtracked inside the bedroom to dress as Horace gave his nephew verbal permission to enter his domain. Since it was the first time Mario had ever been to his uncle's home, he stood in the middle of the living room floor impressed by the sight. Pulled-back horizontal blinds revealed a large balcony displaying a panoramic view of downtown, the Bay Bridge, and San Francisco skyline.

All furniture and appliances in the kitchen, living, and dining rooms were top of the line and definitely expensive. Many of the pieces were exotic and one-of-a-kind items that Mario was unfamiliar with; however, he did assume correctly that his uncle had paid a small fortune to furnish the place and could envision himself living in such lavish luxury.

"Let me show you where you'll be sleeping." Horace snapped him out of his trance.

"You must be Mario," said Harriette, walking out of the bedroom.

"Yes ma'am," he answered.

"It is so nice to finally meet you. Will you be staying long?"

"Uh. . . ."

"I said a few days," Horace answered for him.

The crispness of his words and the death stare he gave his woman let Mario know that Harriette would not be asking too many more questions. Yep, mysterious Uncle Horace, he thought. Harriette headed for the kitchen while Horace took Mario to his room. It was larger than both his and his mom's bedrooms at home and housed a giant king-sized bed that sat so high Mario guessed there were at least four mattresses on it.

"Listen," Horace looked his nephew squarely in the eye, "stay out of my room. I don't want anything missing when you leave, don't bring any of your friends here, and no dope. Cool?"

"Yeah, awight."

"Now, are you hungry?"

"Starvin'."

"Okay, I'll have Harriette go pick us up something. Meanwhile, you can take a bath and change into some clean clothes."

Horace left his nephew alone and went to the kitchen, where his woman was pouring them both a glass of wine. Mario emptied out his duffel bag and found clean underwear, socks, and a warm-up suit to put on. Crossing the hall, he discarded his worn-out rags on the bathroom floor before entering the shower butt-naked. The water cascading down his body was both soothing and refreshing, which resulted in him staying under the shower nozzle much longer than necessary. After toweling off Mario wandered into the living room to find his uncle sipping on wine while flicking playing cards across the room into a can.

"Harriette went to get our dinner," he said, steadily flicking the cards.

"Wow Unc, dass off da heezie. How you know how to do dat?"

"It takes practice, young blood, hand/eye coordination, and a steady wrist."

"Can I try?"

"Have a seat."

Mario did as instructed then accepted the card his uncle handed him and flicked it wildly, but the card dropped on the other side of the coffee table a mere three feet away. Horace grinned, handing him another, with which Mario employed a different tactic, attempting to flick it like a frisbee. This time the card ricocheted across the room but missed its mark badly.

"What you have to do," his uncle coached, "is to keep your hand steady yet flick the wrist with power."

Horace flicked another card, which rotated through the air as if guided by a puppet string, then landed directly inside the can. Mario looked on in amazement as his uncle went through the deck, dropping card after card into the bucket. Eagerly heading to the can, Mario retrieved the full deck then sat back down to try, again continuing to miss badly.

"It's almost like a bowler lofting the ball down the lane near the edge of it, then midway having it curve to the center for a strike. It takes skill, nephew."

"Yeah, ah seen dem do dat befoe."

"You need to practice your vocabulary, dude—we do not speak that way around here."

"You sound like mah momma, what way?"

"Ghetto slang. Have a little class and dignity about yourself. You youngsters wear your pants hanging down your butts but can't even tell someone why you do it or what's the meaning, reasoning, or logic behind it."

"Ah ... I mean, I do it because that's the style—you old folks don't know dat. . . . I mean that."

Horace was ready to educate his young nephew on the revolving door of life when Harriette marched in with their grub. She carried a giant bag with the aroma of barbeque wafting through the air, causing Mario to subconsciously rub his hands together. She wore a flimsy sundress, and blended with the cool evening air it had her nipples stretching the fabric. Mario felt himself gaining an erection and hoped his uncle did not catch him drooling.

"I got us some ribs and links, baby," she said. "Mario, I was not sure what type of sauce you like so they gave me containers with mild, medium, and hot. You can just pour it over your meat."

"I like hot," Mario stated.

"You better taste it first," his uncle warned.

Mario opened the cup housing the hot sauce and dipped a finger in it. Within seconds he was gasping for air and gratefully accepting the glass of water that Harriette handed him. Horace doubled over in laughter at the sight of his nephew trying to be hard.

"I told you, their hot is just as they say, *hot!*"

Harriette giggled watching the scene unfold, then prepared their meals on real plates with stainless steel silverware. Mario wolfed his meal down with the quickness, using mild sauce, then helped himself to seconds. After finishing he retired to his room, leaving the adults alone to finish their meal. He couldn't understand why they had to engage in non-stop chatter while eating, which caused their food to get cold and make the dining experience last too long. Once Mario was out of earshot, their conversation turned to him.

"So he will stay with you for a few days?" Harriette asked.

"Yes," Horace responded, "the boy thinks he's grown and is sending Crystal through the wringer."

"What do you plan on doing?"

"Not much, just raise his consciousness level and use a little psychology, hoping to rattle his brain into understanding that he's the only one responsible for his actions. Eliminate the weak excuses he often uses to blame others for his own shortcomings."

"Honey, it's none of my business, but since you really haven't been a part of his life, do you think he'll listen to you?"

"I don't know, but I will give it a shot. You ready for bed?"

"Not really, but Juicy *is* ready for Brunis."

"Is she wet?"

"Soaking."

"Help me put the dishes away."

Harriette assisted her man with cleaning up the mess then marched into the bedroom. When he walked in she was on top of the covers with legs gapped wide open and pink pussy lips staring him in the face. Horace dove his face onto her crotch and slowly began kissing her vagina like he would her lips. She closed her eyes, enjoying the sensations flowing through her body as it shook uncontrollably.

Within minutes her legs were lifted high in the air, with fluids from her hole saturating his chin and running down the crack of her behind. Passion swelled inside her as he ate with skill and precision, leading her on to a violent climax. Suddenly her body became rigid, her legs plopping down onto the sheets with a thud. She grabbed a pillow, biting deep into it in order to stifle the scream that accompanied her eruption.

Exhausted, Harriette lay still with legs spread apart as he inserted his dick into her steaming hole. Slowly stroking her with controlled rhythms, he rode her body like a jockey would a racehorse until releasing a generous amount of cum inside it. Knowing his nephew was in the next room caused Harriette to continue stifling her moans by biting down on the pillow. Once his load of cream had been deposited inside her, they both drifted off into a peaceful night's rest, locked in each other's arms.

Mario rose at noon and went into the living room, where a note along with a door key was left on the coffee table. Wiping sleep from his eyes he read it.

> *Nephew, we went out. The key is for you to get back in the pad if you leave. If you do go somewhere, don't come home too late. I am not one for late-night visitors.*
>
> Uncle Horace

After a quick shower Mario dressed then headed out the door. Instead of doing as his uncle had suggested and using the money for clothes, he decided to go home and retrieve some of the new duds his mom had purchased for him. Hopping on the 51 bus line, he later transferred to the 83 at 14th and Broadway in downtown's City Center.

The bus was crowded as usual, picking up and dropping off passengers at each stop on the route. By the time it reached High Street Mario's stomach was talking to him. Bouncing off, he strutted rapidly into Taco Zamorano for a burrito, knowing he had time since his mother never missed her hair and nail manicure appointments on Saturday. Once inside, a broad smile creased his face as Mario was greeted by two old friends.

19

PROMISES KEPT

"Willie, Marcus, whatup dawg?"

"Well, ah'll be damned, if it ain't ol' hoop-playin' Mario!" Willie grinned. "Where you been hidin' out at, boy?"

"Jus chillin', bro, tryin' ta keep out of trouble."

"Shidd," Marcus chided, "trouble yo middle name. Where you headed?"

"To mah mom's crib, den ah'mo recop."

"Recop?" Willie asked. "You may as well spin dat money wit us, homes—ah'll break you off sumptun propah."

"Like dat?" Mario asked.

"See what ah'm sayin'," Willie answered by flashing a wad of cash.

"Oh, yaw doin' it, huh?"

"Dat ain't da word.... Marcus? Tell dat niggah sumptun."

"If ya don't know, ya bettah ask somebody," Marcus stated.

All three burst out in laughter as Willie placed their orders then footed the bill. Since his cousin Ronnie's death Willie had inherited his ride, bankroll, and drugs, taking over his rapidly growing business. He had found the drugs and money one month after Ronnie's death, hidden under the spare tire in the trunk, while changing a flat.

Overnight Willie's life changed from small-time dealer on his cousin's payroll to major player on the city's west side. Marcus had risen just as large due to his lifelong friendship with Willie but still understood that Willie was the boss. Mario was more than impressed by the fancy Roca Wear outfits they wore, elephant-choking stacks of cash in their pockets, and enormous amounts of jewelry on their necks, arms, wrists, and grillz. The amount of dope Ronnie's killer lifted from his crib was peanuts compared to what Willie had stumbled across.

Sitting down at a back table to eat, the threesome reminisced about the good old days when they were incarcerated at the Youth Authority. They had no idea that once they walked out the door it would be on—that Junior, Dread, and the rest of their crew were patiently waiting to inflict severe punishment on them. Initially Junior and Dread only saw Mario heading inside the restaurant, but upon peering through the window they noticed their other two rivals already in line.

Dread's eyes lit up at the sight of Willie because he'd always felt like there was unfinished business between him and Willie Glasper.

"Listen, y'all," Junior spoke, "y'all just make sho nobody tries ta stop me from whuppin' da niggah's ass. Ah'mo tell ya now, I'ont need no help 'cause ah wont his ass ta know it's all me."

"Yeah," Dread chipped in, "an Willie's ass is mine. As for Marcus, I'ont give a damn what ya do ta his punk ass."

"Ah'mo beat da niggah so bad he gone vomit up dat shit he eatin'," Junior growled through clenched teeth.

The corner of High and International was one of the busiest in the city and always heavily saturated due to the many Hispanic establishments sprouting up. There were street vendors with push carts peddling everything from popsicles and fruit to corn on the cob and tamales, along with hustlers repairing windshields, doing body work, installing stereos, and peddling stolen jewelry from the trunks of their cars. Of course, packs of Mexicans stood lining both sides of the block, seeking day labor near the bumper-to-bumper automobiles displaying crudely written "For Sale" signs, along with prices painted on their windshields.

Junior could care less about any of that or the heavy police presence in the area, because his eyes were fixated on Mario enjoying his super burrito while shooting the breeze with Willie and Marcus. After what seemed like an hour but in actuality was a mere fifteen minutes, the trio rose to leave. Hiding in front at a spot that concealed his body, Junior waited.

Mario walked out first, rubbing his belly, only to be greeted by a thundering right hand that effectively knocked him on his ass. Before he knew what was happening Junior was raining blows to his face and body, causing him to cover up for protection. A crowd swarmed over to the action, blocked off by Junior's henchmen, leaving the two men in a circle.

Willie had it no better because the moment he exited the eatery after Mario, his face was introduced to Dread's fist and their battle began. Marcus, meanwhile, was ambushed by three goons who instituted a serious beat-down on him. Helpless to defend himself, he attempted to cover up also but still received several punches and kicks that landed squarely on the side of his head, ass, and legs.

Police cruisers rolling by noticed the melee and moved in forcefully to stop the madness, radioing for back-up units in the process. The element of surprise worked exactly as Junior had planned, with Mario never knowing what hit him. By the time the dust settled, Junior, Mario, Dread, and Willie were hauled off to jail in separate squad cars, but only Willie and Mario looked as if they had been in a rumble. Marcus was taken to the hospital suffering from broken ribs and a fractured jaw.

Besides a few scars on their knuckles, Junior and Dread had no damage. Mario did not regain his faculties until two hours later from the knockout blows Junior inflicted on him. Willie, on the other hand, suffered only a busted lip, for which he spewed promises of a payback to Dread while being escorted to his own personal squad car.

Normally, Mario and Willie would not have been hauled off to jail, being victims and all. However, since Willie fit the profile of d-boy by having over four grand in his pocket plus an equal amount of jewelry on his person, the cops figured it was a turf battle that just happened to occur on a main street. They would bring in Willie and Mario as victims needed to identify the suspects, Junior and Dread, along with searching for any evidence or information that would lead to their arrests.

The streets returned to normal, with most shoppers zooming home to tell their families about the street brawl they had just witnessed. Of course, many would flat-out lie about their spectator involvement, causing their wives to think they had participated in the brawl, kicked a little ass, and blended back into the crowd before Five-O arrived.

Mario regained his senses and peered around the room intently. Realizing that he was inside an interrogation unit at police headquarters and wondering what for resulted in his meal rocketing up his chest and out of his mouth. Vomit splattered on the floor with an awful stench from the mixture of onions, cilantro, jalapeño peppers, and meat permeating the confined room.

As if on cue the door slowly opened. Mario recognized the first person through it on sight. It was none other than Dennis Branch, the same officer who had arrested him several years earlier. Branch, now a desk sergeant, worked the gang detail and was just as surprised to see an almost full-grown Mario.

"Let me give you some water and a fresh room," Branch stated, aiding Mario to his feet.

"Hey! I remember you," Mario whispered.

"How's your mom?"

"She cool."

Branch secured a new room for Mario and after locking him inside returned a minute later with a bottle of water. Mario gulped it down thirstily, more than relieved by the fact that it had been refrigerated and was ice cold.

"You want to tell me what happened?" Branch began the proceeding.

"Man, ah had just finished mah lunch and walked out when dat fool stole own me."

"What fool is that?"

"Niggah name Junior—ah had a couple uh beefs wit his ass in YA."

"When was the last time you saw him?"

"Several years ago, when he got out."

"And you've had no contact with him since." It was more of a statement than a question.

"Ah ain't seen da fool til ta-day," Mario seethed.

"What about the other two, Willie Glasper and Courtney Adams?"

"Willie's mah friend and Dread, or Courtney as you call him, is a punk-ass niggah det hang wif Junior."

"Let's back up and clarify—Junior would be Edward Grissom?"

"I'ont know what his real name is. We just call him Junior."

"So you would consider this retaliation for a long-past beef in jail."

"Naw, ah consider it a coward scared ta face me straight up."

"How is your mother again?"

"She be cool, but mad at me right now."

"Why is that?"

"Man, she be tryin' ta control me an dat ain't gone happen. Why am I here anyway? Ah ain't did nuttin' wrong."

"The reason you're here, Mario, is because you guys were fighting in public, and all had enormous amounts of money and no visible means of support to justify the cash. Add in the fact that each one of you has been incarcerated and is known to skirt around the law. We just need to get to the bottom of this and make sure no turf war is the reason you were out there engaged in fisticuffs."

"Da only fisticuff gone happen is when ah see dat punk-ass bitch again."

"So you're willing to go back to jail?" Branch was calm.

"Fa da shit he done did, hell yeah." Mario was serious.

Branch folded up his notebook and left the room for Junior's interrogation cell. The next two hours were spent with Branch jaunting from room to room, attempting to gain some sort of clue as to why all of these young black men would participate in a street rumble knowing that the consequences included returning to jail. It did not make sense to him that petty beefs from years ago in prison would still fester inside them, gnawing at their psyche until revenge was had.

Naturally Branch could never fathom their fury because he had never lived in their world, where pride and ego took the place of decency and common sense. Since no formal complaints had been filed, all four were charged with disorderly conduct and disturbing the peace, then released, free to roam the streets once more.

20

SURPRISING REVELATION

Crystal sat in a padded chair lined neatly in a row with six others on the second floor at police headquarters, sandwiched in by parents waiting, like her, for their offspring's release. She replayed the message on her answering machine, which had sent shock waves throughout her body, because even though she had not seen her son in weeks, she felt he would be safe with her brother Horace. She did not understand how he could get into trouble so quickly.

Other mothers sat in solitude with worried looks on their mugs. But directly to Crystal's right was a heavyset, brown-skinned sister who, while dressed nicely, displayed all the characteristic stereotypes of a ghetto-fabulous mom. She yakked constantly on her cell phone for all within earshot to hear, was loud, and her language was laced with profanity. Hanging up her latest call, she directed her rap at Crystal.

"Girl, they arrest these young black men for any violation of the law they can come up with while the real criminals roam the streets."

"Oh really." Crystal could hardly care.

"Yeah, ah mean, all da boys was doin' was fightin'. Now tell me, how many fights do you see in the hood where nobody goes to jail?"

"Well," Crystal paused, "I'm just glad there was no gunplay involved."

"You too? Girl, if dey had had guns, we wouldn't even had to come 'cause dose niggahs would be havin' da book thrown at 'em by now."

"Wit da key thrown away," said another mom.

"Mah name is Shirley, and dey got mah baby Junior in dare." She held out her hand.

"Crystal." They shook.

"Yo son wadn't in da fight, was he?"

"I believe he was," Crystal stated.

"Well, let's just pray everybody's alright. What's yo boy's name anyway?"

"My son's name is Mario."

"Ain't dat a bitch?" Shirley suddenly boomed, getting every-one's attention.

"What?" asked Crystal.

"Ain't nobody's daddy here, if ah ain't mistaken—all ah see is females. Dass why dem lil' niggahs don't act right—nobody at home ta stomp a mudhole in dey ass."

"My son's father is dead," said Crystal.

"Mine is too," blurted out Shirley, "but dat don't excuse dat sorry-ass excuse for a man ah got now fa not brangin' his ass down here."

Dennis Branch's timing was perfect because Crystal had grown bored of the obnoxious woman sitting next to her. She secretly hoped that her son had not been the one fighting Shirley's boy because there was no doubt in her mind that if that were the case, this would not be the last conversation between them. She and Branch immediately recognized each other for the same reasons. He remembered how fine she was, and she remembered him as being extremely handsome.

"Miss Hayes," he greeted her, ignoring the other women.

"Oh, you remembered?"

"How could I forget?"

"Offisuh, excuse me," Shirley interrupted, "but when is you gone let mah son go?"

"And your son is?"

"Edward Grissom."

"That would be Junior?"

"Exactly."

"Are you ladies also waiting for the youths involved in the free-for-all on High Street?" he asked the group.

"Uh huh," they replied in unison.

"Here is the deal." Branch got official. "No one filed charges so all four individuals were cited for disturbing the peace, disorderly conduct, and instigating a riot. Each will be released on their own recognizance and will have their day in court."

Shirley was just about to ask another rude, dumb question when she saw Junior walking down the long corridor in their direction. She did not recognize the young man with him. As they got closer she realized that it was not Junior, but Shirley was shocked by the striking resemblance. Willie approached his mom, giving her a hug, then Mario hugged Crystal. Shirley became the quietest person in the group, peering intently at Mario, whose face displayed several lumps and bruises.

Willie and his mom headed for the exit, with him filling her in on the ambush while repeatedly stating his innocence.

"Where is mah son at?" Shirley asked Detective Branch rather rudely.

"We'll let the other two participants go in thirty minutes," he said, returning his attention to Crystal. "It's so nice to see you again, Miss Hayes, and if you need any assistance in the future, feel free to call me." Branch handed Crystal his business card then swiped his access card down the scanner and disappeared through the metal door.

A thought formed in Shirley's brain while steadily peering at Mario's uncanny resemblance to her son. As Crystal and Mario prepared to leave, Shirley spoke up.

"Excuse me, sis," she said to Crystal, "you said his daddy was dead, right?"

"Yes, he is," Crystal responded, turning to face her.

"What was his name?"

"His name was Edward."

"And how did he die?"

"He was murdered."

"In Las Vegas?"

"Yes—how did you know?" Crystal felt a lump form in her throat.

"Last name Tatum?"

"Yes, it was, how—"

"Yaw wait right here."

Shirley continued to make eye contact with them while ringing the buzzer outside the metal door like a maniac. Crystal stood frozen in her tracks. She secretly hoped that her worst fear would not soon be realized, but there was nothing she could do to prevent the inevitable. Detective Branch returned, followed by several officers ready for battle, but upon seeing Shirley at the door, he frowned while waving off the back-up.

"May I help you?"

"Yes," she said, "I'd like you to bring my son out here right now."

"Ma'am, I told you he would not be released for another thirty minutes."

"No offisuh, you don't understand."

"Understand what?"

"See, mah boy Junior's daddy died in Vegas and so did hers," she pointed at Crystal before resuming. "Both of their dads' name was Edward Tatum, an' ah know for a fact det he had some moe chillin foe he died, an dey wadn't by me." She emphasized the last point.

"Let me see if I follow you." Branch closed the door, stepping into the hallway. "You have reason to believe that Mario and Junior have the same father?"

"Exactly."

"Miss Hayes, what do you think of all this?"

"I'm not sure, but if it's no problem, I would like to see her son."

After a long pause Branch spoke. "Alright ladies, I'll grant your request on one condition."

"What?" they both asked.

"That I be allowed to handcuff your sons on opposite ends of the table. I cannot risk having them go at each other in here."

"Agreed," Shirley stated, staring at Crystal.

"I agree," she responded.

"Wait here, I'll be back shortly."

Branch swiped his card key on the panel to re-enter the office and was out of sight within seconds. Crystal stood gazing at the floor while Mario stared at Shirley, who was busy on the phone again, yakking away.

"Hey girl," she spoke into her receiver, "ah got some big news but cain't tell you right now. Ah'm downtown at da police station—ah'll call you back later."

No sooner had she hung up than Branch reappeared and casually slapped a set of cuffs on Mario's wrists. The group entered with Shirley, Crystal, and Mario following slowly behind the cop as he led them to the lineup room. Seated at a long table with handcuffs securely fastened to his wrists and ankles was Junior, looking angry.

The tension inside the spacious room was increased ten-fold by the silence among everyone, and when Branch noticed Mario's body stiffen upon seeing Junior, he calmly gripped the cuffs behind Mario's back with his right hand. Leading him to a chair on the opposite end of the table, Branch pulled another sets of cuffs from behind his back and clamped them down on Mario's ankles. The women sat next to each other while Branch closed the door and took up a position directly between Mario and Junior.

It was the first time he had a chance to see the two side by side, and Branch had to admit to himself that they did indeed resemble siblings. Mario's brain was reeling one hundred miles an hour as he remembered the many occasions when people in the Youth Authority commented about how he and Junior looked alike. Junior, on the other hand, had no clue as to what this was all about, thinking maybe they wanted to get him and Mario to call a truce with their mothers present.

"I'll have to admit there is a striking resemblance between the two," Branch said. "Miss Hayes, what do you think?"

"I agree, they do look alike."

"Ah knew, ah knew it!" Shirley hollered.

"Miss Grissom?"

"Yes, offisuh?"

"While there does seem to be an uncanny physical resemblance, that is really not enough to prove your point of them being brothers."

"BROTHERS!?" Junior screamed, attempting to jerk off the cuffs. "Dat fool ain't no kin ta me!"

"Shet up, boy," Shirley admonished. "Proof? I'll give you proof. Was your Edward six feet four?" She directed the question at Crystal.

"Yes."

"Drove a Mercedes?"

"Yes."

"Murdered in Vegas?"

"Yes," she stammered.

"Had a wife and children?"

"He was divorced."

"Mother lived in Hayward?"

"I think so."

"Offisuh, what else do ah need ta say? Dey got da same daddy an everybody here knows it."

"Maybe so, but the one way to be certain is by taking DNA samples," said Branch.

"Man, ah ain't takin' no DNA," growled Junior.

"What you scared of?" Mario asked.

The question Mario posed took everyone by surprise, including Junior, who did a double-take at his most hated enemy. Now he began recalling the multiple comments made by even his closest friends, including Dread, about his and Mario's many similarities. Mario now had all eyes on him and seized the moment.

"I always knew I had a brother, and coming up as an only child I wished that one day we would meet. My mom never told me much about my daddy because I don't think she knew him or his family for too long, but she did tell me his name was Edward Tatum. I used to ask everybody with the last name Tatum all about their father because I never knew if they might be my brothers or sisters." Mario looked at the floor the entire time he spoke, then continued. "When I met Junior in YA . . . I just knew we had the same dad."

"How did you know that?" asked Branch.

"Because we look alike, talk alike, both got mad game on the court, scared of nobody, and I just know he's my brother." Looking directly at a now-passive Junior, Mario continued. "I know you're my brother but never knew why you hated me so much. I never did anything to you, and it seemed like you've hated me from the start. I'm willing to take the test, but I already know what it's going to say."

Mario and Junior continued to stare at each other as both their eyes began to cloud with moisture. Shirley and Crystal openly wept, while Detective Branch used all the will power he could muster not to do the same.

"Awight," Junior spoke softly, "I'll do it."

"Then it's settled. I'll see if I can arrange it," said Branch. "Be back in a flash." Detective Branch walked out, leaving the foursome alone. Five minutes later he returned with Jimmy Chang, who walked over to Mario and inserted a swab inside his mouth before placing it into a ziplock baggie. After repeating the procedure with Junior, Jimmy walked out. The process took seconds, but what amazed everyone present except Branch was the fact that Jimmy never spoke a word.

"We'll know the results shortly," stated Branch, who then trailed Jimmy to the lab. No one said a word as the room remained eerily silent.

21

SUDDEN TRANSFORMATION

Horace and Harriette returned to his crib from shopping, loaded up with groceries and clothing. It had been a pleasant day. They had driven out to the city of Vacaville to shop at the Outlet Mall, which housed more than one hundred and twenty stores. Horace stocked up on discounted slacks, dress shirts, and shoes, while Harriette purchased everything from business suits to casual dresses, sandals, pumps, panties, jewelry, and make-up. She tried to convince Horace to buy a few items for his nephew but he declined, stating rather forcefully that Mario would not wear any of them.

Stopping at a grocery store, Harriette purchased an assortment of snacks and finger foods. She would be playing hostess that evening for a dinner party at her house, where the invited guests were family and close friends. Horace declined to attend because he did not particularly care for most of her relatives, who subtly displayed hints of being racist.

Since Harriette had driven her car, Horace had her drop him off at home. Kissing her goodbye while promising a wonderful day tomorrow that he had planned, he retrieved his packages from the back seat. Walking through the entry door on the first floor, Horace was greeted by none other than Jerry, the building's security guard.

"Oh, I see Miss Thang took you on a shopping excursion today, huh?"

"Yes, Jerry, we picked up a few things."

"Not the right things, I bet."

"It was okay—hey, any packages for me?"

"No, not today, but there is one waiting for you that comes gift-wrapped."

"I'm sure it does," he said, while opening his mailbox.

"Let me know when you want it delivered," stated Jerry to his back. "By the way, I met your nephew today."

"Oh really."

"Yes, and judging from Mario, I now know that good looks run in the family genes."

"You're very observant," said Horace while stepping inside the elevator.

"Let me know when you want that package delivered."

Horace laughed as the door closed, knowing full well that the package Jerry spoke of was in essence an open invitation for sex. Gerald Givens, or Jerry as he chose to be called, had served as the building's daytime security guard for ten years and had been propositioning Horace the entire time. He stood six-foot-two on a solid two-hundred-and-thirty-pound frame and always adorned himself in tight-fitting uniforms. He had a smooth butterscotch skin complexion that complemented his oval face and pearl-white teeth.

All the tenants knew he was gay and unashamed of his sexual preference, but they did not mind because Jerry protected the property as if it were his own. Nothing slipped past him, and anything out of the ordinary was noticed.

Jerry also knew all the tenants' business by serving as a listening ear when they retrieved mail or packages. The one person in the building he did not know much about was Horace, who always seemed to be quiet and reclusive. Jerry wrote it off as either Horace was still in the closet, or he had something else to hide. Regardless, Jerry felt that sooner or later the day would come when he would find out, and when that occurred, Horace Boudreaux would be accepting his big black dick while begging for more.

Having held his urine for the past two hours, Horace entered his unit and dropped the packages on the floor to run to the bathroom. Re-entering his living room relieved, he walked over to a corner bookcase located next to the trash can used to catch his cards and pushed a hidden button on top of it. Slowly the entire case rotated, opening up to reveal a custom-built closet.

Inside were several shelves full of knives, fake identification badges and credit cards, outfits, and cell phones. Lifting a chirping phone from its resting spot among numerous others, he walked back out and sat down on the sofa. Flipping it open, he smiled upon seeing one missed message. Dialing his voice-mail number while reaching for a writing tablet and pen, Horace listened intently as the caller talked.

> *"Shawn Daniels, five-ten, one-eighty-five. Hangs out on the east side and operates as a pimp near Foothill Square. Drives a burgundy Caddy.... The money has been deposited along with a generous bonus for immediate action."*

The voice was that of a regular client, but of course neither man knew the other. Walking back inside the closet, Horace gathered up a basketball referee uniform, whistle on a cotton rope, official cap, soft-soled black shoes, white socks, phony driver's license, and matching fake credit card. Marching into the bedroom, he stuffed the getup inside a small travel bag, returned to the living room pocketing the cell phone, and activated the bookcase button. The unit quietly closed as he headed out the door.

He was now in full Sweetpea mode with his brain on Shawn Daniels. Whoever he was and whatever he had done was of no concern to Sweetpea because after tonight, the target would never be heard from again. Sweetpea's dick began stiffening up as he waited for the elevator and heard his house phone ringing but decided not to re-enter and answer it. The call was one he would have wanted to hear, because Crystal was on the other end of the line with important news.

"Horace, I have some great news. Mario has a brother and sister. I'll fill you in on the details later. We're having dinner with them tonight. Call me when you get this message."

Sweetpea pulled out of the garage and drove over to Lake Merritt, where he did a Superman changing routine inside a park restroom. Now looking like an official referee, he toted the travel bag housing his original clothing back to his Mercedes and tossed it into the trunk. Cruising through downtown, he hit the 880 on-ramp with his destination being the airport.

Once there, Sweetpea pulled into a parking stall in the long-term lot, but instead of going inside the terminal, he hopped on a shuttle bus taking travelers to rental-car row. Using the fake license and credit card, he rented a black Pontiac Grand Am and headed for the east side. It was now on and Shawn Daniels, whoever he was, was as good as dead.

22

FAMILY REUNION

The corner of 83rd and Olive was saturated, with at least fifty people plus an equal assortment of fancy rides. Many were of the classic varieties from the sixties, such as Mustangs, Impalas, Camaros, and Falcons, all of which were restored and included the latest accessories. Young lovers embraced, sharing kisses while their bodies conducted serious bump 'n' grinds more suited to the confines of a bedroom.

Several people were huddled in groups of three or more, drinking alcohol and smoking dope while bobbing their heads to very loud rap cuts. Parking was at a premium, yet one spot in front of the Grissom household remained empty. It was reserved for the guests of honor who had yet to arrive. Children frolicked inside a large helium-filled jumping gym on the front lawn as parents watched the proceedings, making sure that no one got hurt.

Inside the home Al Green's soulful tune "Love and Happiness" reverberated throughout the small yet stylishly decorated crib as Shirley reveled in the role of hostess. The living room was full of family and friends drinking assorted liquors while adding to the already festive atmosphere. In the kitchen, women whipped up side dishes such as baked beans, potato salad, candied yams, mac and cheese, and cakes and pies.

The aroma wafting throughout the house normally would have stomachs churning, but with the booze being guzzled like there was no tomorrow, no one seemed to care about eating. There was some truth to the myth that alcohol curbs the appetite, but the real drinkers would eat before, or while consuming their poison. Flat-out alcoholics would bypass meals opting to get sloppy drunk, make a fool of themselves, then wake up the next morning with humongous headaches and empty bellies.

Out back, barbeque was being cooked by some of Junior's crew, with the scent engulfing the entire neighborhood. Pay for the right to play big-money domino and card games went on everywhere in the spacious yard, with arguments few and far between. No one wanted to upset Junior on his special night, so the feuding was kept to a minimum. The designated cookers did as cooks do, which is sample food while cooking to make certain the ribs, links, chicken, and hot dogs would be tasty to all.

Shirley's big mouth could be heard in the front yard and back, drowning out the music both inside and out. She was on cloud nine, proudly bragging about her sleuthing technique in revealing Big Ed's long-lost son. Junior could hardly care what his mother said because he was too consumed by the fact that until a few hours earlier, he had wanted to kill his own brother.

Guilt overwhelmed him, and he vowed to himself that he would right that wrong by taking Mario under his wing, exposing him to the finer things in life, along with giving him free street game. He paced the living room, occasionally sneaking peeks out the front window while checking his watch for the time. His sister Edwina had learned of the news from her mom and was still in shock by it all. She sat on the sofa surrounded by home girls telling her how excited they were for her and Junior.

Built in the same mold as Junior and her dead father, Edwina stood six-foot-one on a two-hundred-and-twenty-pound frame. Unlike many tall women who had funny builds, she was stacked with long thick legs, nice mouth-watering behind, large breasts, and a beautiful cocoa-butter face. She was a combination of Shirley's looks and her father's build, with tight-fitting jeans and top accenting the obvious.

Shirley noticed the time rapidly heading toward seven and became worried, thinking maybe the guests had changed their minds.

Glancing out the window yet once again finding the reserved spot in front of the house empty, she decided to call Crystal on the cell phone number she had been given at police headquarters. Before she could retrieve the phone, Junior yelled out to everyone present that the guests were pulling up.

All activity in front, out back, and inside the home ceased as people patiently waited for Crystal to park her ride. Mario hopped out, impressed by the welcoming party, while Crystal secretly grimaced at the sight. She had disliked Shirley's ghetto tendencies at the station and, judging by the goings-on outside her crib, Crystal realized that agreeing to come to the party was a big mistake.

It was the same environment she had tried to protect her son from his whole life, and now he had a new band of people who lived it on a daily basis. As Mario bounced up the walkway to the front door, she slowly trudged behind, uncertain what was in store. Everything was quiet, which surprised her, yet the moment he entered the front door a raucous shout of **SURPRISE!** greeted him, along with a plethora of smiling faces.

Shirley was the first to embrace Mario in a bear hug, which was instantly followed by many more as introductions were underway. Crystal entered, receiving the same treatment along with jealous eyes from most of the women, who were upset that, first, she was fine, and second, she probably knew Big Ed had a wife yet still gave up the pootnanny to him, producing Mario.

Even though Shirley's friends and sisters wanted to grill Crystal with an interrogation, they agreed not to spoil Junior and Edwina's party by doing it tonight. The music resumed, with the party taking off in earnest as couples began dancing to the funk cut "Slide" by the show band Slave. Junior gripped Mario in a vice lock hug, lifting his large frame off the ground while immediately whispering more "I'm sorrys" into his ear.

"Man, ah'mo make it up to you," Junior promised.

"Don't worry 'bout it, bro—you didn't know," Mario responded.

"Naw, ah mean, ah wonted to bump—"

"Junior," Edwina snapped, standing in front of them, "let me meet my brother."

Releasing his bear hug, Junior took a step back while Edwina wrapped her arms solidly around her brother, squeezing him tightly. Mario hugged her just as tightly, as all eyes focused on the threesome. Crystal took a seat on the sofa next to Shirley, who immediately pulled out a family photo album and handed it to her. Crystal opened it and began flipping the pages as Shirley gave a detailed description of each picture, including where it was taken, the occasion, and who was in it.

Junior, Edwina, and Mario retreated to an empty bedroom, closing the door behind them as everyone began lining up out back for their meals.

"Isn't it wonderful that we found each other?" Edwina stated to Mario.

"Yeah, it's cool."

"We have so much catching up to do. What do you know about Daddy?"

"I'ont know nuttin' 'bout him."

"Well, we were little when he died so we don't know too much either, but let me tell you what I do know."

Edwina began filling Mario in on the little bit she knew of their father, which wasn't much but enough to keep him and Junior listening intently for the next thirty minutes. They peppered her with a dozen questions but, truth be told, she answered by telling them what she thought instead of actual facts. The only thing Junior knew was that his old man ran the EDE, ruled it with an iron fist, and didn't take mess from no one.

Mario told them about his family, mother, and growing up an only child with no clue as to his father. All three held hands the entire time, promising to stay in each other's lives forever. Walking out of the room they found the party still going on, with Shirley and Crystal in the same spots as before. Edwina introduced Mario to her husband James and three kids, while Junior headed for the kitchen.

James, or Jimmy as she called him, stood no more than five-foot-six on a solidly built hundred-and-fifty-pound welterweight body. Mario instantly recognized that Jimmy had a great sense of humor, and furthermore, he could tell that Edwina ruled their house by the sarcastic remarks she made and her tone of voice. Junior returned from the kitchen holding hands with a super-fine sister who stood a tallish five-eleven, with curves in all the right places.

"Lil' bro, dis mah gurlll Monique."

"Nice to meet you," Mario greeted her.

He stuck out his hand to shake, but she startled him by stepping into his arms and giving him a sensuous hug. Junior and Edwina laughed loudly before patting Mario on the back as most observers became eerily silent.

"She likes you, bro," Junior said. "But don't get no ideas 'cause mah girl don't hug nobody but me."

"He ain't even lyin'," Edwina co-signed.

Next, Edwina introduced him to all of her home girls, many of whom, although older, had been ogling Mario flirtatiously from the time he entered the crib. Junior rode many of them and would fill his brother in on the details later. Grabbing Mario by the elbow, Junior whisked him into the back yard, while Edwina retreated to the front with her girls.

"Man, ah wont you ta meet mah boyz."

All activity stopped as Junior introduced each and every one of them to his little brother, with Mario recognizing several of them as former enemies from the Youth Authority, yet now they all greeted him as family.

"Listen up, yaw," Junior said. "Ta-marraw we gone meet at da park, two o'clock ... Ah got some impotant bidness to discuss."

Gambling and getting high resumed as Junior headed out the

back gate with Mario. "Less take a ride," Junior said while de-activating the alarm on his Navigator.

Mario hopped inside, impressed by the massive vehicle, while Junior acted as though it was no big deal. Driving over a few blocks to Bancroft with rap music shaking the pavement beneath them (along with providing future hearing impairments), Junior pulled up at the neighborhood store. The scene was like all others in the hood, with dealers and freeloaders saturating the tiny storefront, while fiends both on foot and pulling up in their cars spent money.

All of the dealers worked for Junior and had already heard through the grapevine that he had found a long-lost brother. Just like at the house, Mario was greeted with dignity and respect as Junior warned everyone within earshot that his brother was to be treated in the same fashion they treated Junior himself. Inside the market he scooped up several twelve-packs of beer, a variety of hard liquor, and a box of Black and Milds.

"Thank yo momma gone let you spend da nite?" he asked Mario while paying.

"Ah cain't call it, bro, she be hella square, see what ah'm sayin'?"

"Yeah, ah do, but mah moms don't get down like dat; ah'll put a bug in her ear den let her ask yo moms. If she do like ah know she will, she'll put her on blast in front uh everybody."

"If dat happen, moms gone let me do it 'cause she hate ta be own front street."

By the time they returned to the crib, the party had slowed down considerably, with many of the guests gone. The two brothers entered the living room and were surprised to find Crystal holding a foil-wrapped plate of food while jingling her keys. Shirley and Edwina were cleaning up, so Junior made his play as soon as his mother went into the kitchen.

"You ready?" Crystal asked Mario.

"Not really but if you are. . . ."

"Crystal, honey?" Shirley shouted, heading in her direction with

Junior on her heels, "you thank it's alright for Mario to spend da night wif his brother an' sister? Ah mean, dey do have a lot of catchin' up ta do."

"Well, I don't think so. I mean, I wouldn't want him to wear out his welcome so soon."

"Aw, baby, dat ain't a problem—he needs ta know his kin. Ah'll tell you what: ah'll be personally responsible."

"Please, Mom," Mario begged with Junior and Edwina staring at her for a response.

"Oh okay," she reluctantly agreed, "but you behave yourself!"

"Thanks, Momma." Mario gave her a kiss on the cheek.

They all walked Crystal out to her car, with each person giving her her hugs. Setting her plate on the front passenger floorboard, she pulled away from the curb. The moment she was out of sight she reached down, picked up the food, rolled down her window, then tossed it outside. She had no intentions of eating because the people just didn't appear to be that clean and sanitary. Next, she lifted her cell phone from her purse, speed-dialing her brother Horace. Receiving his answering machine, she left a message:

> *"Hi, Brother, it's me. Those people are crazy and I know I should not have, but I agreed to let Mario spend the night. He better make it good because it will be the last time he stays there. That Shirley is something else, mouth vulgar, drinks like a fish, and I'm sure she was selling dope out of her house. Anyway, where are you? Call me as soon as you get this message. I love you."*

Crystal ended the call, tossed her phone onto the passenger seat, and cried all the way home. She just did not feel good about Mario's newfound relatives and knew if he hung around them, he was headed for trouble.

23

PIMP NO MORE

Sweetpea entered the self-service car wash on MacArthur Boulevard after receiving a tip from one of his many informants that Shawn Daniels hung out at that location. Just as he had been told, the mark was standing outside his ride, watching his stable of whores ply their trade. The assassin's initial plan had been to arrange a deal to buy some pussy, hold the prostitute hostage, then kill Shawn once he came to find out what was taking so long.

After surveying the set, Sweetpea scrapped the plan altogether, opting to keep an eye on his intended victim. He pulled into a stall at the vacuum area, got out, and dropped four quarters into the machine. The rental was clean as a whistle, so basically he just went through the motions. Four minutes later he re-inserted more change and repeated the process. This time when the vacuum cleaner stopped Sweetpea grabbed a bottle of window cleaner along with a roll of paper towels and methodically cleaned every window both inside and out.

The stroll between 101st and 106th featured some of the ugliest whores in the city, many of whom freelanced for spending money to support massive drug habits. Some were downright nasty-looking, carrying an assortment of sexually transmittable diseases, a fact that a sane person could deduce from just one look.

Pretty Boy considered himself the biggest pimp in the neighborhood due in large part to his having the most females in his stable. He had a total of six working the stroll, with one strategically placed on each corner. They shared two rented rooms at a flea-infested motel. The going rate ranged from twenty for straight-out intercourse to forty for a double-up of a blow job and some pussy, with Pretty Boy raking in a cool thousand nightly.

Real pimps scoffed at the notion that a fool like Pretty Boy Shawn considered himself pimpin', when simpin' was more like it and the tag given clowns like him. With that many bitches in tow, he should have been working them near downtown on San Pablo Avenue, in San Francisco, or another big city like Los Angeles or Vegas, just to name a few. That was where real money could be made, but along with it came the possibility of your whore dumping you by choosing a real pimp to manage her.

Shawn stood a meager five-foot-nine on a one-hundred-and-eighty-pound frame with an olive-oil complexion. A peanut-shaped head with low-cropped doo was covered by a royal blue fedora, which matched his Italian-designed suit and shoes. Hazel-colored, sleepy-looking bedroom eyes instantly caught your attention, and the brother did possess a required element of the trade, which was a gift for gab. However, his pimping career was stuck in neutral, and he was the last to know that he would be forever small-time.

His bottom bitch was an eighteen-year-old named Cherry who would be the sorriest whore on any other stroll in the county. Yet on the east-side strip she was the finest, with a nice booty, softball-sized tits, and a decent popcorn-yellow shade. Similar to the rest of his crew, Cherry was dressed in cheap shorts and tank top purchased from Wal-Mart, along with fake-designer high heels from Payless Shoes.

Pretty Boy had snagged her into his stable one night four months prior while having cocktails at The Sports Page nightclub, his favorite watering hole due to its location one block from his "office." A bad girl, Cherry was down on her luck with nowhere to sleep when Shawn rescued her from her predicament. Instantly becoming the star attraction in his stable, Cherry considered herself smarter than the rest of his girls and knew she was raking in twice as much cash nightly.

Slowly she began skimming from the take, and with Pretty Boy being no dummy, he set out to nab her red-handed. His plan was simple: her first customer would pay for a double-up then Shawn would collect the money. The guy was a childhood friend named Moses, and since he was getting some free pussy plus fifty dollars for the charade, he was all for it.

"Whatup, Pretty Boy?" Moses asked.

"Here's what you do: pay the bitch forty for a double-up then come back and I'll take care of you for your troubles."

"Dass a bet, dawg."

Sweetpea washed windows while noticing a frail-looking dope-fiend approach Pretty Boy, who handed over what appeared to be cash. Ten minutes later he returned, and Pretty Boy gave him more money before hopping into his ride and driving off in the direction of the motel. Sweetpea knew the game was about to begin and got into his own vehicle, trailing by one block.

Pretty Boy inserted his key into the lock, entering the room just as Cherry was ready to exit. "Bitch, give me my money," he demanded.

"Okay, Daddy." She gave him a dove.

"Oh, you think I'm a fool, don't you?"

Without warning he fired off a straight right hand, which connected squarely to her mouth, dropping her in a heap on the dingy, faded carpet. Cherry attempted to get up, only to be greeted by another thundering right hand to the forehead. Mouth bloody and indentations from his rings on her face caused Cherry to panic. She had never been struck so hard in her life, and the fear of a beat-down engulfed her body.

"Bitch trying to play me!" he yelled. "I'll kill your ass!"

"Wait, Daddy, don't hit me no more!" she pleaded through bloody lips. "I'll give you your money." Cherry snaked her hand under the mattress, pulling out a twenty and cautiously handing it to him.

"Now see, that wasn't so bad, was it?" he softened. "Here, let me look at you." Pretty Boy surveyed the damage. "Go get yourself presentable."

"I'm sorry, Daddy, it'll never happen again, I promise."

"I know it won't, bitch!" he screamed, causing her to jump. "'Cause if it does, I'll kill you!" Once again he softened his tone: "Any of them other bitches doing this shit?"

"I don't know."

"How long have you been doing it?" He rubbed her head.

"It started three days ago."

"And how much have you stolen?"

"Two hundred."

"Give it up," he demanded.

Without a word Cherry headed to the corner of the room and lifted up the carpet, retrieving two c-notes she had pilfered. Pretty Boy was counting the cash when an idea struck.

"Here"—he handed it back to her—"put the money back then run your game on the rest of my bitches. I wanna know which ones I can trust."

"Okay, Daddy." She returned the cash to its original hiding place then went to the bathroom to wash the blood off her face.

He hollered instructions to her from the bedroom. "Don't tell them bitches I know the deal, just see who's willing to go for your scheme then tell me. Got it?"

"I got it, Daddy." Cherry said as she exited the bathroom. She kissed Pretty Boy on the cheek then marched out the door, secretly vowing never to return. No man was going to hit her and get away with it because even at that young an age she knew that after the first beat-down, many more would follow. Pretty Boy began lifting up the mattress, pulling up carpet from every corner, and searching the entire room to see if there were any more hiding places stashed with "his" cash. When he turned to leave he was caught off guard by an older black man wearing a referee's outfit. He was closing the door.

Pretty Boy's extrasensory perception warned him of impending danger, causing his body to square up into a defensive fighting stance. With all senses on alert and dude closing the door, he still tried to remain cool. One of the neighborhood taboos you learn quickly growing up in the ghetto is never to display fear in the face of adversity. Besides, he felt he could easily handle the old guy and, just like all youngsters, the aspiring pimp thought himself invincible.

"What can I do for you, bro?" he asked Sweetpea.

It was only after Sweetpea turned to face him that Pretty Boy spotted the knife gripped tightly inside the palm of his hand. Snatching a pillow off the bed, Pretty Boy flicked it at his assailant then bum-rushed him with the force of a linebacker. Sweetpea, initially startled by Pretty Boy's ploy, deftly stepped to the side like a matador evading an onrushing bull, then gripped his mark's head in a vice lock while slicing his neck from ear to ear.

Roughly slamming the young pimp face first to the rug, he folded up the blade and exited as quickly as he had entered. Heading to his car, he drove a few blocks away before pulling out his untraceable cell phone and dialing the given number. "Hello" greeted the receiver.

"Mission accomplished," Sweetpea said then hung up.

Pretty Boy Shawn died instantly as blood oozed out his neck, ruining the dirty carpet. The motel owners would now be forced to replace it, and Oaktown cops would have another unsolvable homicide on their hands. Once back in rental-car row, the professional hit man exited his vehicle in the return lot and disappeared to the front of the building.

Taking the shuttle bus back to the airport, he located his car in the long-term lot, changed on the spot (dumping the killing clothes plus phone into a garbage can), paid the attendant, then drove away. Retrieving his regular cell phone from the glove box, he called Harriette.

"Hello," she said.

"How's the party?"

"It's winding down, dear. There are only, like, five people here."

"Get rid of them because I have a special treat for Juicy."

She knew that meant his dick was hard. "Okay, I do feel a headache coming on," she laughed.

"Be naked."

"I will."

Sweetpea ended the call then sped onto 880 with a raging hard-on. Killing always magnified his erections and tonight was no different. He knew Harriette would be both naked and soupy wet, but of course by morning all her juice would be on him. Harriette was sure to be served proper.

24

SECRET DISCOVERED

The party had dwindled down to eight people engaged in a serious game of poker, with five more waiting their turn. Unlike most games where one particular style was played the entire evening, this one was played under Grissom house rules, with whoever dealing at the time allowed to call out the format. Thus strategies and betting habits changed dramatically on each and every hand. One game would be seven-card stud, followed by deuces wild, or follow the queen, or Doctor Pepper, or the more famous Texas hold 'em.

As players lost their money and exited for home, their seats were immediately occupied by fresh gamblers ready to break the house. Being an excellent card player, Shirley was extremely talented in all styles and knew when to hold, bluff, or fold. She had the largest bankroll, which in effect gave her the power position, allowing her to scare opponents into throwing away winning hands for fear of losing giant sums of money.

Unlike card parlors or casinos where liquor was barely consumed by players seeking to keep their head straight while attempting to win pots, all of these players were wasted. The advantage Shirley held by continually providing spirits was that she could consume enormous amounts of beer while steadily being in control of her faculties.

With the children peacefully asleep, Mario, Junior, Edwina, and their spouses sat comfortably in the living room engaged in conversation. Most of it was dominated by Edwina's husband Jimmy, who had everyone cracking up from the jokes he told. Edwina, however, was hardly amused and as the clock struck midnight, she informed Jimmy of her desire to leave.

Initially he balked but when she repeated her request more force-fully he obliged by first heading to the kitchen to say goodbye to "Miss Shirley" as he called her, then rousing the kids from their sleep and hoisting them one by one to the car. Junior told Monique that he and Mario would meet her at the crib later after taking care of some business.

She dutifully wrapped their girl Monica inside a blanket then followed her man and his brother inside the kitchen to say good-night. Shirley whisked them all off just as quickly as they had entered because her mind was focused on the game at hand. Outside, Monique pulled off in one direction with Junior and Mario going in the other. She never pestered him regarding his whereabouts due to the nature of his job.

Junior worked twenty-four/seven, with the majority of his money being made while normal people slept. He and Mario hopped inside his ride, Junior rambling on about the big time he had in store, when Mario suddenly realized he did not have anything to wear.

"Can you run me by my uncle's crib, bro?"

"No doubt. Why you wanna do dat, dough?"

"Ah need ta get mah clothes. Ah got some dare, an some at Mom's crib, but ah ain't even tryin' ta let her see me, see what ah'm sayin'?"

"Yeah, ah feel ya. Where yo unc stay at?"

"He stay over by the lake on Fairmont."

"Ah thought you said he don't like nobody comin' ta his pad?"

"He don't, but wit him, ah ain't gone have no mama drama."

"Here, call him first."

Junior handed his phone to Mario, who dialed Horace's number. Receiving no answer, he returned the phone to his brother, inform-ing him of the result.

"He prolly at dat grey gurl's house he be fuckin' wit," Mario said sarcastically.

"Is she phine?" Junior asked while passing a half-smoked joint.

"Thicker dan a muafucka, dude—if he wadn't mah uncle, I'd try ta get some uh dat."

The remainder of the ride to Horace's crib was spent with the brothers sucking away on weed while finding any and everything hilarious. Mario told Junior of his encounter with Jerry the security guard, and by the time he was done, Junior was busting at the seams.

"Maybe he liked what he saw, playa!" Junior roared at his own wit. "You know, dose big greasy Kentucky fried chicken-eatin' muafuckas like healthy young broncos lack yo ass!"

"Shidd," Mario retorted, "all ah got fa dat fool is a mutha-fuckin ass-whuppin', see what ah'm sayin'!"

"I'ont know, bro, some uh dem niggahs can throw dose thangs, ya know."

"Man, ah'll beat dat tight pants-wearin' muthafucka ta death! Let his ass say sumptun outta line an see!"

Having to park nearly two blocks away, Junior signified so hard on his brother that by the time they reached the condo complex Mario was in a rage. The last person he wanted to see was Jerry and so he let out a sigh of relief upon spotting an elderly white dude sitting at the security desk reading a magazine. Walking past the main entrance, Mario scanned the garage, feeling a huge sigh of relief upon seeing his uncle's stall empty. Returning to the front, Mario unlocked the door and headed for the elevator with Junior on his heels.

Wilbur Ramsey had served the complex nearly as long as Jerry after retiring from a thirty-year career at the post office, yet hardly knew any of the residents. He worked the graveyard shift, spending an equal amount of hours fighting sleep as opposed to providing security. His face was shrunken and full of wrinkles, with thick bifocals covering his gray, glossy-looking eyes. Thinning white hair topped his dome, with bald spots peeking through the patches.

With the time being rather early in his shift, he was still awake and sat up in his chair, eying the two young black men as they entered the building. He had never seen them before but he knew many of the condo owners rented their units out, which caused a high occupancy turnover.

"New here?" he questioned the pair.

"Ah live wit mah Uncle Horace in da penthouse," Mario answered.

"What's your name?"

"Mario Hayes."

Wilbur scanned the tenant list but did not see Mario's name on it. Setting down the magazine while replacing it with a clipboard pulled out of the top drawer, he turned it around on the desk and handed Mario a writing pen.

"You'll have to sign in, sir."

Mario snatched the pen, signing his name then handing it over to his brother, who did the same. The guard placed the visitors log back inside the desk then resumed reading his magazine, unaware that Mario was giving him a death stare-down while inserting his key into the penthouse slot on the elevator panel. The door quietly closed and the siblings rode up silently, each absorbed in his own thoughts. Before it opened Mario broke the ice.

"Hope he ain't here."

"You said his car gone, right?"

"Yeah, it's gone."

"Den he ain't heah, and if he is, you just came ta get yo shit an give him his key back," Junior stated convincingly.

"Yeah, dass why I came," Mario thought out loud.

All the scheming was for naught because once they entered the penthouse it was both dark and empty. Mario flicked on the lights while Junior immediately walked over to the window, staring out into the brightly lit downtown skyline.

"Man, look at dat shit," he whistled. "See, dis day way a niggah spose ta be livin', bro."

"Cool, ain't it," Mario agreed, more of a statement than a question.

"Bro, dat ain't even da half of it—yo uncle must be makin' some big-time cheese to affode all liss."

Mario headed for the room, returning with his clothes stuffed inside the duffel bag his mother had given his uncle earlier. Junior remained stationary at the window, gazing out at the awesome view.

"Whatcha thankin' 'bout, bro?"

"Mario, dis da kinda livin' ah be tellin' mah gurl 'bout. Ba-leave it or not, ah'mo be livin' large like dis real soon."

"Ah know, man, hopefully me too."

"Ain't no hope, pahtna—stick wit me an yo ass goin' straight to da top—feel me?"

"Yeah, ah feel you."

They turned to leave when Junior spotted the playing cards on the coffee table. "Oh, dude play cards, huh?"

"Naw, man, he flicks dose muthafuckas into dat can." Mario pointed at the trash can.

"Dass dumb, man." Junior frowned. "Why would he waste time doin' dat?"

"I'ont know." Mario shrugged his shoulders. "But da fool makes every last one—man, you should see dat shit. Ah mean, he sits right heah on da couch and one by one, every card sinks into the can."

"No shit?" Junior was impressed.

"No shit, dawg."

Out of curiosity, Junior picked up the deck and flicked a card toward the can, missing badly. Embarrassed, he tried over and over, continuing to do worse than the time before. Mario accepted the deck from his brother, explaining to Junior the way Uncle Horace had explained it to him.

"See, it's in da wrist, bro. You gotta have a steady hand, and a lot uh control."

Mario flicked one, which sailed on top of the bookcase out of sight. Junior laughed a hearty laugh, for now his embarrassment was minor compared to his younger brother's poor attempt.

"Man, fuck dis shit!" Junior bellowed. "Less raise da fuck outta heah!"

"Okay, let me put da cards back first," Mario said.

Picking up all the loose cards off the floor, Mario then snaked his hand on top of the bookcase, blindly searching for the last one. Suddenly the entire unit began rotating a quarter turn as the brothers stood watching with mouths agape. Looking at each other in astonishment, they then looked inside the open closet, amazed at the sight. Junior was the first to investigate, with Mario peering in over his shoulder.

"Man, look at dis shit!" Junior said to Mario. "Da niggah got enough knives to supply an army. Hey, check out da cell phones an fake IDs. Dude, yo uncle into some big-time shit. This remind me of a James Bond-type setup wit fake closets an thangs, see what ah'm sayin'?"

"Yeah, dis shit off da hook, huh?"

"Dat ain't even da word—man, less get out dis spooky-ass place foe he catch us!"

Mario ran to the kitchen and grabbed a chair from the dinner table. He stood on it in front of the partially open bookcase while Junior followed his lead, getting a chair of his own. Now they both were in position to view the hidden activation switch, whistling at the sight.

"Damn, dude, see dat shit?" Junior now whispered.

"Yeah," Mario answered, just as softly. "His ass paid good money for a hookup like this."

Pulling the chairs out of range, Mario deactivated the switch, watching along with Junior as the bookcase silently rotated back to its original position. Replacing the chairs at the table, they bounced toward the door rapidly. Mario set the keys on the kitchen table when Junior advised against it.

"Keep dose," he warned. "We might need um later own."

Mario retrieved the keys then they cut out quickly for the elevator without a word spoken. Inside, Mario hit the garage button, opting to avoid the security guard as Junior nodded his head in approval. Practically running through the garage to the exit gate, they hit the street feeling relieved by the cool air striking them in the face. Passing the entrance, both of them laughed upon seeing Wilbur fast asleep at the front desk.

"Man, dass what ah call some po-ass security. He cain't protect a damn thang," Junior said.

"Ah know," Mario returned, "but from da looks of it, Unc don't need no goddamn protection no how."

"Dat niggah must be doin' sumptun illegal," Junior stated convincingly.

"His ass might be a spy, or a double agent," Mario said.

Hopping into Junior's ride, each brother now felt safe and wondered if Horace would know they had been inside his crib. Or better yet, located his secret closet. Regardless, they would get to the bottom of it, and at worst, Uncle Horace's game had been exposed. Junior drove away sucking on a phat joint before passing it to Mario.

25
A DIFFERENT APPROACH

The murder scene at the motel was similar to all the rest, with technicians methodically collecting evidence and snapping photos while uniformed police cordoned off the area. Newspaper reporters questioned anyone willing to give a statement, while television personalities practiced their lines off to the side and out of range from curious onlookers. As usual, two men from the coroner's office sat at the back of their van waiting for it all to be done so they could remove the body from the premises and haul it downtown for an autopsy.

It was a circus-like atmosphere that surprised neither Boston nor Jimenez as they maneuvered past the proceedings, waiting patiently while beat cops removed makeshift barricades to allow them access. Pretty Boy's stable of whores, minus Cherry, stood in a circle off to the side waiting for the inevitable questioning from police detectives. They had already decided Cherry had to be involved, for she was the last person to use the room, and with her whereabouts unknown, it did not take a genius to deduce that she knew something.

Boston headed for the beat cops to get their reports and information while Jimenez questioned the prostitutes. Five minutes later they met outside the motel room door and compared notes before entering.

"Neither the women nor motel proprietors saw or witnessed anything," she said to her partner.

"It figures," he responded. "I scored a zero too."

"There is one girl missing, and she was the last person to see the victim alive."

"Let me guess, she only has a street name, right?" Boston was sarcastic.

"They call her Cherry, but I'm sure the boys down in vice can probably provide a name for her."

"Okay, then we'll—"

"I know," she cut him off, "I've already requested it."

"Good work, detective," he chided.

"I was trained by the best." She played the game with him.

"Shall we?" He motioned toward the door.

"By all means."

They entered the overcrowded room, noticing several pieces of rug lifted up from the corners. The mattress had obviously been shifted, alerting them to the fact that someone was definitely searching for something. Pretty Boy lay on the floor face down in a pool of his own blood, outlined by white chalk markings. Technicians inspected his fingernails for skin fragments, snapped photos of his prone body, and collected blood samples for DNA testing.

"Anybody got a name for this guy?" Boston blurted out.

"Shawn Daniels," Jimenez answered. "Street tag of Pretty Boy, lightweight pimp who obviously has retired."

"Well, judging by the loud attire, he had to be flamboyant."

"Colorful is more appropriate," she corrected.

"Let's see what method was used," Boston said while slightly lifting Pretty Boy's head.

Getting down on his knees while making sure not to get them soiled from blood, he called his partner down to view with him. They gave each other knowing looks.

"The Knifeman," they blurted out in unison.

"Notice the precision cut," he said.

"Obviously the hit was swift and without witnesses—I know it's our boy."

"We really need to nab this creep," Boston growled.

"I agree wholeheartedly, but without clues, we'll be just as dumb-founded as our predecessors."

"Wait a minute!" Boston removed the latex gloves, holding an index finger up to each temple.

"What?" Jimenez asked, animated.

"I have an idea!"

"Not another one of your bright ones, I hope."

"Hold on before you jump to conclusions—"

"Alright, lay it on me."

"This guy has been operating for years under a cloud of secrecy, right?"

"Yes."

"Well, what's say we expose him to the public?"

"Now how are we supposed to do that, Holmes?"

"Elementary, my dear—we get the department to agree to an in-depth profile in a series of stories in the papers and on the news."

"Then someone, somewhere, may know the guy," she answered for him.

"Exactly!" he yelled. "Let's run it by the boss first."

"I'm down with that."

The detectives left the crime scene, making a beeline toward their service vehicle and ignoring questions from reporters. Rolling to the station, they arrived in ten minutes, barging in like there was no tomorrow. They had been discussing Boston's idea the entire time and felt that they were onto something. Edgar Lewis sat behind his desk, engaged in what appeared to be a serious conversation on the telephone.

He raised a hand up to them, which they recognized as a signal that the call was important. They both sat down to wait as he finished the conversation.

"That was the Chief saying in no uncertain terms that since it's an election year, the Mayor is on his ass for results. The murder count is almost double the average, and with our thirty percent conviction rate, things don't look rosy for our elected officials. Now, what can I do you for?" Lewis was calm.

"I, we, have a plan," Boston spoke.

"Lay it on me."

Boston relayed the entire media blitz on Lewis, with Jimenez adding her two cents' worth from time to time as he listened patiently. Once done, he and his partner sat waiting while Lewis seemed to be absorbing the idea. They each felt that it was a good plan that could effectively flush out the notorious Knifeman, and when their boss began speaking, the detectives were ready to congratulate one another for their brilliance.

"The plan is decent," Lewis said, "but does have a few flaws."

"Flaws?" Boston couldn't believe what he heard. "What kind of flaws?"

"First, if it backfires, and it possibly could by people seeing uncanny similarities in previous crimes, the department will take a beating for withholding knowledge of a known killer from the general public. Second, the city would undoubtedly receive a slew of lawsuits resulting in a public relations nightmare. And last but not least, the already shaky trust we have within the community will be destroyed."

"But if it works, we will have in custody one of the deadliest killers in the city's history!" Boston pleaded his case.

"I agree, yet before I can approach my superiors with this plan, you'll have to tie up all loose ends. Look"—he stood up—"in two hours I have a political function to attend with the Chief, and if you give me a foolproof plan to lay on him, then I can broach the subject. The mayor, city manager, and city attorney will all be present, so we can line up our ducks in a row. But I will need answers for their arguments, which I'm sure will be similar to mine."

Lewis walked out of the room and left them alone in the office with their heads down. Boston was angry while Jimenez provided the voice of reason.

"He does make some valid points," she surmised.

"Points my ass," he raised his voice. "What do you want, points or a fucking killer?"

"Calm down, Derrick, he's just covering his behind."

Boston stormed out of the office to his desk, where he remained the rest of their shift doodling while appearing to be busy. Jimenez, knowing he was on one, gave him his space by occupying her time scouring her notes regarding the Knifeman. Bored to death by his lack of enthusiasm and conversation, she exited the office with the vice unit as her destination. There she would attempt to get a line on their mystery woman, Cherry.

Half an hour later Jimenez returned with the name Chamiqua McGuire, plus a last known address and phone number. Dialing it up, she was not surprised that it was no longer in service. She also knew the address would be useless, because ladies of the night never stay in one place too long.

Once the detectives' swing shift ended, they left the office and headed to Maria's place, where Derrick immediately undressed and went to bed.

Initially she was upset with him, but as she drifted off into an uncomfortable sleep, her anger was directed at the Knifeman. It was unusual for her lover to not want sex, so as far as she was concerned, if it wasn't for the Knifeman, they would be doing it right now. She awoke the next morning pleasantly surprised to find his penis inserted deep inside her hole, banging away.

He was stroking with such fury that she closed her eyes, accepting his meat with a smile. Raising her legs high in the air while spreading them apart as wide as they would go, she kissed his chest repeatedly while he plowed violently into her steaming hot hole. Once he released a shotglass full of cum, her legs plopped down onto the bed and she gripped his body tightly.

"Not that I'm complaining, because I'm not, but what got into you?" she whispered.

"I never like to go to bed thinking about another man," he spilled through clenched teeth.

"Don't worry, baby, it's like Jimmy always says, you never know what will happen."

They both drifted off into another slumber until one hour later when she got up and inserted a Barry White disk into the stereo. The music began with the telephone ringing simultaneously. She lifted the receiver and spoke softly.

"Hello."

"Hi Maria, it's me, Edgar."

"What's happening, Boss?"

"Good news—I spoke with the Chief and the Mayor, and they both agree that if we do a story on the Knifeman it will more than likely provide us with some solid leads."

"Ooh, that's wonderful! Have you told Derrick?" She knew he had not.

"No, I'll call him as soon as we are done. There is one catch, though."

"What is it?"

"The article in question has to be crafted in a manner where the public will only know about the recent killings, and specific details of the crimes cannot be given."

"So that means we'll only mention the past three which include the pimp, the double homicide on Dimond, and two on the west side."

"Exactly," Lewis said. "Now, our boy Harold was at the event, and the Chief got him to agree to write a feature series. He started on it this morning and will be waiting for you two at his office for input."

"I'm getting dressed."

"Good, I'll telephone Derrick."

"Bye," she said, "and Lieutenant—?"

"Yes, Sergeant?"

"Thank you."

Rousing Boston from his nap, Jimenez had time to give him a one-minute rundown on her phone call with Lewis before his cell phone rang. He answered it, talking briefly with the boss, while she took a shower. After hanging up he bounced into the shower with her, and with newfound vigor began soaping down her back before receiving the same treatment.

Lewis sat behind his desk grinning because the same tune he had heard while talking to Jimenez was playing when he talked to Boston.

His office radio was tuned to the Quiet Storm, which was also their favorite station, so he knew they were together because they had to be listening to a recording. Picking up the phone once again, he called Harold at the *Tribune* to inform him that the detectives would be arriving within the next hour.

26

MIXED EMOTIONS

Horace pulled into his assigned parking stall, surprised to see Jerry heading his way in the underground lot. He held a sheet of paper in his hand and was not smiling, causing Horace to instantly recognize bad news on the horizon. After grabbing the bag of leftovers Harriette had given him from where he'd transported it on the back floorboard, he waited at the door for Jerry to reach him.

"Hello, Jerry," he greeted him casually, "what brings you to the dungeon on a vibrant Sunday morning?"

"I have some disturbing news."

"Lay it on me."

"From the sign-in log it seems you have a couple of visitors."

"A couple?"

"Yes, your nephew and someone with him."

"What time did they arrive?"

"At twelve-twenty in the morning."

"Who is the other person?"

"Now that's where it gets sticky." Jerry paused. "The name on the visitor log says Peter Pan."

"Peter Pan." Horace was his usual stoic self.

"We know that's not his name, but my problem is with Wilbur. I mean, he at least could have looked at the damn paper then asked for identification."

"And they're still up there?" Horace asked directly.

"They never signed out."

"Thanks, Jerry."

"Do you need any backup?"

"No, I'm quite capable of handling a couple of juvenile delinquents."

"Call down if you need me."

"Will do."

Jerry marched through the garage exit gate and up the front steps to his post while Horace took the elevator to his crib. Walking cautiously to his door, he pulled a switchblade from inside his coat pocket, palming it in his hand, then entered the pad silently. Finding the house dark, he tiptoed through the living room into the hallway leading to the bedrooms, using the darkness as his element of surprise.

Flicking on the light switch, he found Mario's room empty with the bed untouched. Next, he opened the closet then repeated the process in his room. Wandering back into the living room he noticed the message display button showing he had missed three calls, but before he could play them his phone rang.

"Hello," he greeted.

"Is everything okay?" Jerry asked.

"Yes, I guess they failed to sign out. It looks like Mario has taken his belongings."

"Oh, a night crawler, huh?"

"You could say that."

"Call me if you need me."

"Thanks, Jerry."

Horace hung up the phone then pressed the playback button on his messages. The first one was from Harriette, thanking him for a wonderful night of sex; it had been left ten minutes earlier. He punched the forward button then headed for the kitchen, retrieving a can of coffee along with a fresh filter. Crystal's voice froze him in his tracks but she was not making sense. He sat the can down then pushed the replay button, listening intently.

"Hi Brother, it's me. Those people are crazy and I know I should not have, but I agreed to let Mario spend the night. He better make it good because it will be the last time he stays there. That Shirley is something else—mouth vulgar,

drinks like a fish, and I'm sure she was selling dope out of her house. Anyway, where are you? Call me as soon as you get this message. I love you."

Still without a clue as to what she was talking about, he waited for the next message.

"Horace, I have some great news. Mario has a brother and sister. I'll fill you in on the details later. We're having dinner with them tonight. Call me when you get this message."

Closing his eyes, Horace's body trembled with emotion while his hands subconsciously lifted the deck of cards off the table. His hands easily flicked them one by one into the trash bucket. It was then that he noticed all the footprints mashed into the carpet, with most leading to his killing closet. Upon further inspection he saw the imprints left by chair legs, which caused his heart to thump violently against his shirt.

Hitting the activation button on top of the bookcase, he paced the floor while it quietly rotated open. One look inside was all it took for him to know that he had indeed been violated because he had installed a special piece of rug on the floor that he never stepped on. Footprints were all over it so he knew someone had been in there. Mario, and whoever he had with him—possibly this newfound brother—had discovered his hole in the wall, as he called it. Now he was in a rage, with his mindset assuming the alter-ego role of Sweetpea, assassin for hire.

He knew that in order to avoid jail time, his secret could not be revealed, and if that meant bringing severe heartache to his sister Crystal, then so be it. Mario should not have been snooping around inside his crib; and had he behaved like a normal teenager, this could have been avoided. Of course his uncle felt like a fool for giving the young buck a key but did warn him never to bring anyone inside his place.

Stepping inside the closet, he selected an all-black outfit consisting of khaki pants, turtleneck sweater, tennis shoes, waist-length leather coat, and beanie cap, plus several killing knives. Packing the clothes he had just taken off inside a duffel bag, Horace changed on the spot, then selected a fake identification complement of driver's license and credit card. Storming about, he snatched his phone with such force that he nearly ripped the entire unit from the wall socket.

"Jerry," he spoke boldly into the phone.

"Yes, Horace. Is everything alright?"

"Nothing I can't handle," he said. "It seems Mario and his guest stole some money from me, so I will need my locks changed."

"Consider it done," Jerry stated, "and as far as this Peter Pan, I've already informed the boss that Wilbur was sleeping on the job again. You know that ass gives my profession a bad name and the sooner we get rid of him, well, it won't be soon enough!"

"Handle your business, man."

Horace ended the call without so much as a goodbye, activated the bookcase button, and marched to the stairwell. Knowing Jerry as he did, he knew that his phone call downstairs would result in Jerry taking the elevator up for a nosy investigation. By that time he planned on being long gone. It worked perfectly because as Jerry stood outside his unit banging on the door, Horace was pulling out of the driveway.

Ten minutes later Horace was marching up Crystal's front steps with the solitary purpose of learning Mario's whereabouts. She answered her door on the first ring, and it was obvious to him that his sister was on her way to church. Decked out in a light-blue dress that ran down to her knees along with a matching hat, Crystal was surprised by her brother's visit. Clutching her purse in one hand while dangling the house and car keys in the other, she stepped to the side, allowing him to enter.

"Hey Sis, what's going on?" He kissed her on the cheek.

"I don't know where to begin...." They both sat on the sofa.

"Mario has siblings, right?"

"Yes. While at the police station yesterday we found out the boy he was fighting is his brother."

"He was fighting?"

"Yes, him and some other boys had a big brawl at a Mexican restaurant on High Street. Anyway, while I was waiting for him to be released this crazy woman kept on yakking, and when they brought Mario out, she began claiming that his father was also the father of her son."

"That would be the one you call Shirley?"

"Yes, it is. Once Officer Branch sat them side by side, it was obvious to all of us that they did resemble one another."

"So where is the proof?"

"They did a DNA test and it came back ninety-nine point nine percent positive that they indeed are brothers." Crystal began crying.

"In your message you said that Mario was spending the night with them."

"I should have never agreed to that."

"Where do they live?"

"Shirley lives on 83rd and Olive. I told Mario to come home today."

"I don't think that's going to happen."

"Why not?" She dried her eyes with a sheet of tissue.

"Because last night while I was with Harriette, Mario came to my place and took his belongings."

"WHAT?" Crystal screamed. "Horace, we've got to find him!"

"I know, I know, just leave it to me."

Horace planted another kiss on Crystal's cheek then walked out. Now mentally exhausted, she undressed then lay down on the sofa in a fetal position, crying her eyes out. He drove to the airport, parked his car in the long-term lot, then caught a shuttle bus to rental-car row.

27

FACT FINDER

The Tribune Tower sat on the corner of 13th and Franklin, six blocks from police headquarters. It was one of Oaktown's greatest landmarks, complete with a monstrous tower atop the three-hundred-and-ten-foot-high structure. It housed giant clocks on all four sides that were visible from any angle throughout the entire city. Since it was Sunday morning and the office closed to the public, the only people inside were reporters working on new stories inside the sixth-floor newsroom.

Boston phoned from outside the locked building to announce their arrival, then he and Jimenez waited to be let in. Moments later, Harvey Underwood pranced off the elevator and hurriedly rushed to the door. Boston and Jimenez both smiled broadly as Harvey made his way to them. He was family to most cops, having served as a crime beat reporter for nearly thirty years, and he knew everyone on the force on a first-name basis.

A little man, Harvey stood a meager five-seven, weighing in at one hundred and fifty pounds. He fit the classic reporter stereotype in appearance with beige cotton Dockers, rumpled white with red stripes button-down shirt, no tie, brown corduroy sport coat, run-over light brown shoes, with a stained peanut-butter fedora tilted beyond his receding hairline.

Fifty-five years young, Harvey had been writing the stories of murder and mayhem in the city as long as anyone could remember; he could recite criminal names along with the crimes they committed rapid-fire off the top of his head. His pale-white skin complexion instantly gave off the notion that he didn't get out much, and his conversations always centered on a writer's creed consisting of the five W's and an H—that being who, what, when, where, why, and how come?

On first assumption one would label Harvey a nerd from his clean-shaven face, bifocal glasses covering his aqua-blue eyes, mismatched attire, and square conversations. Yet the more he engaged you in rap, the better understanding he would gain of your mentality and/or perspective. He took his job seriously and was very good at his craft. Had it not been for his weakling body, he surely would have been a cop and probably the best interrogator they'd ever known.

"Hey, you guys," Harvey greeted the pair as he opened the door. "Let's go up to my office. I've already prepared a couple of rough drafts but need to ask you a few questions to gain a better insight into this creep's mindset."

"Harvey, how are ya?" Boston shook his hand.

"Sorry to have you working on your off day, Mister Underwood," Jimenez blurted.

"No apology needed, Maria. My job is twenty-four/seven, and last night when the Chief and Mayor asked me to do a feature on the Knifeman, to be honest, I began salivating at the mouth."

Boston and Jimenez laughed loudly at the last quip, and all three headed for the rickety elevator. On the ride up Harvey began his interrogation of the cops, flipping out his trusty notepad.

"So tell me, what do you think of this person?" he asked Boston.

"Well, he's—"

"How do you know it's a he?" Harvey cut him off.

"It's gotta be," shot back Boston.

"The assassin has never been seen, correct?"

"You're right about that."

"So how are you so sure it's not a female?"

"Because," Boston got instantly irritated, "some of the murders had violent fights that I just don't think a woman could have been involved with."

"Meaning...?"

"He's getting sloppy," Jimenez aided her man. "We have DNA matches, but the guy—I mean suspect—doesn't show up on our radar."

"Still, how are you definite it is a man?"

The elevator door squeaked open, with all three people becoming silent. Harvey marched through the office to his corner unit, with Boston and Jimenez trailing. He did not even have to look back to know that they were surprised at all the activity going on around them. Reporters typed away furiously on their stories, occasionally gulping down cold cups of coffee. Stacks of empty pizza boxes sat in a corner next to fresh bagels, donuts, and continental breakfast trays full of fruit.

Most ignored the detectives as they glided past, heading to the far corner of the floor where Harvey's office was located. Generally, reporters such as he would be assigned to a crummy desk in the overcrowded newsroom but Harvey, being widely regarded as a superstar of his craft, along with possessing the most seniority of anyone at the paper, had a private office all to himself.

It was the corner unit of a row consisting mostly of editors and bigwigs from the advertising and sales divisions. On the door was a brown nameplate with the word "Underwood" on it, which was odd since all the other offices had both first and last names plus titles. The threesome entered with Boston and Jimenez copping squats in two well-worn leather chairs. Harvey walked around to his desk, passed each one of them a different rough draft, then picked up his coffee mug.

"Would you guys like coffee, water, or something to eat?" he asked.

"No, we're fine," answered Jimenez.

"Okay, I'm going for a refill so you can read those and tell me what you think when I get back."

They only faintly heard his statement because the detectives were already reading his rough draft. The reporter strolled past them dangling his mug and returned several minutes later to find they had swapped drafts and were finishing them.

"Well, what do you think so far?" Harvey asked.

"I think they're both great, but you should print mine," Jimenez answered.

"I think mine catches the nuts and bolts better," Boston surmised.

"Actually," Harvey said as he sat down, "I'm going to combine the two along with whatever tidbits you guys give me and create a complete profile of this criminal that will run as a three-day series. As you already are aware, we will only mention the most recent crimes. That's where you come in."

"What do you need?" asked Boston first.

"I need to get your take on why everyone murdered has ties to, lives now—or rather, used to reside—in the city, and if the murders are that of an assassin, a hired professional."

"He has to be getting paid," Boston shot off.

"You said 'he' again," Harvey corrected. "Why do you think it's an assassin?"

"Because there is no set pattern. If it were all prostitutes, drug dealers, or business types then I would agree that we have a serial killer on the loose, but since the people come from all walks of life, it has to be an assassin."

"But two of the last three murders involved dealers."

"Agreed, yet the other was a pimp and you can't forget the girl. She just happened to be in the wrong place at the wrong time. As a matter of fact, the Rivers killing was classified as a robbery gone bad due to the fact that for several days leading up to that homicide, the victim had been spending money like it was hot."

Maria nodded approval at her partner's theory as Harvey scribbled away furiously onto his notepad. Once done, he fired off another question. He still had issues with the *who* but would save that for later; now he moved on the *what*.

"The tool of choice is a knife, so the suspect always gets pretty close to the victims—how is that possible?"

Being the ace reporter that he was, Harvey already had the who, knew that the when and where were public knowledge of past crimes, and would not only get the what from this query but could delve into how come. Meaning, why is this person murdering people and has been doing so for the past twenty years? Boston took him up on the issue.

"The suspect gets close because he has to be someone who does not appear to be a threat. Since he's been doing this crap for over two decades, he has to be an older individual now, and I would bet good money that he's an African American."

"Derrick, you said 'he' again." Harvey looked him directly in the eye. "If I were to state it's a male without proof and it winds up being a female, my credibility is lost forever."

Suddenly a light bulb lit up in Jimenez's head, causing her to blurt out, "We know it's a man!"

"Oh, you do? How so?" Harvey pushed up his bifocals.

"Because Jimmy Chang found evidence at two of the previous three homicides positively identifying the killer as a male."

"He has DNA samples?"

"Yes." Boston looked at his partner with pride as Jimenez continued: "We have no doubt it's a male of African American descent, but the DNA didn't help identify him because the suspect had no matches on file in the national database."

"Okay, I'll need to change the story a bit and talk with Jimmy. The suspect is now officially a he."

Boston and Jimenez laughed broadly as Harvey made the last statement, and they felt victorious for the simple fact that she had come up with proof that they had been right all along in their assessments. The look he shot in her direction caused her to change seating positions, pussy become soaking wet, and feet tap on the floor uncontrollably. She knew she would be served heartily after they left and could already see his meat stiffening up inside his pants, revealing a delicious imprint to her salivating eyes.

"I guess that'll do it," Harvey said, continuing to write.

"When will the first installment hit the racks?" Boston asked.

"Tomorrow morning."

Harvey answered without even looking at them, for he was busy typing away on his laptop. They said goodbye, receiving only a nod of his head, and walked out grinning. Jimenez had a dark, smoky look in her hazel eyes that Boston knew oh so well. Her gait was a bit unsteady, prompting him to cup her arm at the elbow. Once inside the confines of the elevator, he kissed her passionately.

"Where to now, the office?"

"Hell no," she answered defiantly, "I want you to fuck me."

They rode home with her bobbing away on his rock-hard pole as he drove. Ten seconds after entering the unit she was undressed with a steaming hot pussy waiting to be filled. Ten seconds after that, she got her wish, with him banging away deep inside her willing body. They could hardly wait for the morning paper.

28

EYES WATCHING

It was two in the afternoon on a cold and windy day, yet the crowd assembled at Arroyo Park could care less. They were engaged in the usual madness of making some money, and others getting high. All of the major players in the EDE were patiently passing the time while waiting for their leader and his brother. Some were visibly angry because just like any other organization, legitimate or shady, the grapevine was active. Rumor circulated among them that Junior was planning to give somebody's turf to Mario, and of course that gossip created a negative atmosphere.

On cue, Junior rolled up to the lot in his Navigator with rap music blasting so loud the ground beneath the vehicle shook. He and Mario hopped out wearing identical canary-yellow Lakers warm-up suits. From their height, physical appearance, and fancy ride they could easily be mistaken for ballers.

Junior began dancing right outside the vehicle, pumping his hands in the air while bouncing up and down in rhythm. Mario, just as amused and surprised by his brother's theatrics as everyone else, laughed up a storm. Instantly surrounded by a large group of approving onlookers, Junior put on a show. He grabbed the closest female, spun her around where her booty faced him, then began lightly whacking that ass in the manner of a jockey whipping a racehorse to increase its speed.

His impromptu partner Tasha played the perfect foil, bending over and allowing him to have his way while seeming to enjoy the grinds he banged against her shaking butt. The skin-tight black spandex pants she wore quivered with every slap, and when she reached both hands back and pulled him closer, the gawkers hooted their approval. Playing it to the hilt, Junior clutched her hips on both sides with his massive paws and imitated a bronco buster riding his steer.

Tasha Leslie had a body built for sex and never hesitated to show it off. She was a stoutly built five-foot, ten-inch thorough-bred weighing a strong hundred and sixty pounds with long legs, thick sprinter thighs, round booty, melons for titties, and a beautiful charcoal face. A stripper at The Bus Stop nightclub, the girl had no inhibitions when it came to flaunting her assets and was propositioned nightly at the club by married, single, and "in the process of breaking up" men.

She hung out at places like Arroyo hoping to satisfy her secret desire of being the first lady of a baller and, needless to say, was ecstatic that Junior had grabbed her for his partner. Now she was a part of the featured attraction and no doubt would receive curious double-takes from her friends. In less than ten minutes the grapevine would label her as Junior's sidepiece, and she knew once he debunked that myth, other men would line up to get with her.

When the song faded on his compact disc player Junior reached inside the ride, turning the volume down, then stuffed something inside Tasha's palm, with her sashaying away like the winner of a talent show. No doubt everyone wanted to know what he had given her but she wasn't telling, even with a stable full of home girls following her to their car. Junior told Dread, who was just as entertained as everyone else, to park his ride, then he and Mario headed for the bleachers.

Dread hopped inside and parked the vehicle before joining Junior and Mario in front of the crew, who had all assumed their positions on the bleachers. Seating was by order of status, meaning the higher your rank, the closer to the top you sat. Mario, Junior, and Dread were the only ones standing on the concrete, and after Junior conducted a visual scan of staff to see who was missing, he called the meeting to order.

"Listen up, yaw—most uh you done heard ah found mah long-lost brother, but some uh yaw probably don't bah-leave it. Well, ya bettah know it's true and Mario"—he pointed at him—"is family now. We took a DNA test ta prove it. Now foe yaw say sumptun, ah know da rumor goin' 'roun det ah'm gone hand over somebody's turf to him ta-day, but dat ain't true. What is true dough is det he will have a spot in da family—anybody got a problem wit dat?"

With no response Junior continued. "Good, 'cause I'ont need nobody havin' issues and fuckin' shit up behind mah back. Most uh yaw know Mario from YA and know he's a bad muthafucka, ain't afraid uh shit. So yaw can now understand with him bein' family an all, why he was da only one in dare crazy enuff ta fuck wit me!"

The entire group erupted in laughter, with Junior leading the charge. Comments were coming rapid-fire from everyone, with those who had not heard of their rumble inside the Youth Authority getting full details from others who had witnessed the now-legendary battle. Junior playfully shoved Mario then cut the conversations short with a swift wave of his hand.

"Now, mah lil' brutha gone be hangin' wit me an Dread so he can learn da bidness from da groun up. If he ever come an tell you ta do sumptun, act lack ah tole you, dig? 'Cause if you rebel, or don't do it, don't be sa-prised when ah start whuppin' yo ass. Anybody got issues wif what ah just said?"

No one cracked a peep so Junior concluded the meeting: "Now, ah wont each one uh yaw to introduce yo-self ta Mario an tell him what set you grindin' own. Ah'll be back in a minute. Dread, you start it off."

Junior walked away toward the parking lot, where he would seek out Tasha's fine ass. He knew of her from endless nights spent watching her undress at the club yet had never met her formally. After the sexually enhanced dance, he now desired to know her better. Of course, she would be pleased and willing to give him some pussy once she realized that he had placed five crisp one hundred dollar bills inside her palm.

Tasha spotted him first, exiting her girlfriend's vehicle and walking in a straight line toward him. Junior grabbed her in a loving embrace then began chatting away freely while she laughed and posed. Her chickenheads looked on with envy, dissing her as a gold-digging tramp.

At the bleachers, Dread told Mario his name and rank in the empire, then gave him a brotherly hug. One by one, starting with the lieutenants who sat on the bottom row, each man followed suit. By the time they were done Mario realized the enormity of his brother's operation. They controlled every area of the "killing zone," which spanned from 73rd to the San Leandro border, including the hills.

That area was dubbed the "killing zone" because fifty percent of the city's murders happened in there, and the EDE crew was partially responsible for eighty percent of them. Junior returned happy to see Mario meeting his crew, unaware that his every move was being watched by an interested observer.

Sweetpea sat in his rental car on the other side of the park, which was a dead-end street, peering through binoculars at the gathering. He had received information from informants that Arroyo was Junior's main operation site, so he set up shop there and would begin his usual task of bird-dogging from that point on. His mission would be to get a line on Junior's daily activities, then catch him in a surprise ambush when he was most vulnerable.

With the meeting over, Junior and Mario hopped inside the Navigator and headed for Shirley's house, where they would inform her of their secret find the night before. As was custom, she was sitting in a rocking chair on her porch listening to the Sunday oldie-but-goodie jams on her radio while guzzling down one beer after another. Normally she cooked big-time meals on God's day, but all the leftover food from the party granted her the day off.

Junior and Mario hopped out of the Navigator and casually strolled toward her. She rose from her rocker, giving them each a hug and a squeeze, then resumed her throne.

"What brangs y'all out heah? June-yah, ah ain't seed you on a Sunday in so long ah know it must be good news."

"Mom, check dis out—lass night when we left here we went to Mario's uncle's crib ta get his shit, ah mean stuff, right?"

"And...?" she waited.

"Now Mom, how come a man need a secret closet full of knives an fake IDs, huh?"

"What you mean, knives an fake IDs, boy?"

"Ah mean what ah'm sayin', Momma, is da man had a closet where when you touch a secret button on top, it open up to a room full uh fake ID, clothes, and enuff knives to kill an army. Now why would somebody need all lat?" Junior was animated in his words and movements.

"Mario?" she questioned, "what dis fool talkin' 'bout?"

"Just like he said, mah uncle got dis secret closet full uh all dat stuff."

"What he need wit dat?"

"I'ont know, Mama Shirley, but he do got it."

Shirley sat back in her rocker contemplating what she had just heard with her mind seeming to be far off in the distance. They stood waiting for her to give it some thought, shuffling from one foot to the other.

"Yaw stay 'way from dat man—he sound dangerous."

"Oh, we ain't never goin' back dare," Junior said.

"Ah juss went ta get mah stuff," Mario co-signed.

"Awight, but remembah, stay ya black asses 'way from dare, yaw heah me?" Her voice rose two octaves.

"Yeah, we got it, Moms—ah'se juss lettin' you know, see what ah'm sayin'."

The brothers strutted down her walkway, re-entering the ride when she called out to Mario's open window.

"Ah luw y'all, an be safe, ya heah?"

Junior sped off, heading for home, where Monique was preparing a menu of spaghetti, tossed salad, and garlic bread. She also had a friend there waiting to meet Mario, who had no idea about the surprise in store for him. After stopping at the liquor store for cognac, soda, rolling papers, and smokes, the brothers cruised to the crib. Sweetpea trailed slowly from a block behind.

29

TABLES TURNED

The morning paper arrived with an eye-popping headline and sub-title:

KILLER STALKING CITY STREETS
SUSPECT RESPONSIBLE FOR FIVE MURDERS

The second-floor hallway at the police station was packed with relatives of Shawn Daniels. Many were openly sobbing while others sat with their heads down, contemplating the path of life they had chosen. His parents sat stoned-faced, waiting for department officials in order to claim their dead son's possessions, which included more than four thousand dollars in cash, keys to his ride, and mountains of jewelry left on his body.

News cameras set up shop outside on all four corners as reporters and newscasters sought out officials for more details on the story. Harvey's article was instantly considered a blockbuster scoop, so naturally the media would increase the hype by covering any and all angles. Some questioned angry family members as citizens protested loudly behind them about police brutality, along with incompetence when it came to solving real crimes.

Inside the homicide unit all detectives on duty had their noses glued to the article, absorbing every word like a sponge. Boston and Jimenez sat stationary at their desks, reading with more than a passing interest. They were double-checking to make certain the facts reported were indeed accurate. Once done, Boston tossed the paper onto his desk and waited until his partner finished reading hers. The moment she did so he engaged her in conversation.

"Nice article," he said.

"Yes, Harvey outdid himself," she responded.

"Now all we have to do is wait, and the phone will be ringing off the hook."

No sooner had the words left his mouth than they became prophetic, as phone lines jammed with people calling in to the precinct. Every detective on duty fielded calls while jotting down notes, with many of the calls from people who provided what appeared to be solid leads. Others claimed to be the killer himself, with even more who ranted and raved about nothing while wasting valuable time. It was a circus-like atmosphere, yet all Five-O needed was for one call to be on the mark. When that happened it would lead them to the killer, so they treated every call as legit.

Two hours later a list was compiled on an easel board with all tips, possible suspects, follow-up calls to be made, and informants. In the bottom portion was a space for prank calls, which would not normally be considered. Boston and Jimenez now had more work than they could handle, so two additional teams were assigned by Edgar Lewis to assist them on the case.

Harvey entered the office, instantly greeted by all as a celebrity, with hoots and catcalls booming throughout the tiny room. Of course, to him it was just another report where he wrote about the facts and mysteries regarding the suspect. Dressed in his usual bland apparel, the reporter obliged the smiling cops with an entertainer's bow at the end of a performance then made a beeline to Boston and Jimenez.

"Well, what do you guys think?" Harvey asked.

"The phones tell it all," Boston answered, pointing at the full switchboard.

"Harvey, you are the greatest," Jimenez chimed in.

"Thank you," he said before continuing, "you got anything new for tomorrow's installment?"

"There's more?" Boston asked, failing to hide the excitement he felt.

"Indeed," Harvey answered. "The second installment of this three-part exposé will run tomorrow. I'll talk to you two later, and call me if you get a line on the case."

"You got it," Boston said.

Harvey Underwood glided out of the office and hopped inside his company vehicle, heading for the Trib Tower, where he would complete the next edition of his series. The opening installment listed the crimes committed, their location, names of the murder victims, and methods used to kill them. Tomorrow's story would delve into the psyche of the killer, the varying patterns in which the murders were carried out, and the fact that none could be tied together.

On the east side of town, Shirley sat on her front porch drinking beer and enjoying the morning paper. While reading, she sat her beer down and consumed the Knifeman story voraciously, noticing that all the killings had been carried out by a knife-wielding assassin. Her extrasensory perception kicked in, with her replaying the conversation yesterday with her two sons. Could it be possible that Mario's uncle and Big Ed's murderer were one and the same? She could not stop asking herself questions.

Upon further reflection, she began tying up the loose ends. Big Ed's killer definitely could have been upset that his sister had a child by a married man who had no intentions of getting with her. Edward, as she called him, did die from an ear-to-ear knife slashing of his throat. And last but not least, Mario's uncle was from the city and so was her dead husband. All of a sudden Shirley had a headache, and the beer she was drinking no longer tasted good. Lifting her telephone from the pouch in her muumuu dress, she called Junior.

"Momma, wuss up?"

"Where yaw at?"

"We 'bout ta take care uh some bidness—wuss up?"

"Yaw come over heah rat now."

Shirley hung up without even saying goodbye, then waited on the porch for them to arrive. Junior did not disappoint, arriving in ten minutes flat at the crib, and upon seeing his mother's mug instantly assumed she was sick. Mario ambled up the walkway feeling just as helpless as his brother, wondering what was wrong.

"Yaw read da paper yet?" she asked.

"Naw, not yet." Junior did tell the truth even though he never read the paper.

"Read dis."

Shirley flicked the paper at her son, who made a futile attempt to read it. Actually, he just looked at photos of murder victims then passed it on to his sibling. Mario began reading aloud, and once it became apparent to Shirley that he was just as illiterate as Junior, she took the paper from Mario then read the entire story to the both of them. By the time she was finished all eyes were misty, and there seemed no doubt that Mario's uncle Horace was responsible for Big Ed Tatum's murder.

"You thank he killed Daddy?" Junior asked forcefully.

"Yeah, ah do," Shirley answered.

"Den we gotta get his ass!" Junior hollered. "You down wit dat?" He looked at Mario.

"Hell yeah, ah'm down," Mario sneered. "Never liked his ass no way."

"Hey yaw, don't look right now but dat car pulled up soon as yaw came an it's parked on da wrong side of da skreet."

"What color is it?" Junior asked his mom.

"Is black an somebody in it—look lack dey be watchin' us."

On Junior's cue Mario followed him to the Navigator's trunk, where he popped it open. On their walk, they too noticed the black car parked on the wrong side of the street with an occupant sitting crouched down in the driver's seat. Junior handed Mario a Glock semi-automatic while arming himself with an Uzi assault rifle. Walking boldly down the block in the direction of the car, they took dead aim.

Sweetpea saw them coming with weapons drawn and started the ignition, revving the motor full throttle. Pulling off violently, he maneuvered a u-turn, speeding off with the sound of gunfire ringing in his ears. Mario and Junior were emptying the clips while running in the direction of the vacating vehicle. Bullets bore into the body and blew out windows as they continued to fire away.

Realizing that the driver was safely escaping, they ran to Junior's ride and sped off in hot pursuit. Shirley along with several neighbors witnessed the entire episode, yet no emergency call was made to police. It was just another ugly scene in the hood and besides, if someone was dumb enough to tell, they would surely be labeled a snitch and suffer the consequences.

Sweetpea could hear bullets whiz by his earlobe and drove as if his life depended on it, which it did. The moment he felt relieved, he caught a slug in the shoulder, grimacing as blood stained his shirt. Driving like a maniac he conducted a series of right then left turns, winding up near 74th and International. On the next block he pulled into the lot of a chicken chain, parking in the far corner. Leaving the key in the ignition, he flagged down a taxi headed to the airport, hopping inside while covering his bloodied shoulder with his jacket.

The three-minute ride seemed to take forever as Sweetpea constantly peered out the back window to make sure he was not being followed. At the airport he handed the driver a dove then walked rapidly to his Benz. Inside, he surveyed the wound and was happy to see that it was superficial. He knew a shady doctor who could treat it quickly, along with keep his mouth shut, so he paid the lot attendant then drove there.

Sweetpea's mind was moving a mile a minute, yet he never thought about the rental car because he knew if he were to take it back in that bullet-riddled condition, police would be called and questions asked. His hope was that some teens or vagrants would stumble across the vehicle, notice the key in the ignition, then take it on a joy ride.

Junior and Mario drove recklessly around the neighborhood searching for the vehicle when Mario unloaded a bombshell.

"Dat was mah uncle, dawg."

"You show?"

"Yeah ah'm show, dat was his ass awight. Niggah know we done found out 'bout his secret."

"Well, it don't matter now, bro, 'cause his ass good as dead, see what ah'm sayin'?"

"No doubt."

The brothers devised a plan, with Junior calling all of his boys and instructing them to meet at his cooking house immediately. There, they would fill in the crew on the details of Sweetpea then locate, flush him out, and kill him. The hunter was now officially the hunted.

30

TAIL BACKFIRED

Sweetpea sat on a table in the makeshift examination room at the home of Doctor Charles Turner, a one-time respected physician who was banned from practicing medicine for unethical conduct. Charlie, as he preferred to be called, was convicted of heavily sedating his female clients, then having sex with them while they were drugged and unconscious. After serving a five-year prison sentence the doctor couldn't buy a job, so he resorted to treating criminals.

Having met many of them inside the pen provided him a plethora of clients, plus a six-figure annual income for his services. His medical skills also saved him from getting his booty busted while locked up, because he served as the unofficial resident doctor of the joint.

Charlie was a fifty-six-year-old black man who stood five-foot-eight, weighing a mere one-sixty. He had a peanut-shaped bald head, sunken jet-black eyeballs, and frail body, yet possessed the skills of a master when it came to medicine.

His house was located in the Montclair hills, a plush neighborhood of the city where million-dollar homes were the norm.

"Now, change the bandage daily and in a week's time you'll be fine," he told Sweetpea in his high-pitched voice.

"Thanks, Doc," Sweetpea answered.

"I've given you some medicine to ease the pain, but feel free to call me if you have any discomfort."

"I will."

Sweetpea handed him ten one hundred dollar bills for the five-minute patch job, then when he walked out retrieved his original clothing from his duffel bag and changed inside the cramped quarters. With the medicine ceasing all pain, Sweetpea exited a side door and walked down a concrete path to his car. Tossing the bag housing his bloodied clothing into the back seat, he drove to the nearest park and poured the contents in a garbage bin.

Arriving at his complex, he was met by a young white dude changing the lock on his door. He looked to be in his mid twenties, had long stringy dirty-blond hair, acne pimples covering his face, and was rail-thin. Judging from the dirty jeans he wore plus filthy white t-shirt, Sweetpea instantly stereotyped him a punk rocker.

"Your place?" the guy asked.

"Yes, it is," Sweetpea answered.

"I'll be done in a sec."

"Oh, take your time."

That was the only conversation between the two, as Sweetpea was not in the mood for chatter. The young locksmith tightened up the remaining screw then put away his tools.

"What's the damage?" Horace asked while holding a money clip stuffed with greenbacks.

"Oh, no charge," the guy said. "Your complex will cover it."

Sweetpea forced a fifty on him his for his troubles then entered the unit and plopped down on the sofa. He was exhausted and needed rest yet could not because there was work to do. He did not realize he had indeed fallen asleep until five minutes later when the sound of his doorbell roused him awake. Slowly rising up, he grabbed a butcher knife from the kitchen drawer and cautiously looked through the peephole.

"*Damn,*" he mumbled to himself before opening it.

"Saw you drive up," announced Jerry. "Is everything okay?"

"Yes, it's fine, dude, I'm just tired. Oh yeah, thanks for the lock."

"No problem, Horace, that's what they pay me for. Well, I was just checking to make sure you're alright."

"You're a class act, Jerry."

"I'm glad you noticed."

Jerry walked away with his chest poked out, happy that Horace appreciated his rapid service. Jabbing the call button on the elevator panel, he stepped inside, smiling at Horace's now-closed door. The unexpected visit seemed to invigorate Horace as his alter-ego Sweetpea once again took over. He marched into the bedroom, grabbed an overnight bag, and stuffed it full of clothing.

Activating the switch on his hole in the wall, he entered and retrieved several killing items. Being the true professional, Sweetpea never used a gun, but realizing he was now the hunted forced him to lift a .357 Magnum from the back shelf. Guns were all young people seemed to know, and since he was definitely outnumbered, this time it would be a necessary tool he would more than likely need.

Tapping the button once again, he exited the crib as the unit slowly rotated to a close. Inside the garage Sweetpea scanned the parking lot, wary of someone possibly staking out the joint. Satisfied that the coast was clear, he got into his ride and used the garage remote control switch to open it. Pulling onto Fairmont Drive, Sweetpea again scanned the area, peering up and down the block to be certain that no one was watching.

The five-minute ride to Harriette's house took thirty due to Sweetpea driving around aimlessly while constantly checking the rear-view mirror. He felt weird by his actions and now understood the feeling he had given many people who knew their life could be over instantly. It was a feeling he would never forget, and it caused him to promise himself that if he lived through this, he would surely retire.

It was the same promise he had made on many occasions yet never lived up to, due to a burning desire to kill. For some reason, this time Sweetpea felt as though he would keep it. Pulling into Harriette's driveway, he parked behind her Camry then entered through the back door. She was curled up on her sofa reading *Soul Mates Dissipate* by Mary Morrison and was extremely aroused from the highly erotic novel.

Hearing the key inserted into the lock caused her to place the book face down and rise up to meet him in the dining room. "Hi, baby, I didn't know you were coming over," she greeted while planting a wet kiss to his mouth. Horace felt his manhood stiffen to full strength immediately and returned the favor by slapping his tongue against hers with urgency.

She was dressed in a skimpy lavender negligee that barely covered her private parts, and the pleasure her kiss provided made it easy for his hands to grab her milk-white butt, pulling her closer. Without a word spoken between them he backpedaled her to the bedroom still engaged in a tongue lock, then shoved her on the bed and began undressing. Harriette lifted the nightgown over her head and got under the covers, watching her man with a lustful look they both knew so well.

"Ooh baby, what happened to you?" She sat upright, noticing the bandage.

"Nothing major," he reassured her. "I nicked myself on the edge of the kitchen cupboard," he lied. "Guess I just wasn't paying attention."

She was more than satisfied with his answer because as he talked her eyes were glued to the fat-ass weapon dangling between his thighs. Horace crawled under the covers with his main squeeze and resumed their kissing session while gliding his sausage up and down her soaking wet slit. Content that she was ready, he penetrated, letting out a pleased sigh as she released a soft moan from her vocal cords.

Outside, half a block away, "Squirrel" was on his cell phone giving Junior some wonderful news.

"Boss, I got a line on the fool," he barked.

"Where he at?" Junior boomed.

"Over here on Mandana between Lakeshore and Grand."

"Don't move, we own our way." Junior ended the call then

announced to all his crew: "Squirrel pegged da niggah—his ass holed up own Mandana."

"Dass where his grey gurl stay at!" Mario shouted.

"Good," Junior responded, "ah hope he gettin' some pussy 'cause dass gone be da lass piece his ass ever get. Come own y'all, less go."

The hoodlums drove caravan style to Mandana Avenue with murder on the mind. Squirrel had located their victim, and he would certainly die before daybreak. Ronnie Drummer, with a street tag of Squirrel, was the best in the business when it came to playing private eye. Twenty-one years old, Squirrel was a small short man who stood five-foot-three on a lightweight hundred-and-thirty-pound body.

Sweetpea never saw him because the moment the nose of his vehicle pulled out of the parking garage, Squirrel lay down in the front seat of his twenty-year-old Honda Civic and slowly counted to ten. When he completed his count and looked up, Sweetpea was merging with traffic on Harrison Street. By the time he arrived at Harriette's home he had shaken the tail but Squirrel patiently, and slowly, cruised the neighborhood until spotting his ride in the driveway.

The caravan of EDE crew members pulled up behind Squirrel's ride, with Junior and Mario getting out. What they saw was a sight Mario would remember for the rest of his life.

"*Damn!*" Junior screamed, causing several of his boyz to exit their vehicles.

Mario vomited in the streets as everyone inched closer for a better view of what all the hoopla was about. What they saw was Squirrel lying down in his seat with an icepick protruding from his temple. He was dead as a doorknob, and the manner in which the murder was performed caused Junior to reassess the plan. The commotion resulted in several residents of the community wandering over to see what it was about.

Horrified by what they saw, people ran home to place emergency calls to the police as Junior, realizing the situation, ordered his henchmen to vacate pronto. When cops arrived on the scene, they were provided with vivid descriptions and license plate numbers of all the cars that had abruptly sped off. The neighborhood residents, nor cops for that matter, had no inkling that the perpetrator of the crime stood among them.

31

KIDNAPPED

Horace woke up at six in the morning to the sound of Harriette's alarm clock rattling away. He had no intentions of working that day, so he picked his cell phone up off the floor and placed a call to his day job, claiming illness. Returning to the bedroom he smiled upon seeing Harriette's naked ass peeking out from the sheets, which prompted him to roll her over and insert his suddenly rock-hard meat into her wet hole.

Her eyes remained closed but a smile creased her lips as she was awakened from a peaceful slumber by his dick batter-ramming her body. Squeezing his waist tightly, she allowed him to rock her world, professing her love while enjoying the sensations. He blasted off a load of cream then rolled to the side and dozed off. Harriette got up to take a shower and, upon returning to the bedroom, roused her man awake.

"Baby, we have to get ready for work," she said.

"I'm not going." He pulled the bedcovers over his head.

"You don't feel good?"

"I feel terrible—let's play hooky today."

"Mister Boudreaux, I would love to play hooky with you and enjoy your fantasy, but the lights have to remain on."

"Baby," he continued to speak with his head covered up, "they will not miss you and the work will still be there when you return."

"I know, dear, but I have a few deals that must be closed."

"Fine, you can go without me."

Horace looked up from the covers, getting an eyeful of Harriette's pink swollen nipples. She sat on the bed so close they nearly slapped him upside the head, causing his manhood to regain full strength. Lightly pulling her down onto the sheets, he spread her legs wide and she willingly allowed him to roll over and plow deep inside her again. Once he was done and they both were satisfied, she took another shower and got dressed.

"I'll see you later, honey—you will be here when I get back, right?" she asked, fully clothed.

"Yes, I will," he answered, accepting yesterday and today's morning papers from her before embracing her lovingly.

Harriette strutted out of the room then returned one minute later.

"I need you to let me out."

"Damn" was all he could muster.

Horace put on his pants, shirt, and shoes, then followed her outside, where he got into his car and pulled it into the street. When she drove off he pulled back into the driveway, parked, and sleep-walked into the home. Getting back under the covers he removed the rubber band from the previous day's paper and opened it up. The headline-grabbing article regarding the serial killer instantly killed any thoughts of sleep he had in mind.

He read the story four times, searching for any clue that could possibly lead the police to him, and once confident that the story could not, Horace browsed through the local and sports sections. Retrieving Tuesday's edition from the floor, he sighed upon seeing another article regarding the city's unknown killer, whom the report referred to as "The Knifeman." Again unfazed, he scanned the rest of the sections, taking particular interest in a murder story on page one of the Metro section.

It described a victim named Ronnie Drummer, who had been killed in the 2600 block of Mandana the previous day. Instantly realizing that the murder occurred just doorsteps away and the victim resided on the east side caused his heart to thump loudly against his chest. The article stated that Drummer did have prior arrests and convictions for drug selling and was a reputed member of the notorious Eastside Drug Empire. It described in detail the icepick that punctured his temple and informed readers that the police had no idea why Drummer was on that side of town nor who had committed the crime.

The next paragraph caused Horace to bolt upright into a sitting position, for it blamed the murder on the now-infamous Knifeman. After finishing the story Horace bounced out of bed, screaming at the walls in a fit of rage.

"Now the bastards are blaming me for everything!" he yelled. "I don't even use icepicks!"

He needed a foolproof plan, he thought while pacing the floor, and needed it fast. Reverting to the Sweetpea role, he took on the mindset of assassin even though, in this case, he was dodging assassination. Suddenly an idea clicked inside his brain, causing him to wander into the bathroom and take a well-deserved shower. Having no appetite, he dressed, hid a few weapons under and inside his clothing, then headed out the back door to his ride.

Hopping inside his car, Sweetpea drove around for two hours on busy city streets, all the while checking his rear view with the hope of singling out a trailer. There were a few times he felt that he might be onto something, but in each case the vehicle he assumed to be following would turn off, leaving him back at square one. With no other options, he headed back to Harriette's, replaying the article about Ronnie Drummer in his head.

"Residents of the neighborhood provided police with detailed descriptions and license plate numbers of several cars seen speeding away from the crime scene. The police are treating the case as a contract hit ordered by a rival gang."

Sweetpea entered Harriette's home then attempted to call her, receiving no answer. After her secretary informed him that she had failed to arrive for work, his heart rate increased ten-fold. Pacing the floor he tried her cell phone again and again, still receiving no answer. Next he phoned his sister Crystal.

"Hello," she answered.

"Hey girl, how are you?"

"I'm okay, Brother, and yourself?"

"I'm cool—have you heard from Mario?"

"Not a peep."

"So we still have no idea what that dude is up to."

"Horace, I know it may seem like I'm paranoid or overly concerned, but I just don't like those people. Did you have a chance to go by Shirley's?"

"Yes I did—struck out, though."

"Damn, that boy doesn't know what he's getting into!"

"I agree, Sis—hey look, if you find out anything, call me."

"You know I will, and you do the same."

"Talk to you later."

"Bye bye."

Horace ended the call then decided to drive to his job with the hope of tracing his woman's movements. Arriving at work, he entered the underground parking lot and noticed her car in its assigned stall, but something was amiss. First, there were thick tire tracks on the pavement, which meant someone had pulled away from that location with urgency. Second, one of her shoes lay on the ground right behind her car.

"*Shit!*" he growled, stomping violently on the concrete. He knew they had his woman and would use her as bait to lure him in. Caught in an unfamiliar predicament, Sweetpea drove back to Harriette's crib, where he would remain until receiving the inevitable phone call.

32

ABUSED

Harriette drove peacefully to work, listening to an all-news radio station. She did not understand why Horace refused to come to work, even though he appeared fine. Still feeling the effects of his dick planted firmly inside her body, she had a contented look on her face while parking in her assigned stall. The underground parking structure was both damp and poorly lit, and with her spot on the opposite end from the elevator, she had no idea of the danger she would soon encounter.

After getting out of her car, Harriette retrieved her attaché case from the back seat then activated the alarm. The minute she turned around, a large sport utility vehicle accelerated, screeching to a halt right at her feet. Mario hopped out the front door while Dread opened the back. Instantly recognizing her assailant, she attempted to question why he would scare her in such a manner.

"Mario, what are you doing?" she asked, receiving a powerful right hand to the jaw as his response. The force and viciousness of the blow knocked her to the ground, breaking a tooth in the process. Terrified, she felt herself being lifted up like a rag doll and tossed head first into the back seat. While Dread reached over her prone body to close the door, Mario scooped up her purse and attaché case, hopping into the front seat as Junior peeled rubber pulling out of the lot.

Dread strapped duct tape over her eyes and mouth while eyeing her delicious-looking thighs, which were clearly visible due to her skirt being hiked up over her behind.

"Ooh boy, ah know he be wearin' dis shit out—look at dis ass, dawg!" he yelled to no one in particular.

"Ah tole you, bro, da bitch got a tight-ass body!" Mario hollered at Junior excitedly.

Junior glanced back over the seat, gaining an instant erection at the sight his eyes rested on. Harriette lay sprawled on the seat face down, with her dress resting on her back and pussy lips parted open by Dread, who had yanked her panties off after closing the door. He was already inserting a finger inside her, and with her eyes and mouth taped shut, along with fearing for her life, she had no choice but to let him have his way.

"Man, look at mah fangah!" Dread shouted while proudly displaying a well-lubricated index finger. "Ah'm fitna get me some uh dis."

"Save a little for us, Homes," Junior laughed while merging with traffic and blasting the music.

Dread climbed on top of Harriette, positioning his rock-hard dick directly at the base of her slit, then proceeded to fuck her doggy style on the back seat. Harriette felt both violated and humiliated by his actions, screaming her heart out with each thrust, but with her vocal cords muted by the duct tape, her screams for help went unanswered. Mario watched the entire episode, roughly rubbing his crotch. He knew that Dread would not be the only one hitting that quat so he patiently waited his turn.

Letting out a contented sigh after blasting of a load of cream inside her pussy, Dread zipped his very wet and now flaccid dick back into his trousers then watched grinning as Mario hopped over the back seat for his turn. Assuming Mario's spot in the front seat, now it was Dread's turn to watch as Mario flipped Harriette on her back and plowed his ten-inch link sausage into her, thoroughly working over her hole.

Harriette wiggled and squirmed, which Mario took to mean she was enjoying his meat. Her action spurred him to lift her butt off the seat and bang away violently inside her helpless body. Her brain was in shock mode, and she was powerless to prevent the onslaught being wracked upon her body. The tape prevented tears from rolling down her face yet she was secretly crying her eyes out.

In what seemed like hours to her but in actuality was a mere ten minutes, Harriette had been raped twice and knew more of the same lay ahead. She had no inkling as to why it was happening but felt it was the reason Horace did not come to work. They were after him, she thought, and using her as a trap. Mario completed his assault, blasting off a gob of cum inside her thoroughly abused hole, then zipped up his trousers and used his shirt to wipe the perspiration from his forehead.

Harriette remained motionless with her legs spread apart and pussy juice bubbling out of her hole. Having no clue as to their location or where they were taking her, she realized that if she panicked it would be over. She had to remain alert and pray for the opportunity to escape. In a matter of minutes her world had collapsed, and even if she survived this ordeal, her life would never be the same.

The deafening rap music was giving her a migraine, and the scent of marijuana being passed among the three made her nauseous. After hearing the vehicle's engine shut off, she felt herself being gently lifted off the seat and her skirt pulled down to its rightful position. Next she was led through a series of doors and roughly shoved onto a bed.

Suddenly and without warning, her clothes were ripped off her body then her wrists and ankles roped and tied to the bedposts. She lay still on the bed stark naked and shivering from the cold, musty air.

"*I must be in a warehouse,*" she guessed, then listened intently as her captors began talking.

"Give me da bitch's phone," Junior ordered. Mario retrieved it from her purse "Yeah, we gone get da niggah now 'cause ah know he gone come lookin' fa dis fine thick-ass hoe."

"Dawg, good as dat pussy is, no doubt eyed be tryin' ta track you fools down, too," Dread capped, laughing at his own joke.

Junior and Mario roared in agreement, with all three men ogling Harriette's fabulous frame. Her legs were parted invitingly in a vee shape, with her arms outstretched, leaving her at their mercy. Junior began scrolling down her contact list on the phone and smiled when he came to a listing simply titled "Home."

"Uh huh, ah got it," he boomed.

Harriette heard the statement also and in her darkened world wondered whether or not Horace would attempt to rescue her after receiving the call. She didn't have time to think about it though, because seconds later she felt the biggest dick she had ever taken plunging inside her body. As Junior banged away with his cucumber-sized penis, Harriette's vocal cords worked overtime.

Her neck veins were clearly visible, with the tape covering her mouth expanding upon each thrust. Junior was tearing it up violently, with Mario and Dread urging him on like cheerleaders at a football game. Try as she might not to, Harriette was moaning loudly, along with hoping he would finish quickly. Unlike his brother and best friend, who came inside her body, Junior pulled out at the last minute, spraying his cum over her face and breasts, then rubbed it in like lotion.

"Okay, less call da niggah." He now spoke softly, gasping for breath.

IT'S ON!!

Horace sat on the sofa examining Harriette's shoe, which had been left in the underground parking lot. He knew that when this was all said and done, Crystal would be shedding many tears. What he was unsure of was if those tears would be for Mario, him, or both of them. Now he had no choice but to take out his nephew, along with anybody else involved.

The phone finally rang, with caller ID displaying Harriette's cell phone number after the second ring. He inhaled then exhaled strongly before answering.

"Hello." He was calm.

"Uncle Horace, it's me, Mario."

"Mario, what are you doing?" His tone was more intense.

"Hole own a minute."

Sweetpea heard shuffling sounds and muffled voices in the background.

"Yea, check dis, dawg." The voice was unfamiliar.

"Who is this?" he asked.

"Fuck dat, niggah, we got yo grey bitch an gone kill her ass if you don't do as ah say, DIG?" Junior yelled.

"You must be Junior?"

"Yeah, ah'm Junior, muafucka, an if yo ass don't do what ah say to a tee, yo bitch gone get what you got comin', see what ah'm sayin'?"

"Lay it on me, bro."

"Ah ain't ya bro, you honky-lovin' muthafucka!"

"Let me speak with Harriette."

"Ah ain't 'bout ta let you do shit!" Junior screamed into the receiver. "Now, you killed Squirrel an we got yo hoe, so ah thank yo ass can figure out da rest."

"What do you want me to do?"

"Shet da fuck up an listen, Knifeman." Junior was now in control and talked the walk, leaving Sweetpea no option but to hear his play.

"Come again?"

"Niggah, we know you da Knifeman 'cause we found yo lil' closet where you got all lat shit. Fool be thankin' we stupid or sumptun. Da only reason ah ain't turned yo ass in foe da reward is 'cause you killed mah daddy, so ah'mo make yo ass pay." He paused for effect then continued. "By da way, ah know why dis bitch got yo nose open 'cause she got some good-ass pussy—see what ah'm sayin'." He let out a sigh.

"If you lay a hand on her—"

"If ah lay a hand on her WHAT? Niggah, you ain't callin' no shots heah—yo ass bettah get wit da fuckin' program, see what ah'm sayin'?"

"Okay, what do you want me to do?"

"Take ya black ass home an wait foe further instructions. Ah'll call ya back when we ready ta make a deal."

The phone went dead, leaving Sweetpea to ponder how they had captured Harriette, to blame himself for not joining her for work, and to wait for the next call at home. Rushing out the door, he drove home with tears in his eyes and a hole in his heart. Harriette had not done anything to anybody and should not be involved, yet because of him, she was the pawn. He would go to the crib and await the next move in what was now a cat-and-mouse game of chess.

Ten minutes later he pulled into his assigned parking stall, relieved to see Jerry's usual spot empty. The last thing he needed today was to interact with the nosy security guard, who no doubt would have questioned him about the puffiness under his eyes. Trudging to the elevator slowly, Sweetpea suddenly felt old, worn out, and tired. One minute after entering his unit, the phone rang, which he answered immediately.

"Yeah."

"Okay, dis what you gone do." Junior barked instructions. "Ta-nite at eight, you gone come to da old Mother's Cookies warehouse on 83rd, then drive 'roun da co-nah and pull in the back gate. Next, ah wont yo to pull up to da back uh da buildin' an wait in yo car. Somebody gone come get you, den we'll take it from dare."

"Before I can agree to that, I'll need to speak with Harriette to be certain she's still alive."

"BE CERTAIN?" Junior yelled. "Man, yo ass been 'roun white folks so long, you sound like 'em."

"Just put her on the phone."

"You got yo instructions!"

After another round of shuffling noises with Sweetpea listening intently, Harriette's voice echoed through the receiver.

"Horace?"

"Baby, what have they done to you?"

"Oh baby, it's terrible, you have to help—"

"You got yo instructions," Junior repeated before ending the call. "It's own," he said seriously to Mario and Dread.

Placing calls to several of his top lieutenants, Junior ordered them to arrive at his warehouse by four o'clock that afternoon, then mapped out a strategy where each corner would have a look-out man posted to monitor all activity surrounding the perimeter. Once Mario's uncle arrived he would be escorted inside, then both he and Harriette would meet their maker.

She remained tied to the bedposts shivering while the threesome entered an adjoining room to discuss his plan. The cookie plant had been shut down for two years, with the city still trying to figure out whether to build affordable housing or retail space on the lot. Junior had received keys to the place shortly after its closing from a former employee, and he'd used bolt cutters to pop open giant padlocks on the gate and back door.

In honor of their turf being dubbed the "killing zone" by police and the press, and since they only used this location to murder people, Junior dubbed this area of the warehouse the "killing floor." There was no way possible for someone to sneak up and make a surprise attack without being spotted, and with their vehicle parked safely behind a closed roll-up gate inside the facility, the entire area appeared deserted to passing motorists.

"Man, is it juss me, or is yaw hungry too?" Junior asked them.

"Starvin'," Mario answered with Dread co-signing.

"Dread, take da keys an go get us sumptun from Giant Burgers."

"You want the usual, right?" Dread asked Junior, who nodded the affirmative. "What about you, Mario?"

"Ah'll take a cheeseburger wit grilled onions, chili-cheese dog, large fry, an strawberry shake."

Dread and Junior glanced at each other then erupted in very loud laughter.

"What's so funny?" Mario asked.

"Tell 'im, dawg!" Junior roared at Dread.

"What's funny is that the shit you just ordered is the usual!" He laughed some more. "Yeah, you niggahs is brothers all right, and I bet a hundred to fifty that yaw still gone be hungry after you eat that."

"Aw fuck you, niggah!" Junior had tears rolling down his face.

"I'll be damned," Dread said while leaving the room, "them two fools even thank alike!" Mario and Junior watched him walk out, with Junior barking, "Brang da bitch back sumptun too 'cause by da time ah'm through wit her ass, she gone be starvin' like Marvin."

"Yaw better save some of that shit for me, man," Dread grinned before disappearing into the darkness.

The brothers sat down in lounge chairs then glanced at one

another before exploding in laughter once again. Junior fired up a joint, taking two strong hits, then passed it to Mario who did the same. The next half hour was spent with the siblings smoking weed and Junior boasting to his younger brother about how much money he would soon be making. Mario absorbed it like a sponge and felt that with a brother and sister in his life, it was now complete.

34

BURGERS GONE BAD

Dread entered the lot at Giant Burgers on 81st and International with rap music blasting from the sound system. The lunchtime crowd assembled in line heard the commotion, which caused everyone to turn around and wait for the fool inside to get out. Parking near the back of the lot, Dread exited the vehicle then took his place at the back of the line. Recognizing many people already there, he engaged in loud conversation, showboating along with acting as if the seventy-five-thousand-dollar SUV actually belonged to him.

Of course, diner patrons immediately stereotyped him as a drug dealer/bad element from the monstrous vehicle, clothing attire, and gold-plated grill on display each time he opened his mouth, yet they acted normal. Many witnessed this sort of behavior from young black men on a daily basis and knew that their only option was to hurry up and get their lunch, then vacate the premises.

The lot at Giant Burgers was a regular hangout for neighborhood undesirables, ranging from old hustlers still trying to make a buck, boosters selling stolen merchandise, dopefiend whores willing to sell their body for drug money, and young players such as Dread flaunting their prosperity and riches. The best way to avoid their wrath was to ignore them, which most in line did, because if you displayed any animosity toward them, you would no doubt be singled out and beaten down or shot.

Known for the best burgers in the city, Giant Burgers in the past had numerous locations scattered around Oaktown, but this was the last remaining spot open. All the rest had closed down as a result of the influx of fast-food chains enveloping neighborhoods and providing residents with options. The demise of Giant Burgers was also due in part to the fact that each meal was cooked to order, meaning there was always a wait.

Dread placed his order then continued to signify on the smiling crowd of young black men and women. Upon the occasional passing of a police cruiser he would deftly blend in with the crowd, only to re-emerge front and center once Five-O rolled by. He really did not have anything to hide yet avoided confrontation with the police from a built-in lifetime cultivation of "anti"-cop mentality.

After about fifteen minutes the cashier motioned toward Dread that his order was ready, for which he stepped up to the counter pulling out a large wad of greenbacks. Returning to Junior's ride with food in hand, he deactivated the alarm, placed the grub on the passenger side floorboard, then rolled off the same way he had arrived, with the ground-shaking music blasting away and thumping rap beats.

The delicious aroma of food wafting through the vehicle caused his stomach to growl, prompting Dread to reach inside a bag and scoop out a handful of fries. Jetting through the warehouse parking lot, he exited the still-running vehicle and lifted the roll-up gate. After slowly driving inside the building, he got out and closed the gate behind himself, then parked in the center of the room.

Junior had provided battery-powered fluorescent lights for the offices they occupied, yet the loading dock area remained damp, musty, and dark. Dread could care less because he was deeply engaged in satisfying his aching belly by munching on another fistful of french fries. He heard a sound yet wrote it off as rats being startled from their hiding spots by human invaders.

Suddenly he heard another noise, resulting in him slowing his pace. Now Dread heard what he was sure were footsteps approaching rapidly in his direction.

"Dat you, Mario?"

Turning around quickly in the darkened room, he was greeted by a knife to the chest. Dread dropped the bags on the floor then found himself being stabbed repeatedly. The entire sequence happened so quickly that all he could see were news headlines running across his brain, describing his gruesome death to the reading public. Blood poured from his body, sending it into shock. Within seconds, he was dead. The killer yanked the knife out of his heart and disappeared into the shadows until the next opportunity presented itself.

"*One down, two to go,*" the assassin reminded himself.

35

A GIANT SURPRISE

Mario passed the weed to Junior, stifling his sneeze with a grunt while bobbing his head to the music blaring away from a large boom box in the corner. Harriette remained tied to the bedposts butt-naked, providing the two brothers with some serious eye candy. Junior accepted the joint, puffing forcefully along with stroking his rapidly stiffening penis.

"Man, call Dread's muthafuckin ass!" he yelled to Mario. "Niggah shoulda been back."

"Yeah, he is takin' long, huh?"

"Fool prolly out dare fakin', actin' lack mah ride belong to him an thangs."

Calling Dread's cell phone, Mario received no answer, getting his voice message instead. Ending the call before Dread's extra-long music intro was complete, Mario shot a look at his brother that spoke volumes.

"Man, where dat muafucka at? Shit," Junior growled angrily.

Had the music volume not been turned up so loud, they no doubt would have heard the creaky roll-up gate open and close with Dread's arrival. That was five minutes ago, yet to them Dread was still missing in action. Another thirty minutes passed with Mario constantly ringing Dread's phone. The result was the same as each prior call placed: no answer.

"Ah gotta go pee."

Junior paced the floor angrily as Mario walked out, heading for the bathroom, which was to the right down a long hallway. The restroom sat next to the loading dock, and after Mario finished urinating, for some unexplained reason he peeked inside the dark-ened room. To his astonishment, the Navigator sat in the center of the massive loading dock, which caused a smile to crease his face, along with his right hand subconsciously rubbing his churning stomach.

Dread must have arrived while he was pissing, he thought, so now it was time to eat. Eagerly rushing to the main office he found Junior redialing Dread's cell phone while cursing up a storm.

"Da niggah ain't heah?" Mario shouted to Junior.

"Hell naw, da niggah ain't heah!" Junior shouted back. "You ont see da muafucka, do you?"

"But, yo ride is in da loadin' dock," he stated matter of factly, pointing in that direction.

"It is?"

"Yeah, it's out dare right now, ah juss seen it."

"Less go get to da bottom uh dis shit."

Junior picked up the fluorescent light from an office desk, then he and Mario boldly walked out of the room, leaving Harriette in total darkness. Once inside the loading dock, they spotted Dread's lifeless figure in the center of a puddle of blood, their lunch splattered on the floor nearby. Junior screamed out loud while Mario held his stomach, which suddenly felt as though it were full of knots.

Had he eaten anything that morning, the contents of his gut surely would have risen up from his bowels and saturated the floor. On instinct, each man pulled their weapons, cautiously inching closer to the body. Junior grabbed Mario by the elbow then shut off the light while continuing to hold his brother in place until their eyes adjusted to the darkness.

Motioning non-verbally with a wave of his hand, he instructed Mario to search the right-hand side of the room while he went left. They met up with each other on the opposite side, both looking dumbfounded.

"Go get da hoe," Junior whispered into his ear then went to retrieve his car keys off the floor.

Mario picked up the light and headed for the makeshift bedroom where Harriette had been left. By the time he reached it Junior was right behind him, gun drawn and at the ready. The room was instantly illuminated from the light, but the sight their eyes rested on caused Junior to fire off his piece in rapid succession.

"Muthafuckin Knifeman!" he screamed while killing the boom box with a bullet. "You dead, muthafucka!"

The bed was empty, with Harriette gone and only the ropes used to tie her up left on it. The combination of Dread's corpse, Harriette missing, and a killer lurking in the massive warehouse sent shivers down the spine of both Junior and Mario.

"Let's get da fuck outta heah," Junior ordered.

Mario trailed his brother, nearly stepping on his ankles in his rush to leave the place. While Junior started the vehicle, Mario pulled open the roll-up gate. Once the vehicle exited, Mario closed the gate and joined his brother inside the ride as he sped off to safety. Empty-handed with fear gripping their bodies, the brothers hauled ass away from the warehouse, riding in silence.

It wasn't until then that Junior fully realized that his lifelong road dawg lay dead on the killing floor. Tears trickled down his cheek as he drove, with him promising revenge to the murderer of his boy. Now food was the last thing on their minds. They had a new hunger pain—payback.

36

AN UNLIKELY DUO

Horace slammed the phone down and began pacing the floor while attempting to formulate a plan. One thing he knew for sure was that he would not wait until the agreed-upon time to arrive at the warehouse. Very familiar with the place, he also knew that if their game was tight, there would be no way to surprise them without being detected. With his chances of rescuing Harriette bordering on slim and none, he left the crib and headed for the old cookie factory and warehouse.

Dressed down as a disheveled hobo, he parked on 85th Avenue near Tassafaronga Recreation Center and the housing projects located right behind it. Walking down the tracks toward the warehouse, he retrieved an abandoned shopping cart and began pushing it while picking up several cans and bottles along the way. To the casual observer he appeared to be nothing more than a bum trying to gather enough recyclables for drink money, but he was a man on a mission.

Throughout the afternoon, Sweetpea collected cans, bottles, and scrap metal from apartment dumpsters, tossing them into his cart yet staying close enough to the warehouse to watch all activity without being spotted. He had a growing urge to enter the lot, but common sense prevailed so he continued to peep out the place from a distance. At three in the afternoon he watched with amazement as Junior's SUV bolted from a rapidly rising roll-up gate, with Mario closing it then jumping inside the ride.

The vehicle sped out of the lot, zooming down the quiet street. Sweetpea felt like an idiot for parking his own ride so far away. Knowing that by the time he reached 85th they would be long gone, he decided to search the warehouse on the slim hope that Harriette was still inside. Moving with quickness that belied his outfit, Sweetpea left the cart where it stood and ran across the street.

Before he could enter the lot, the same gate they had just exited quickly shot up again, only this time two familiar figures ran out in his direction. *"I'll be damned,"* Sweetpea said to himself as he stood in plain view awaiting their arrival and noticing that Harriette was barefoot and covered by a large pea coat. At the gate, Sweetpea bear-hugged his woman, lavishing her with kisses while her savior hopped into a Toyota Camry and revved the ignition. Screeching to a halt at their feet, the driver popped the door lock switch and urged them both inside.

"Hurry before they get away!" he said.

"What are you doing here?"

"Helping you out of a jam—now which way did they go?"

"They went left down this street." Sweetpea pointed in the direction Junior had driven.

The car lurched forward and as it did so they spotted Junior's ride turning right on International, five blocks away.

"Don't worry, we'll get 'em."

"Thanks for saving my woman," Sweetpea stated gratefully.

"None needed."

"How did you know?"

"Now Horace—how many times have I told you that I make it my business to know everything that goes on with my tenants?"

"Too many!" They both laughed.

"The icepick?"

"I hated to do it, but he got what he deserved." Jerry smiled.

At International Jerry turned right, spotting the Navigator two blocks away at a stoplight. Horace/Sweepea sat gawking at his building's security guard as multiple questions roamed his brain. Harriette sat stoned-faced, quiet as a jailhouse rat.

"What tipped you off?" he asked.

"Not that I'm nosy," Jerry said, "but when you had those visitors, I let myself into your place to see if they had stolen something. That was when I noticed all the footprints and chair indentations around your bookcase. It took me a while to figure it out, but eventually I discovered your closet."

"So you know?" Sweetpea felt the air swoosh out of his body.

"Trust me, I ain't tellin'. Your secret is safe with me."

"What secret?" Harriette butted in with a voice barely above a whisper.

"No secret, Harriette—you need something to drink." Jerry handed her a room-temperature bottle of water.

"Let me ask you something," Sweetpea said. "How did you get inside undetected?"

Jerry maneuvered a left turn on 98th five car lengths behind Junior, acting as if he were on a casual cruise through city streets. While Junior drove in the left lane, he blended his ride with the flow of traffic in the right one. The only way he could be detected as a trailer would be for Junior to constantly scan his passenger-side mirror or conduct many right-left-right turns, thereby exposing him by process of elimination.

"Well, after the Knifeman"—Jerry laughed—"stuck an icepick to Ronnie Drummer's temple, I camped outside Harriette's home until she left for work. I wondered why you weren't with her. Then I noticed she was being followed so I tailed them at a distance. At the job I parked on the street at a meter, got out, and peeked around the entry ramp, then watched while they hijacked her in the lot."

"So you saw it all?" he asked Jerry accusingly.

"There was nothing I could do—it all happened in the blink of an eye. The only thing left was to follow them."

"How did you get inside the warehouse?"

"I saw what gate they went through, so after about fifteen minutes, I did the same. They never knew they had company." Jerry grinned. "I think you should call them on her phone." He got serious, constantly eyeing Junior's vehicle.

Sweetpea lifted his cell phone from inside the coveralls he wore and dialed Harriette's number. Junior answered on the third ring, shouting loudly into the receiver.

"Muthafucka, you gone pay!"

"Give it up, Junior, we don't need any more bloodshed."

"Aw, fuck you, niggah, ah'mo kill yo ass if it's da lass thang ah do, see what ah'm sayin'?"

"Let me speak with Mario."

"Kiss mah ass, bitch!"

The phone line went dead as Jerry hooked a left turn on Bancroft. It appeared to him that Junior was riding in circles but when he made a left at Ritchie Street and zoomed into the parking lot at Arroyo, Jerry conducted a three-point turn and headed back down Bancroft out of harm's way. Junior and Mario were instantly surrounded by a gang of thugs, and in a matter of minutes, eight cars peeled rubber burning out of the parking lot.

Everyone at the park knew from the proceeding that something serious was about to take place, with all spectators grateful that the object of Junior's wrath was not them. The caravan of eastside empire associates followed close behind as Junior drove recklessly to his next destination. Mario sat on the passenger side with mixed emotions. He tried to figure out how his uncle had found them so quickly, and knew that his mother would soon be shedding many tears.

She would be burying a family member real soon, of that he was sure. What was uncertain was whether or not it would be Uncle Horace, him, or both of them.

Meanwhile, Horace finally noticed that his woman was scantily dressed and had a distant, uninterested look on her face.

"What happened, baby?" he asked her.

"It was horrible," she answered, barely above a whisper.

"What did they do?"

"Raped me." She cried softly.

"When I found her she was naked, tied to all four bedposts," Jerry cut in.

"Bastards!" Horace screamed. "I'll kill 'em! Jerry, let's get her to the hospital."

"I just want to go home," Harriette protested weakly.

"No, you're going to the doctor to get checked for diseases, possible DNA samples of those perverts, and to start a paper trail on their asses."

Harriette knew any objections would be ignored, so she did not attempt to persuade her man otherwise. She wondered whether or not he would ever desire her after her ordeal, or if she would ever feel the same way about sex. The girl was a mental wreck, and it would be a long time, if at all, before she regained trust in people. Ten minutes later Jerry rolled into the emergency lot at Kaiser Hospital. He helped Harriette out of his ride.

The emergency room at Kaiser was brimming with activity. Sick patients stood in a very long line waiting their turn to be admitted. Family members of gunshot and stabbing victims paced outside smoking cigarettes, crying, or engaging in prayer while nurses and doctors scurried about at a frantic, nonstop pace. Jerry escorted Harriette to the sliding glass entry doors then abruptly turned around, nearly jogging to his car.

She stood there frozen like a deer in the bright headlights of an oncoming vehicle on a dark country backroad. An ambulance rolled up with its lights flashing and siren screaming as paramedics whisked an obviously injured black male up the ramp. There was a registered nurse named Cheryl passing the triage counter who first noticed Harriette blocking the entry.

Cheryl Ramirez had been employed at the hospital for nearly twenty years and had seen it all. A tiny woman of Hispanic descent, she carried weight around the hospital due to her seniority status and union-related activities. She had a gold mane with brown streaks cascading down past her shoulder blades, a pretty school-girl face accented by a black mole on the right side above her lip, large breasts, and a decent figure for a forty-five-year-old mother of six.

Running over to Harriette, she grabbed an unoccupied wheelchair, sat her in it, then wheeled her out of harm's way just in the nick of time. The gurney flew by as Cheryl began questioning Harriette regarding her condition.

"Are you alright?" she asked, showing genuine concern.

"I—I—I've been raped," Harriette blurted out.

"Oh my God!" Cheryl bit her bottom lip. "Somebody help me, NOW!" she hollered in a voice that belied her tiny physique.

Harriette was wheeled to an examination room, and within minutes an assortment of tests were conducted including swab samples taken from her vagina for DNA testing. Cheryl vacated the room, promising Harriette that she would return shortly, then used the nearest available phone to call the city's rape crisis center. Meanwhile, a front-office medical assistant entered the room and jotted down Harriette's medical number and family contact information.

After two hours and several mini visits by Cheryl, Harriette was finally admitted as a patient and placed in a room on the hospital's seventh floor. At the end of her shift, nurse Cheryl paid a final visit to Harriette, reassuring her that everything would be alright. As she exited the room for home with tears in her eyes, two females entered. One was a detective who would attempt to get a line on the attackers, the other a rape crisis counselor whose job it was to deal with the victim's mental state.

37

A ZILLION CLUES

The old Mother's Cookies warehouse was saturated with cops, media personnel, coroner's staff, and residents. Dread's body had been found by kids playing in a nearby apartment complex who just happened to witness Junior and Jerry lifting the roll-up gate. Kids being of the curious nature they are, they entered the warehouse in search of fun and games. Upon stumbling across the gruesome body of Dread lying in his own pool of blood, they ran home to inform their parents of the grisly discovery. Naturally, parents called the police.

Boston and Jimenez cruised into the lot, parking away from the carnival in a spot where they felt they could enter the warehouse unnoticed. The moment reporters saw them, however, the media mob swarmed over to block their path and bombard them with questions. Boston waved the horde of reporters off with a flick of his wrist, then he and his partner pushed their way past under the now-open roll-up gate.

Jimmy Chang was already on the scene, labeling and bagging evidence along with snapping photos and dusting for prints. On a hunch, he unzipped Dread's trousers and found his flaccid penis covered with dried-up semen. Flicking scraps of that into a ziplock baggie, he tagged it for lab testing. Carefully putting away his work tools inside a carry bag, Jimmy stuffed all the evidence bags into a giant brown paper sack, carrying them in his arms as if the contents were laced in gold.

"What we got, Jimmy?" asked Boston.

"I found shell casings in the office, which the suspects had converted into a bedroom," he said. "I also collected semen samples from the bed and victim's body, plus ropes used to tie someone up, along with fingerprints on the restroom wall and in the room. A funny thing, though—"

"What's that?"

"I also bagged up a couple of very used condoms filled with sperm."

"Good work, man. Has the victim been identified?"

"Yes, he carried a driver's license in his pocket with the name Courtney Adams."

Upon hearing this bit of information, Jimenez pulled out her note tablet and jotted down the victim's name, then followed Boston and Chang into the torture chamber. Jimmy led them to the bed then pointed out a few more clues.

"As you can see here, the bed is full of blond hair, meaning either the woman was Caucasian or Hispanic, or wore a wig. From the fibers, I can tell it was no wig."

"I wonder how the obviously tortured soul escaped this hell hole," Jimenez asked no one in particular.

"She had to have help," Jimmy answered. "Inside the loading dock, I noticed several tracks of footprints encased in blood. However, we will not be able to use that in a court of law so I just measured the imprints and took photos. I guess I'm just a creature of habit."

"And like you always say, Jimmy, you never know."

"I'll contact you guys as soon as I come up with something pertinent."

"Thanks, Jimmy," they said in harmony.

Jimmy Chang walked under the roll-up gate ignored by the media, which was just the way he liked it. Had they known he would provide most of the factual proof, along with solid evidence to break the case wide open, they no doubt would have bombarded him with questions. After a peaceful ride back to the station Chang entered the lab, placed a Do Not Disturb sign outside his door, then began testing all his samples.

While Boston questioned responding officers who were first on the scene, along with the parents and their children who had discovered the body, Jimenez eased to her service vehicle to run a make on Courtney Adams. When she returned inside with a powerful strut plus that familiar gleam in her eyes, Boston knew they had hit pay dirt.

"Okay," he smiled at her, "give me the lowdown."

"Courtney Adams, street tag Dread, big-time dealer and a member of the EDE."

"Wow, the EDE," stated Boston in amazement. "We need to—"

"I know," she finished for him, "get with Vice and the Narco squads for a line on this guy."

"That's my girl," Boston said with pride.

They left the warehouse with Boston satisfying the media's thirst by providing them with the victim's age, race, and method in which the murder had been accomplished. He declined to put a name on the dead body because the family was not yet notified. After fielding numerous questions of the generic variety, Boston concluded the interview with the usual promise to alert the media of any new breaks in the case.

Rolling out of the lot slowly, the detectives headed downtown in order to connect with the Vice and Narc units to see if they had any helpful information on Adams. They were most interested in his current address and known associates. Jimenez placed a call to their boss, filling him in on their activities along with the case, while Boston crept through traffic on a congested 880 freeway. Upon arriving at headquarters, they were greeted by Deputy Chief Lewis the moment they entered the office.

"Hey, you two," Lewis spoke in his normal soft voice, "I have some information related to your case that just came across the wire."

"Not another murder," Jimenez said.

"No, not that," Lewis responded. "We just received a call from Kaiser Hospital regarding a rape victim."

"And you think she's our girl?" Boston inquired.

"No doubt," he said. "The sperm samples taken from her body matched those of Adams, meaning the guy recently had intercourse with her."

"Something tells me that's not all," Jimenez stated truthfully.

"No, it's not, there was an additional DNA hit belonging to one Mario Hayes. Here's his rap sheet."

Lewis handed each of them a one-page crime activity report on Mario, which they scanned like vultures circling wounded prey.

"Look," Jimenez spoke while reading the document, "he was just hauled in here two days ago for disorderly conduct."

"Fighting in public is more like it," Boston stated. "Who else was involved?" he asked Lewis, accepting another paper. "Whew!" he whistled. "Courtney Adams, Willie Glasper, and Edward Grissom."

"Says here the lead detective on the case was Dennis Branch," Lewis deadpanned. "I think you guys should talk with him then head on over to the hospital and question the woman. Her name is Harriette Colbert and she's in room 713B. I've already placed an all-points bulletin out for the other three, so I'm sure we'll have them in custody pretty soon."

"We're on our way." The moment they walked through the door they were standing face to face with none other than Dennis Branch.

"I was on my way to see you two," Branch said, shaking each of their hands.

"Seems we have a certain interest in the same guy," Boston stated.

"Yes it does, only with me it was a public brawl."

"Well, the dude has graduated to rape and a possible murder beef."

"How sad—I know it's going to kill his mom."

"Is there something we're missing?" Jimenez asked curiously.

"No, not really." Branch attempted to avoid the question.

"Come on, Dennis, when did you decide we were stupid?"

"It was just a dinner date we had planned for this Friday."

"A date, huh?" Boston laughed.

"Have you ever seen Pam Grier?" Branch laughed too.

"Like that?" Boston mused, knowing he meant she was fine.

"Like that," he affirmed.

Before Boston and Branch had time to bore Jimenez with more machismo, Jimmy Chang joined the threesome, ruffling his jet-black hair while approaching.

"Hey Jimmy, any good news? Lord knows I've had enough bad for one day," Boston joked.

Jimmy was his usual professional, get-down-to-business self: "The semen samples collected at the crime scene were first-time DNA hits to three of the four people."

"Names?" Jimenez's voice rose three octaves.

"The dead guy Courtney Adams, another belonging to Mario Hayes, a woman's who is not in the database, and the fourth— which I recovered from the condoms—belonged to a guy named Edward Grissom. All three have criminal records."

"And all of them participated in the brutal torture of that woman," Jimenez said somberly. "I have no doubt her sample is one of them."

"Hey, we'd love to chat longer, but if you two will excuse us, we've got our work cut out," Boston blurted out. "Jimmy, thanks for the quick turnaround, and Dennis, we'll get back with you later."

In a flash, Boston and Jimenez headed down the steps and outside to their service vehicle, with Kaiser Hospital as their destination. Jimmy engaged in small talk with Branch for another minute then rode the elevator back to his domain, while Branch entered his office and attempted to call Crystal with no success. Murder was serious business, and deep down he knew that all bets related to his wooing of Crystal Hayes were off. She was fine, without a doubt, but not worth losing his job over.

38

BETTER HIM THAN ME

The caravan of cars rolled up to the corner of 62nd and Majestic, with Junior first out of his vehicle, trailed closely by Mario. It was a quiet block in a working-class residential neighborhood of the east side, where manicured lawns and freshly painted homes were the norm. "Crime Watch" placards were prominently displayed in many windows, and most people felt safe and secure in this area. They had no inkling that drugs were cooked, weighed, and packaged for sale twenty-four/seven in the modest white with green trim two-bedroom bungalow.

Of course, convergence of pimped-out rides caused suspicion but no calls were made to the police because as far as residents knew, no crime had been committed. Maybe they were coming for a birthday, barbeque, or were rappers discussing a new record release party. Regardless, the home would definitely be spied on by nosy neighbors, which was of no concern to Junior. He barged into the place and headed for the family room, where he stood front and center. Once everyone had gathered inside, he began his tirade.

"Da muthafucka killed Squirrel *and* Dread!" Junior screamed. "So we gone kill his ass. Dass fa got-dam sho."

"How we gone do it, boss?" asked Himey, a frail lock-wearing youngster with a grill full of glittering gold.

"I'ont know." Junior scratched his head. "what yaw thank?"

For the next fifteen minutes thoughts and ideas rolled from the mouths of the assembled hoodlums, ranging from the sublime to the ridiculous: camp out at his job, bum-rush his pad, kill his relatives, bomb his car, kidnap the woman again. They were floating around everything they could think of as Junior canceled each idea with logical explanations as to why they would not work.

Suddenly, Matthew Miller entered the room, looking as if he had just seen a ghost. "Milktoast," as he was called, was the head cook in the organization and a good one. Of mixed heritage with a white mother and black father, he was a robust two-hundred-and-eighty-pound, six-three mass of muscle. Bordering on the lighter shade of white after his mom, he was all black at heart.

Unlike the goons who employed his services, Milktoast possessed a college degree in chemistry and seemed to know all the latest techniques in producing dope even before they became common knowledge. He was currently developing a new drug known as "Ice" which he promised Junior would be cheaper, with a longer-lasting effect than crack. Initially Junior balked at the idea of making less money, but the way Milktoast explained it eased his fears.

"Look at it this way," he had reasoned, "with you having the cheapest dope on the streets that will keep their groove on longer, you'll be the fucking man. Not only will your product be the most craved, you'll make all that money, then some. Not to mention even rival dealers will buy from you." Milktoast was excited. "I'm talking legendary status, bro, the kind of shit where they will be talking about YOU until infinity."

Junior realized that Milktoast had the knowledge and skill to pull it off and was thoroughly convinced that since the new drug would be on the streets within a year, he may as well be the first to have it. Just like the shady doctor Charlie Turner, whose only clientele now were criminals, Milktoast had similar unfortunate dealings with the law, resulting in him using his talents to the benefit of organized crime.

Junior knew that whatever brought Milktoast to the room had to be serious business because he never conducted meetings at the cookhouse, and judging from the look on his face, the news he was about to reveal would not be good.

"Milktoast, you look like you just seen a ghost, bro."

"I have some bad news," he said.

"What is it?"

"I was listening to my police blotter when the announcement of an all-points bulletin was called out for you and Mario. You are going to be charged with rape of a white woman, and the murder of Courtney Adams."

"Man, fuck dem, I ain't killed Dread!" Junior shouted, then was struck by a bright idea. "Ah got a plan."

All ears were at attention as Junior relayed his plan to avenge the murders of Squirrel and Dread. He would also bump off the white girl for good measure, and the murders were to be crafted in such a manner as to implicate the Knifeman as the real culprit of the crimes. His reasoning was since Five-O had no idea who the Knifeman was, or what he looked like for that matter, they would never know that they would be blaming him for the death of his own woman.

For the plan to work, it would require Milktoast to use his vast knowledge in electronics to assist in carrying it out. Not only did he major in medicine, he had a minor in electronics and had tapped into the police radio system, guaranteeing that if they ever tried to raid his operation, he would be long gone before they arrived. The dude could wiretap phone lines, bug homes, blow up cars, and was a computer genius.

"Mike, you 'bout ta move up," Junior stated softly, using his given name.

"You know I've never turned down a raise," Milktoast answered, boastfully figuring that Junior needed his services in the worst way. The only time he called him Mike was when he was serious.

"Come own, let me rap wit ya." Junior walked out with Milktoast eagerly following behind. "Ah get wit y'all later, everybody come back at nine. Mario, come wif us."

EDE members exited the cookhouse and headed back to their

assigned turfs, wondering what grand plan Junior had in mind. Within minutes Majestic Avenue was once again quiet as residents returned to their daily routines, thinking the meeting of rap artists was over. Junior, Mario, and Milktoast sat on a bed in an unoccupied room at the rear of the house, with the latter two silent as Junior laid out his plan of attack.

After listening intently while his brother spoke, Mario felt that the scheme would no doubt work, along with pangs of sympathy for his mysterious uncle. Again his mixed emotions overwhelmed him as he thought of all the tears his mother would soon be shedding for her only brother. However, the more he thought about it, the more he convinced himself that it was better that she shed them for Uncle Horace and not her son.

39

WHERE'S MARIO?

Jerry dropped Horace off at his ride near Tassafaronga then promised to meet him at the condo complex within the next two hours. There they would devise a defense for the inevitable offensive assault from Junior, Mario, and their gang. Horace shed his costume then drove back to Kaiser with the purpose of checking on his woman, but when he got there, after garnering her room number from an unsuspecting triage nurse, he realized there was no way he could visit.

The seventh-floor hallway was saturated with cops, along with Harriette's family members who were politely answering questions. Horace peeped out the scene the moment he stepped off the elevator, then just as quickly hopped back inside for a return trip to the ground floor. He wanted no dealings with Five-O and correctly assumed that they had tied loose ends together. As he stepped off at the ground floor, Boston and Jimenez entered and headed up.

Walking rapidly across the street, Horace went to the public parking lot, located his ride, then drove to Crystal's house. Knowing this would be the biggest hit of his career and uncertain of the final result, he had a burning desire to see his sister for what could possibly be the last time. Pulling up in front of her crib, he noticed his other sister Melody's car parked in Crystal's driveway.

That was good, he thought, because now he could visit both siblings at the same time and, who knows, maybe get some fresh information on Mario. Crystal stood in front of the stove cooking spaghetti while Melody sat at the table softly talking to her. Upon hearing the doorbell, Crystal wiped her hands on her apron as she went to answer it.

"Horace, two times in one week, I must be blessed!" She hugged him.

"No, I'm the one blessed," he corrected her. "I get to see both of my sisters at the same time. Where's Melody?"

"She's in the kitchen."

They walked back to the kitchen, and when Melody looked up to see her only brother, she rose out of her seat accepting his skin-tight bear hug.

"Peanut, girl, you look better than ever!" He greeted her using Melody's nickname.

"And you still know how to charm a woman with straight-faced lies!" Both sisters laughed.

Horace leaned back admiring Melody's frame while she blushed openly. Just as fine as Crystal, she had a pronounced permanent curve on the right side of her lip along with a noticeable limp to her walk. They were from a stroke she'd had a year earlier as a direct result of a near-death experience—she had survived a vicious shooting at the hands of an EDE associate named Anthony "Junebug" Grimes.

Melody wore black spandex pants, which accented her powerful legs, butt, and thighs, along with a form-fitting t-shirt. It was obvious to Horace that she had been to yet another physical therapy session, and sympathy engulfed him as he tried to comprehend the pain his sister had to be enduring. She was just as fine as Crystal, and before her mishap had even more suitors. Now a shell of her old self, Melody struggled to hold normal conversations and could not participate in any athletic activities.

"You're just in time for dinner," Crystal stated, slapping plates on the table.

"It smells wonderful," Horace responded.

"Good, I'll place a setting for you."

"So what have you been up to, Brother?" Melody asked.

"Trying to keep my head above water, Sis, and keep tabs on your nephew."

"We were just talking about Mario."

"Has he called?" Horace hoped the answer would be yes.

"No, I haven't heard from him," Crystal answered while spooning spaghetti onto their plates. "I thought you may have."

"No dice, but I did learn that the people he now chooses to run with are bad news."

"See what I told you, Peanut?" Crystal chipped in. "I knew it from the first time I met them!"

"What's wrong with Mario?" Melody drawled out slowly.

"I don't know what's gotten into that boy!" Crystal answered emphatically.

Crystal placed a tray full of garlic bread on the table, along with a tossed salad and bottle of wine, then joined her siblings. Melody led them in prayer then proceeded to chow down along with her sister, while Horace picked at his food without emotion.

"What's the matter? You don't like my cooking anymore?" Crystal asked Horace.

"Not that, girl, I just had lunch before I got here," he lied.

"Horace," Melody interrupted, "how's Harriette? Have you two set a wedding date yet? Or will you die a divorced bachelor?" The sisters burst out laughing again.

"You know I never give that stuff much thought. She's fine, we have no date planned, and I probably will die a divorced bachelor. I think your first sister-in-law wiped out any desire of mine to go through that again."

"Yeah, she was a witch." They all could agree on that.

The remainder of dinner was spent with the threesome reminiscing about the good old days, with Horace feeling refreshed by the "remember when" stories. Glancing at his wristwatch, he noticed that an hour and a half had flown by, so he waited until Crystal wrapped up his plate, kissed both of his sisters on the lips, and walked out of the kitchen. They remained sitting, where they would continue talking for the next two hours.

Horace drove home and began gathering up his arsenal, along with reverting into his Sweetpea alter-ego. Twenty minutes later his phone rang, and upon seeing Jerry's name displayed on the caller ID, he smiled wider than he had for days.

"Hey Jerry," he answered, "I hope you got something."

40

BULL'S EYE

Boston and Jimenez were greeted in Harriette's room by Sybil Evans and Amber Harris. Sybil was a beautiful twenty-five-year-old brick house with thick, mouth-watering legs and thighs that were proudly on display from the black skirt on her body and matching high-heeled shoes on her feet. She had a small waist and very large breasts, with nipples the size of quarters straining to peek through the fabric of her black turtleneck sweater.

Prominent dimples were deeply implanted on both sides of her cheeks, complementing full luscious lips covered with gloss. Her hair was styled in a modest press and curl fashion, with brown eyes looking out through black-rimmed designer glasses. She rose from her chair to shake their hands, and Boston was unable to ignore those baby oil-shined ham hocks.

This was her third year working as a domestic violence advocate for the county, and Sybil felt as though she would not be able to last many more. Dealing with the daily trauma of women beaten down by a jealous man, only to return for more abuse, or like today, attempting to console a rape victim whose life was now forever changed, caused Sybil to constantly re-evaluate her career choice.

Initially she felt as though she could make a difference, but now she was convinced that boys grew up watching fathers abuse their mom, then acted accordingly as adults. She also noticed an increase in the number of teen and young twenty-something males who would help produce a child, then fail to handle the responsibilities that came along with it. The end results were always the same, with minor disagreements resulting in extreme violence including, in some cases, death.

"Hello, Detectives," she greeted them, extending a hand.

"Hi, Miss Evans," they replied.

"How's the victim?" asked Jimenez.

"Well, the doctor gave her some sedatives and she's been resting, but she did give us quite a bit of information on the culprits."

Amber Harris rose from her chair, nodding at the two detectives while pulling a note tablet from her purse. She was a thirty-year-old bombshell who had been on the force for five years and actively campaigned for the domestic violence gig due to her own personal experiences with domineering men. At five-feet-nine, one hundred and forty pounds, she possessed the physique of a body builder, along with black-belt skills in karate.

Amber's hair was golden blond, cascading well past her shoulders, and she had baby-blue eyes along with thin lips coated by ruby-red lipstick. An angular chin and long pointy nose, combined with the hardened glaze in her eyes, gave off warning that this was a serious lady not in the mood for games. She wore a two-piece brown skirt/jacket set with matching heels that accented her chiseled bare legs.

Normally her outfit was a simple combination of blue jeans and button-down shirt, but having worked the past year with Sybil, who dressed stylish daily, caused Amber to improve her wardrobe. However, even with the appropriate attire, she still did not look quite the part of classy dame.

"The victim identified one of the perps as Mario, no last name, who is the nephew of her boyfriend. She didn't know the other two but heard them call each other Junior and Dread," stated Amber.

"Can she identify them?" asked Jimenez.

"Not really. They had her blindfolded and tied to a bed the entire time of the assault."

Jimenez jotted notes as Harris spoke then joined everyone in watching as the door softly opened and the doctor entered. Narinder

Somal hailed from East India and was brought to the States as a child by determined parents who paid a small fortune for the dangerous journey in search of a better life. The trip consisted of a long boat ride in which many on board perished from lack of food and water, a twelve-hour plane flight, then having to live with "sponsors" in a converted basement for nearly five years until his parents could make it on their own.

Young Somal was five at the time and only knew of the trek from eavesdropping as adults discussed it at family gatherings. This knowledge caused him to study longer and work harder than his childhood peers in order to attain his goal. Upon his graduation from medical school he garnered a job at Kaiser Hospital where he remained for the next two decades. Now with more years behind him than ahead, Doctor Somal relished the thought of retirement.

A small dude, Somal stood five feet five inches, carried by a puny one-hundred-and-forty-pound body. His jet-black hair was cut close to the scalp, and horned-rimmed spectacles covered his midnight-colored eyeballs. Holding a clipboard stacked with papers in his hand, he marched directly over to his patient, examining her closely. Scribbling notes onto a sheet of paper atop his clipboard, he turned to face the foursome whose attention was directly on him.

"How is she, Doc?" asked Boston.

"She'll be fine with rest and the proper after-care counseling," he answered.

"Any idea who did this?"

"She gave a statement to Miss Harris"—the doctor nodded at Amber—"and we sent DNA samples to headquarters in order to speed up the identification process."

"I think I'll talk to the guys outside," Jimenez whispered to her partner, then left the room.

Boston continued to ask the doctor generic questions while Amber and Sybil sat back down in their chairs next to the bed. It only required two minutes for his question-and-answer session with the doctor, yet he took five as his eyes greedily devoured Sybil's massive yams the entire time. Boy, did he envision riding that fine piece of meat. Exiting into the hallway, he found Jimenez alone in a corner writing furiously on her notepad.

"Looks like you hit the jackpot, babes," he smiled.

"Don't 'babes' me, I saw you!" she snarled.

"Saw me what?"

"Derrick, do not try to play me. I saw the way you looked at her."

"At who?"

"Sybil, that's who."

"Damn," he growled. "Alright, that's it, let's go."

Boston marched off angrily toward the elevator bank with Jimenez right on his heels just as perturbed. All the way to the hospital he had clowned her about the shifty eyes he assumed she was giving Dennis Branch at headquarters, and now she had effectively turned the tables. Their relationship was built on mistrust from the moment they began cheating on their respective spouses, and now that they were free to be together, they could not trust each other.

It was a simple case of each one knowing what the other was capable of and thinking the worst. Of course, once they left the hospital Boston drove to their sex crib, where they gave each other the silent treatment for hours. In the middle of the night as he spooned up behind her and she felt his throbbing penis, they had make-up sex, which eliminated all anger. At five in the morning his phone rang, arousing him from a peaceful slumber.

"Boston here."

"Good news."

"Lay it on me, Jimmy."

"The semen samples collected from Miss Colbert are a perfect match to our suspects and the samples collected at the warehouse."

"Excellent, thanks, bro."

"No problem."

Boston rolled back over and parted his woman's legs while climbing on top. She awoke to the pounding force of his meat slamming into her juicy wet hole. Her legs remained spread wide while she clutched his shoulders, humping like a bronco bull. They matched each other thrust for thrust when finally he erupted in an explosive climax. After drifting off into slumber, they arose three hours later and took a shower together.

"Jimmy called," he stated while soaping down her back.

"What did he have to say?"

"DNA hits on all the suspects."

"Baby, let's stop all this nonsense, okay? I only want you."

"And I only want you."

She turned to face him, lavishing kisses on his chest while smiling as he regained another massive erection. He closed his eyes, enjoying the sensations while his mind thought about how good his dick would feel implanted firmly inside Sybil's awesome body. Twenty minutes later they were dressed and out the door.

41

PHINE INVESTIGATING

Jerry eased into the parking lot at Arroyo Park, ignoring dealers who assumed he was there to buy dope. A wide grin crossed his face upon seeing the person he hoped to find, and he made a bee-line to the patch of grass where a small group of people sat drinking Night Train. The individual doing the talking had his back to Jerry, who held a finger to his lips using nonverbal communication with the other three in order not to spoil his surprise. When he got directly behind, he placed both hands over the target's eyes.

"Wait a minute, I'd know these strong hands anywhere. Jerry, stop playing!" Tugging his hands away, the target turned around. "Well, ah'll be damned if it ain't old Jerry!"

"I see you still haven't changed, lying to anyone about how great you are!" Jerry chortled.

"Aw, fuck you, niggah, you know first-hand that when I drop the bomb, I do it well."

"Is that right? Everybody gets sprung, huh?"

"I never heard a complaint from yo ass—give me a got-damn hug!"

Cedric Rogers rose up and treated Jerry to his trademark bear hug, which consisted of grabbing him in a vice lock around the small of the back while lifting his feet off the ground. "CeCe," which was her street name, was a very muscular, six-foot two-inch transvestite. She had a chiseled physique, proudly displayed by the skin-tight jeans and painted-on halter top she wore.

The hormone pills she had been taking religiously for the past four years resulted in small baseball-sized breasts poking through her top, and from a distance, she appeared to be all woman. That was due to her pronounced feminine tendencies, including a walk that would stop traffic, with both drivers and passersby greedily devouring her mouth-watering booty.

CeCe wore a shoulder-length brown wig with streaks of gold in it, did not possess an ounce of flab, and had no shame whatsoever regarding her sexuality. At the park she was known as "Queenie" because of her willingness to talk shit to anyone, along with fist-fight them by throwing non-stop windmill punches. CeCe provided strangers with the typical stereotype of transgenders because she openly flaunted her sexuality and would get drunk and act a fool daily.

"Everybody, this is my very dear friend Jerry and we go a longgggg way back." She rolled her eyes. "Jerry, I want you to meet Wanda, Kiana, and Melanie."

"Nice to meet you all," Jerry smiled.

The entire group consisted of trans-sexual individuals in various stages of development and, just like CeCe, they seemed at peace with their lifestyle. Introductions were made then Jerry joined the group by occupying a seat next to CeCe on their spread-out blanket. CeCe resumed yakking away while playfully nudging Jerry from time to time.

"Hey," he interrupted, "did you hear about the dude they found at Mother's Cookie factory?"

"You know nothing gets past your girl," CeCe boasted. "How do you know about it?"

"One of my co-workers was assigned to that location and just called me with the gossip."

"Oh, that's right," CeCe snapped her finger. "I forgot to tell y'all that my Jerry works as a rent-a-cop at a boo-zwa-jay condo complex—he only caters to the high and mighty!"

"I'm a security guard," he stated sheepishly. "Anyway, dude was messed up."

"I feel sorry for whoever did it." CeCe spoke in hushed tones.

"Why is that?"

"'Cause Dread was a part of Junior's group, and they will have revenge."

Everyone nodded in agreement, remembering the chaos that had ensued only one hour earlier when Junior rolled into the park announcing what had occurred at the warehouse along with promising instant death to the perpetrators. Jerry was unfazed by the comment and remained passive in his demeanor.

"That bad, huh?"

"Girl, that ain't the half of it," CeCe warned. "Shit, even I keep my distance from Junior's crazy ass. They picked the wrong group of fools to fuck with this time."

"Well, if it's like that, then I feel sorry for them too."

"Girl, you shoulda seen the way those fools acted! I mean, they rolled out eight cars deep, burning so much rubber a cloud of smoke covered the whole damn lot. Those dicks probably headed to Junior's crib for their assault weapons, or his cookhouse to make a plan. I'm just glad it ain't me they after." CeCe was solemn.

"You'd think in this day and age they would use something like that warehouse to make dope."

"Naw, honey chile, they are not that sophisticated yet. They got a house on 62nd and Majestic where they cook, package, and distribute product. I've been there one time but left soon as I got there."

"Why is that?"

"'Cause one mistake from those fools cooking that shit, and that whole block gonna explode. Shidd, girl, I love myself way too much for that to happen!"

"I can see you still think rather highly of yourself," Jerry laughed.

"Bitch, what the fuck you really want?" CeCe feigned annoyance. "Yo ass just ain't the type to show up unannounced and not want something!"

"Actually, I met this freak who happens to like cocaine and since I'm not one to indulge, or buy that shit, I came to you."

"See, I told yaw he wanted something. So I see you're still using that same old tired ass game, huh?"

"What game would that be?"

"Get 'em high then fuck um with that fat-ass sausage you got."

"I'm spending a hundred."

Jerry peeled a c-note from his roll, handing it to CeCe, who slipped him a package of dope. Kissing her on the lips, he rose to leave. CeCe sat stunned from the kiss, looking as if she had been bitten by the love bug.

"You still have the same number?" he asked.

"Yes," she answered throatily, with a far-off gaze in her eyes.

"I'll call you."

"You'd better."

Jerry returned to his ride with the dealers now ignoring him. Most had witnessed his departure kiss and knew CeCe dominated drug sales to the gay community. Her group of girls gathered around as she began filling them in on all the details of her one-time sexual encounter with "monster dick," as she called him. He drove a block down then tossed the dope out of his car window, knowing some unsuspecting fiend would soon be feeling blessed upon finding it.

He wanted to get a line on Junior's address but knew if he asked too many point-blank questions, she and her associates would become suspicious. With only the cookhouse spot as a lead he drove there, finding a slew of fancy cars lining the block. Now that he had their location, Jerry parked one block down and called Horace on his cell phone. When he answered on the second ring, Jerry ran down the situation then waited, watching all activity to and from the house.

Sweetpea arrived twenty minutes later on foot, having hidden his car one block over. Jerry pressed the door lock switch then shook his hand as he entered the vehicle.

"You got here pretty fast."

"Didn't want to miss anything. What's going on?"

"I'm not sure." Jerry scratched his head. "Most of the gang has left, but there are still some people in the house."

"Which one is it?" Sweetpea asked, eyeing Junior's ride parked on the street.

"The white one with green trim."

"Okay, here's the plan. Take the keys to my car, it's parked around the corner, then drive to the block behind their house."

"What do you want me to do then?"

"Just stake out the back. Maybe they have a window open or curtains drawn where you can view their activity."

"I'm on my way."

Jerry bounced out the ride, tight pants and all, then switched down the street and around the corner. Sweetpea continued to scope out the front of the house and was more than surprised to see several people who he guessed were cookers leaving the crib. He had no idea that only Junior, Mario, and Milktoast remained inside and could care less, because to him, no life would be spared.

42

CLOSING IN

Boston parked the service vehicle crookedly on the curb as he and Jimenez practically ran inside the police headquarters building. Their first destination was the office of Jimmy Chang, who sat at his desk polishing off a bowl of shrimp fried rice. Wiping his face with a napkin, then his hands, Jimmy rose from his chair to greet the two detectives, who were breathing heavily.

"I tested the semen samples from the hospital and they are a perfect match to your suspects," Jimmy said.

"What about the victim?" asked Jimenez.

"Hers was the fourth."

"So now all we have to do is locate them. We have an APB out for the three, and I have a name and address for the boyfriend, who happens to be one of the suspects' uncle."

"You do?" Boston was surprised by his partner's last statement. "Why didn't you tell me?"

"After I questioned her relatives at the hospital, we were discussing other things."

Boston remembered vividly the ensuing argument about Sybil Evans and let the issue go. He was relieved that now they could concentrate on the case at hand, and he could not wait to question the boyfriend about his nephew.

"What's his name?" he asked her.

"Horace Boudreaux, resides on Fairmont Avenue in a penthouse suite."

"Let's go," Boston ordered.

They left Jimmy to his work, thanking him profusely then heading out the door. While waiting for the elevator, they were joined by none other than Dennis Branch. Boston stiffened while Jimenez greeted him warmer than necessary.

"Hello, Sergeant Branch," she said.

"Hey, you guys, I have some information for you."

"What would that be?"

"I have a last known address for Grissom—it's his mother's house."

"We'll take it," Boston snapped.

Branch handed over the piece of paper containing Shirley's address, wondering why Boston was in such a foul mood. They continued to ride in silence in an obviously tension-filled elevator. When the two detectives stepped off, Branch remained inside, watching as people entered and the door slowly closed. The moment it did, Boston started up once again.

"Hello Sergeant Branch," he snarled hatefully.

Jimenez ignored his snide comment and continued walking, not wanting to resume where they had left off the day before. The ride to Horace's home was taken in silence, with each person deep in their own thoughts. At the condo complex they flashed their badges, informing the guard on duty of their purpose, signed into the guest log, then were keyed up to Horace's suite. After ringing the doorbell several times and knocking loudly, Boston stuck a business card in the door and they reentered the waiting elevator.

"Think he's at the hospital?" Boston asked.

"Probably not—her family hasn't seen or heard from the guy."

Back in the main lobby, Jimenez handed her card to the guard, writing her cell phone number on it with instructions for the guard to call them if Boudreaux arrived or had any visitors. Boston shifted the car into gear and drove up Harrison, joining traffic on the 580 freeway. His destination was Shirley's, but as he passed the High Street exit a call blared over the radio regarding a triple homicide in the 6200 block of Majestic.

Lifting the radio transmitter from its holder, Boston informed the dispatch operator that they were on route then zoomed down the

Seminary Avenue off ramp. Rolling to the crime scene, Boston eased up to the block, which was saturated with police cars. The house had been cordoned off with crime scene tape, and media personnel were already gathering in bunches. Getting out of their vehicle, the detectives walked up to the house not knowing what to expect.

43

LIFE & DEATH

A "For Sale" sign sat planted in the center of a neatly manicured lawn of a brown stucco home on Outlook Avenue. Jerry smiled at the sight, parking right in front of it while knowing he had an instant alibi that would enable him to complete his task. To anyone observing, he appeared to be a prospective house hunter because he first lifted an information flyer from the holder under the sign, then peeked curiously through the front windows.

Checking the door and finding it locked, as he knew it would be, he glanced at his watch then walked around the side of the home. The back yard gave a clear view of Junior's cookhouse. While standing on the porch Jerry observed a meatily built half-breed making several trips to a black Yukon parked in the driveway. With his ponytail dangling behind his back, Milktoast was loading up his vehicle with explosives and electronic gear.

Jerry called Sweetpea, giving him a rundown of the situation, talking quietly through his earpiece attachment. Jerry knew he held the element of surprise and waited until Milktoast re-entered the house then jumped the fence. The moment his feet landed on the ground he saw movement in the corner of his eye and turned quickly to see what it was.

"Oh shit!" he yelled.

"Jerry, what is it?" Sweetpea screamed into the phone.

A tan-colored pit bull that had been enjoying a giant piece of red meat noticed the intruder then took off in his direction. He had a gold splotch covering one eye and his chest, and a powerfully built torso. Jerry leapt back over the fence just in the nick of time, as the canine narrowly missed chewing off a chunk of his behind. The dog began barking loudly, along with trying several times to scale the fence, as Jerry ran up the vacant house's back yard toward Sweetpea's car.

"A fucking pit bull!" he panted into the earpiece.

"What?' Sweetpea yelled then heard gunfire.

"Damn near got me!"

Mario, Junior, and Milktoast heard the dog barking and ran to the back yard with guns drawn. "Dass dat punk-ass security guard!" Mario screamed to his brother while unloading his clip. Junior grabbed the dog with two hands, throwing it across the fence while hollering, "Get him, Brutus!" Next, he and Mario climbed over in pursuit, while Milktoast ran inside the crib to get his own weapon.

Jerry got to the Benz but had trouble fishing the keys from his pocket due to a visibly trembling hand. Glancing up, he saw the dog speeding toward him and felt a lump form in his throat. Finally jerking the keys from his trouser pocket he de-activated the alarm and jumped inside as Brutus crashed into the window, saliva from his mouth coating the glass.

Inserting the key into the ignition, Jerry sped away and began talking to Sweetpea. He became alarmed upon hearing no response. Junior and Mario stuffed their weapons inside their waistbands, which were covered by their shirts, then watched as the Benz turned the corner to safety. Junior patted the dog on the forehead and headed back to the cookhouse with his younger sibling right behind.

This time Mario hopped the fence then accepted a key from Junior, which he used to disengage a master padlock clamped down on a custom-built swing gate. After Junior and the dog barged through, he and Mario stormed into the house. The Yukon was still there yet the house was eerily silent.

"Mike!" Junior hollered out. "Mike, where you at?"

Mario headed to the bedroom and found Milktoast lying in a pool of his own blood on the bed. His throat had been slashed with a deep cut from ear to ear, and his body lay peacefully across the sheets. Mario returned to the kitchen looking spooked, which set off shock waves in his brother.

"Mike dead," he softly stated. "Uncle Horace been in da house."

"Well, he gone be dead too!" Junior promised then turned around to find the silver blade of a stiletto rotating directly at him. He tried to avoid it without success, catching it directly through his adam's apple. Sweetpea stood under an archway separating the living and dining quarters, gripping another knife in his hand while watching Mario gasp at the sight of his brother hit the floor with a deafening thud.

"Let's end this, nephew—there's no need for you to die too," Sweetpea pleaded with Mario.

"Fuck you, man, you done fucked up my life. Killed mah daddy and mah brother!"

"Don't do it, son," Sweetpea warned as Mario slowly trained the gun on him.

Without another word spoken Mario closed his eyes and pulled the trigger as Sweetpea flicked his knife simultaneously. The bullet caught Sweetpea directly on his kneecap, sending excruciating pain through his entire body, while the knife connected on a bull's eye to Mario's chest. He was dead before he hit the ground as Sweetpea gathered up his weapons and hobbled out the back door.

The pangs of grief enveloping him caused him to temporarily forget about the dog, and the moment he stepped into the back yard, Brutus attacked with vengeance. Sweetpea saw him leap and used his arm to protect his exposed face, while Brutus clamped down on the arm in the "lock" that pit bulls are famous for. He shook his head violently from side to side while Sweetpea was flung around the yard like a rag doll.

Knowing that pit bulls would hold the lock until you were dead, or until they could get a better grip on another part of your body, Sweetpea frantically attempted to retrieve one of his knives. As blood squirted out from Brutus's clenched teeth and Sweetpea felt himself losing consciousness, he pulled out a dagger and stabbed the dog repeatedly in the chest until the death lock was released.

Brutus rolled over with his entire torso soaked in blood as Sweetpea painfully struggled to get on his feet. Pulling out his cell phone while stumbling through the open gate to the empty house, he smashed in the back door window, let himself inside, then called Jerry.

"Hello!" Jerry was hysterical.

"Yeah, I left your keys under the driver's seat and here's what I need you to do."

"Tell me, man!" Jerry hollered.

"Go get your car . . . and pull all the way back . . . intothedriveway . . . ofthevacanthouse." He was nearly out of breath yet continued, "Then come . . . to the back . . . door . . . andcarryme tothecar."

"I'm on my way!" Jerry shrieked.

"Inside . . . my wallet . . . you'llfindanaddressfor. . . . Doctor CHARLES TURNER," he blurted out. "Take me there—he'll know what to do."

Jerry, who earlier had parked a few blocks over on Hillside Avenue, drove Sweetpea's Mercedes up behind his ride. Hopping inside, he located the keys exactly where Sweetpea said they would be, then went to pick up his friend. Carrying his unconscious bloody body out to the car, he reclined the seat, gently placing Sweetpea inside, then searched his wallet for the doctor's address. Upon finding it he headed for the hills.

"Don't die on me, man!" he cried.

Jerry continued an ongoing conversation with Sweetpea the entire ride, glancing at his passenger repeatedly as if expecting a response. Sweetpea, who was losing tons of blood pouring from his kneecap and arm, did not hear any of it because his life hung in the balance.

Doctor Turner heard his doorbell ring and stomped his foot violently on the carpeted floor. "Who in the hell has the nerve to interrupt me while I'm watching *Law and Order*?" he angrily stated while opening the door.

"Doc, I need your help!" Jerry gasped.

"Do I know you?" The doctor was suspicious.

"Horace Boudreaux is in my car bleeding badly."

"Oh, Horace, let's get him inside. Pull your car all the way to the back!" the doctor ordered.

Jerry did as instructed, then carried Horace into the quack doctor's examination/operating room. Sitting inside a makeshift reception area, he waited three hours until the doctor re-appeared. Turner pulled off what normally would be blue latex gloves, now crimson in color, then spoke.

"I have some good news and bad."

"Give me the good," Jerry said.

"He will live. . . ."

"And the bad?"

"He probably will have a limp to his gait for the rest of his life. The kneecap was shattered."

"Thanks, Doc."

"You can go home, young man," the doctor stated. "Mister Boudreaux will need to stay here and rest for at least a few days."

"Okay," Jerry responded. "Let me give you my number, and you call me if you need anything."

Jerry wrote down his phone number and handed it over to the doctor. He left the house, got into his ride, and slowly backed out of the driveway. Charles Turner watched with more than a passing interest. Not that it was any of his business, or if he cared for that matter, because the only thing which meant anything to him was getting paid. But he was certain Jerry was gay, and now wondered whether Horace was too. From this day on he would view his best-paying, most frequent customer in a different light.

44

EXPOSED

"Definitely the work of the Knifeman," Boston stated to his partner while perusing the grisly crime scene. It was obvious to them both that this was the hit of a professional, and since nothing else in the home had been disturbed, there was little doubt who had conducted it.

Jimmy Chang along with two additional technicians busily labeled and tagged everything remotely resembling evidence, while beat cops and reporters questioned neighboring residents. The bomb squad unit carefully removed explosives from a Yukon parked in the driveway, with additional officers scouring Junior's ride.

The entire block took on a familiar circus-like atmosphere with photographers snapping flicks, television personalities giving citizens their fifteen minutes of fame on camera, and helicopters hovering above with searchlights illuminating the entire neighborhood.

As usual, word spread through the grapevine like wildfire as cell phone calls were made throughout the city by more-than-curious onlookers. When the news made it to Arroyo that Junior had been murdered, EDE members instantly began brewing secret plots to seize control of the empire.

There was no doubt a violent turf war would soon engulf the east side, because when a drug lord was killed without a pre-named successor to the throne, violence and death surely followed.

"Any identification on the victims?" Jimenez asked her partner.

"Our two guys," stated Boston, "Grissom and Hayes."

"And the third?"

"Driver's license lists his name as Matthew Miller, no criminal record, but the SUV in the driveway registered to him is full of explosives."

"Looks like whoever they were after got them first."

"By hiring the Knifeman," Jimenez concluded.

Narcotic officers hauled out pounds of dope, along with enough ether to blow up the whole neighborhood, while Animal Control staff carted away the pit bull. From all the blood in and around the dog's mouth and face, they knew he had been chewing on someone, or thing, and alerted police to the trail of blood leading out the back gate.

Officers followed the trail to the vacant house's kitchen then returned outside to find it ending at the driveway. Summoning Jimmy Chang, who was in charge of the techs on duty, they waited while he assigned one of them to collect samples from inside the vacant house and the dog's mouth. As good as Jimmy was, this was a monstrous job and he needed every available tech on duty to assist him with it.

When Junior's mom and sister finally arrived, the sideshow began in earnest. Edwina parked her Lexus haphazardly, hopping out along with her mother and demanding to identify the dead body.

"Dey tole me mah baby got kilt!" Shirley hollered to a cop manning the crime scene.

"You'll have to calm down, ma'am," the officer said.

"Fuck dat!" she screamed. "Ah wont ta see mah boy!"

"Who's in charge here?" shouted Edwina as she bolted for the front door.

"Wait a minute!" said the cop grabbing her by the collar.

Edwina and Shirley began wrestling with the cops, attempting to get into the house, while the crowd looked on amused by the sight. Normally laughter would be had by all, but since everyone knew who they were—and feared later retaliation for finding the scene funny—no one did so much as crack a smile.

After the women had calmed down and the bodies were carted out, they were allowed to view Junior's. A member of the coroner's staff was instructed to lift the blanket covering Junior's body slightly for Shirley and Edwina to view.

Both women broke out in mournful tears upon seeing Junior's lifeless form on the gurney as quiet otherwise ruled the cool night air. Their sobs verified the rumor that Junior was indeed one of the murdered victims inside the house. Slowly, onlookers began easing away, and within ten minutes the crowd had dwindled to a handful.

Shirley and Edwina began making loud promises of death to the Knifeman, who they knew had committed the crime. Inside the home, Boston and Jimenez were unaware of the outside drama, continuing to gather facts, clues, and evidence.

"I'm certain the Knifeman is responsible for this," Jimenez said with conviction, "but I do think he almost got his due from the dog."

"I've already alerted all the local hospitals to be on the lookout for someone coming in with dog bites," Boston stated while acknowledging Jimmy Chang, who was headed in their direction.

"I'll go test these blood samples and see if we get a hit," Jimmy said.

"We'll wait for the call," Boston responded softly.

Jimmy packed up his bags and walked out, with the detectives following shortly. Outside, they were directed over to Shirley and Edwina, who provided them with much-desired information on the notorious Knifeman.

"Yeah, dat bastahd was Mario's uncle," Shirley muttered. "If yaw don't get 'im, we will!" she promised.

"So why do you think he's the Knifeman?" Boston asked quietly.

"'Cause Junior found a secret closet in his condo det had nuttin' but guns, knives, and costumes in it."

"Where was this secret closet located?"

"In his livin' room, behind da bookcase."

"And how did they get it to open?"

"Dare was a button on top of it."

With this newfound bit of information, the detectives would secure a search warrant for Horace Boudreaux's condominium, locate the secret closet, then use any evidence found as proof in court against him. Their adrenaline was running on full speed as they headed to the car.

Hopping inside their service vehicle, Boston and Jimenez first went to Crystal Hayes' home with the devastating news that her son was dead. After that, they went to Matthew Miller's parents. Being the bearers of bad news was the hardest part of their job bar none, but this time the sting wasn't as severe because they had what they considered to be a solid lead on the Knifeman.

45

FUNEREAL FAREWELLS

Not by coincidence, both Junior and Mario's funerals were held on the same day at different locations. Shirley left numerous unreturned voice messages on Crystal's answering machine requesting a joint service, with them being brothers and all. However, Crystal was having none of that, opting instead to have a nice, quiet ceremony for her one and only child.

Junior's service was held at one of the largest churches on the east side, which was rented by Shirley for the occasion. It was attended by at least a thousand people, with standing room only, and speakers placed outside for those who came late.

Going all out with no worry about expenses, Shirley hired the best musicians, wonderful singers, and even had the body conveyed in a horse-driven carriage. What normally would be an hour and a half service lasted nearly three, along with a slow-moving, two-hour procession to the cemetery.

During the walk-around song, many of Junior's boyz placed gold rings, hundred-dollar bills, sacks of weed, or packets of cocaine inside the casket. The battle for control had already begun in earnest, and most of them had not spoken to each other since their leader's grisly murder.

Tension was high, yet everyone remained civil in honor of their fallen leader. Cops lined the block outside the church, taking notice of everyone attending the funeral. They arrested at least a dozen people on outstanding warrants ranging from failure to appear, parole violations, and expired license plates on their vehicles.

The official repast was held at Shirley's home, attended only by family members and close friends. There were several other gatherings throughout the city including Arroyo Park, top east-side drug empire members' homes, and Junior's favorite watering holes.

The homegoing for Mario was held at Crystal's house of worship on the west side in a small chapel seating no more than one hundred and twenty-five people. One hundred at best attended, with most of them being family, church members, or close friends.

Mario was dressed up in a blue suit with matching necktie, which was complemented by a white button-down shirt. Crystal and Melody wore black dresses, their constant sobs of grief echoing throughout the tiny temple. Horace, who had not been seen since Mario's murder, hobbled into the church aided by Jerry, whom neither Crystal or Melody had ever met.

Horace wore a black two-piece designer suit with matching tie, shoes, socks, and white shirt. The sisters noticed his pronounced limp, loss of weight, and heavily bandaged body, yet attributed it to the car accident he told them he had been involved in on the day of Mario's death.

He also lied to them about Harriette, who since her rape and torture had refused to respond to his repeated phone calls at the hospital. Horace told his sisters that she was a passenger and suffered multiple injuries too. Midway through the service Horace could take no more of his siblings crying, which caused him to erupt in loud, mournful sobs.

His pain was a combination of sorrow for the misery brought on to Crystal and Melody, along with guilt rumbling throughout his body for being the cause of his nephew's untimely death. Detectives Boston and Jimenez eased into the church, occupying seats on the last pew, with their eyes zooming in on Horace.

Harriette had given them pictures of Horace Boudreaux, and they matched the ones provided in the family photos with the obituary. After finding the secret closet loaded with assault type weapons and colorful disguises, Boston and Jimenez knew Boudreaux was the Knifeman.

Upon receiving results from a background check on Boudreaux, they were not surprised to find his record squeaky clean. The man had never received so much as a parking ticket, yet remained the one person on their list who had deftly avoided answering their questions.

Call it cop's intuition if you will, but after Jimmy Chang revealed news that blood from the cookhouse matched that of the Dimond and Campbell Village murder scenes, they knew if Boudreaux came into the chapel injured, he was probably their man. If that proved to be true, Boston also knew that he and his partner would instantly secure their spots in OPD lore.

Armed with a signed search warrant to secure DNA samples of his blood, they waited right outside the church house doors until Jerry wheeled Horace out.

"Horace Boudreaux?" Boston asked him discreetly.

"Yes," he answered.

"I'm Detective Boston and this is my partner Detective Jimenez." They flashed their badges. "Could we have a word with you?"

"Can't it wait until after the burial?"

"No, not really."

"Okay, make it quick, please." Horace felt the familiar lump form in his throat.

"How did you get your injuries?"

"I was in a car accident."

"Oh really?" Boston felt he was lying. "When and where did this accident occur?"

"Last week, up in the hills."

Boston and Jimenez stood at the ready, he with a hand placed on his weapon inside his coat and her directly behind Boudreaux's wheelchair. Jerry stood off to the side of Jimenez as if he were just a casual observer.

"I need to ask you to come downtown with us to the station," Boston stated.

"For what reason?"

"I have a warrant requiring you to give us a sample of your DNA."

"Man, look, we're trying to bury my nephew here—can't that wait?"

"I'm afraid not, sir."

Before the words could leave Boston's mouth, Jerry had Jimenez in a vice lock with a gun barrel planted forcefully on her temple. Seizing the moment, which caught Boston totally off guard, Sweetpea rose from the wheelchair, casually lifting Boston's revolver from its holder inside his jacket. Next he took Jimenez's weapon and handcuffs from her purse while motioning with a head jerk for the cops to re-enter the chapel.

They abandoned the wheelchair directly inside the church, with Jimenez's purse hidden behind the seat, then exited a side door leading to the nearly deserted parking lot. The cops were in front, with Jerry and Sweetpea trailing closely behind.

Outside, Jerry accepted the pair of cuffs from Sweetpea then used one set to connect the detectives' wrists to each other. With the remaining pair, he clamped one to Boston's free wrist then attached it to a chain-link fence behind the church and out of view.

"You won't get away with this," Boston promised.

"I already have," Sweetpea answered before hopping inside the vehicle with Jerry.

Nearly two hours elapsed before the cops were discovered by the church custodian while emptying trash. Upon freedom, Boston placed an all-points bulletin out for Horace Boudreaux and his unnamed accomplice. Yet as the weeks rolled by without a lead, he and his partner never gave up hope that the Knifeman would be nabbed.

They received kudos and commendations from the department for bravery, along with going above and beyond the call of duty. Along with providing definite identification of the infamous Knifeman, the department enlisted the aid of the *America's Most*

Wanted television show, hoping that someone, somewhere, would recognize those two. It was now only a matter of time until they were captured.

46

A BOLD ESCAPE

Carl, as Horace called himself now, sat at the table of a beachside Jamaican restaurant, sipping on Bahama Mama cocktails while Earl, Jerry's new tag, gave eyes to the waiter. Surrounded by Nubian queens along with freeloaders, they were the men of the hour.

Being bald in the States, Earl now sported shoulder-length dreads, tattoos exposed on his ripping muscles and chest, and a native tongue. Carl had a clean-shaven head, wore the finest of duds, and looked to be a retired bodybuilder from his powerful physique.

Word had it that they were filthy rich looking to invest, and once they began purchasing property and businesses like it was the thing to do, no one questioned them. Those two had it going on, and everybody wanted a piece of the action.

Their escape from the States was just as elaborately planned as everything else associated with the Knifeman. After gaining freedom by handcuffing the cops, they caught a plane to Los Angeles. There, Sweetpea provided Jerry with a dreadlock wig, had a local barber shave his own head bald, bought fake passports from some Mexicans, got a change of clothing, then headed for Jamaica. By the time Boston and Jimenez were free to place an all-points bulletin out for their arrest, they were on a plane headed to the Caribbean, with new looks along with new identities.

It was a Saturday night and the restaurant was full, with party-goers lingering and waiting for the festivities to begin. Flies were swarming as usual, which Carl had a problem with, yet everyone's eyes were glued to the bar's television set.

America's Most Wanted was about to air and, people being people, the customers hoped to see someone they knew in order to turn them in and receive a handsome finder's fee. The top-of-the-hour criminals displayed were Horace Boudreaux and Gerald Givens, a.k.a. Jerry. As their story was told with graphic, sensational details of their escape, the night air loomed quiet.

Boston and Jimenez could be seen giving their thoughts on the two criminals, while host John Walsh ended by promising capture. They had reports that the two were spotted in New York and Chicago. The episode ended with pleas for help in nabbing the fugitives.

"Mon, I glad ees not me," stated Earl when the show ended.

"Let's party!" shouted Carl.

Televisions went off, music went on, and the party took full effect. They looked nothing like the photos and would never be captured.

ABOUT THE AUTHOR

Renay Jackson has published six urban lit novels based in and around the city of Oakland. *Sweetpea's Secret* is his sixth novel, following on the heels of *Crack City* and the popular Oaktown Mystery Series, which includes *Oaktown Devil, Shakey's Loose, Turf War,* and *Peanut's Revenge*—all published by Frog Books in 2004 and 2005.

Recipient of the 2002 Chester Himes Black Mystery Writer of the Year Award, Jackson is currently working on his next as yet untitled book. He resides in the Bay Area.